CECIL COUNTY
PUBLIC LIBRARY
301 Newark Ave.
Elkton, MD 21921

P9-CLF-399

NIGHTKILL

NIGHTKILL

F. PAUL WILSON AND STEVE LYON

FORGE®

A TOM DOHERTY ASSOCIATES BOOK
New York

This is a work of fiction. All of the characters portrayed in this novel are either fictitious or are used fictitiously.

NIGHTKILL

Copyright © 1997 by F. Paul Wilson and Steven G. Spruill

All rights reserved, including the right to reproduce this book, or portions thereof, in any form.

This book is printed on acid-free paper.

A Forge Book
Published by Tom Doherty Associates, Inc.
175 Fifth Avenue
New York, NY 10010

Forge® is a registered trademark of Tom Doherty Associates, Inc.

Library of Congress Cataloging-in-Publication Data

Wilson, F. Paul (Francis Paul)
Nightkill / F. Paul Wilson & Steve Lyon. — 1st ed.
p. cm.
"A Tom Doherty Associates Book."
ISBN 0-312-85910-4 (hardcover: acid-free paper)
I. Lyon, Steve. II. Title.
PS3573.I45695N54 1997
813'.54—dc21 97-16824

First edition: October 1997

Printed in the United States of America

0 9 8 7 6 5 4 3 2 1

CECIL COUNTY
PUBLIC LIBRARY
301 Newark Ave.
Elkton, MD 21921

OCT 0 7 1997

To the regulars at NECon,
where we first cooked up this story

PART 1

HITS

1

FREDO

August

Jake heard from Fredo Papillardi the usual way: a typically verbose note to Jake's Atlantic City post office box: "Call Fredo."

So Jake called. But instead of Jake telling Fredo the where and when of the meet, as was customary, Fredo insisted on next Tuesday at 4:00 P.M. in a place with a TV. Jake didn't like that. One of the rules—Sarge's rules—was always set the conditions of a meet. But Fredo was insistent this time, said it had to be this way—"Totally necessary"—so Jake gave in. Fredo pushed for a hotel room but Jake wasn't giving in that much. He told Fredo the address of a place on Fairmount in AC. Leonardo's Bar & Grille.

Jake got two drafts from Ernie at the bar and settled himself at an isolated table in a dark corner. Next best thing to being invisible.

Leonardo's was a particularly dingy dive, which was one of the reasons Jake liked it. Always night inside; so dark the afternoon regulars winced and cringed like vampires every time the front door swung open. One of a hundred just like it spread across the Atlantic City you didn't see on postcards.

AC wasn't Jake's favorite city, but it was the closest to his place on the Bass River. He thought of AC as two cities, really. First was the new Atlantic City, the one you *did* see on postcards, crowded up against the ocean with its high, shiny casinos and boardwalk-treading tourists. Then the old AC that the gamblers' buses had to pass through to get to the casinos, with its dirty, crumbling sidewalks, empty storefronts, shuffling residents, and old, leaning buildings that rarely rose above two stories. Beirut on the Jersey Shore.

Leonardo's was in the second AC, in a working-class neighborhood four blocks west of TropWorld, in another time zone, another climate, another country. Jake liked it not only because it was dark, but because it was never crowded, and because Ernie, the owner-barkeep, had selective Alzheimer's—knew every stat about every guy who'd ever worn a Phillies or Eagles uniform, but never knew nothing nohow about nobody who was ever in his joint. Try to talk to Ernie about his clientele and you'd swear the place was empty day and night.

Jake watched Fredo breeze in from the bright afternoon and stand, lost and disoriented, in the gloom. Watched him stumble to the bar, an island of dimness in the dark.

"I'm lookin' for a guy."

Ernie gave him a hard look. "This ain't that kinda bar, sweetie."

"Very funny. Name's Jake."

"Jake who? I don't know no Jake."

Good old Ernie.

"Over here," Jake said, flicking his Bic and raising the flame like a metalhead during a ballad. He kept it burning until Fredo had groped his way to the table.

"Jesus, Jake, it's like a fuckin' cave in here."

"Your eyes'll adjust."

"Look, I thought we agreed to meet where there's a TV."

"There's one over the bar."

"Yeah, but it's got the fuckin' game on."

"That can be fixed. What are we supposed to see at four?"

"The whackee, if you know what I'm saying."

Jake thought about that. Four o'clock was too early for news. So who was the target? A talk-show host? He stared at Fredo. He knew he had dark hair, dark eyes, and olive skin, liked shiny shoes, thousand-dollar sport coats, and heavy gold, but all he could make out here in the dark was slicked-back hair, a bulky build, and a sport shirt. Light glinted faintly from the thick gold chain around his throat. Fredo was a made man and proud of it. Jake wouldn't have been surprised if his license plate read MOB-1.

Jake, on the other hand, was careful to make sure he'd never be mistaken for one of the Boys. Straight blond hair streaked with barely noticeable gray, long, straight nose, blue eyes, sharp chin, lean, wiry build, jeans, sneakers, work shirt. And no gold. *No* chains, nothing that reflected light.

He pushed the extra eight-ounce draft toward Fredo. "This one's yours. We've got a couple of minutes to kill."

"Don't they have any wine?"

"What do you like?"

"A Cabernet or something'd be good."

"Ernest, my good man!" Jake shouted, flicking his Bic again and waving it in the air. "A bottle of your best Cabernet Sauvignon, if you please."

Ernie barked a laugh and raised his middle finger in front of the TV screen.

Jake put out his lighter and pushed the draft closer to Fredo. "Maybe you'd better stick with beer."

Fredo took a pull on the draft and jerked his head toward the bar. "That guy don't exactly strike me as the sort who'll jump at the chance to change the channel at four."

"Ernie's all right," Jake said, draining his beer. It could have been colder and the glass could have been cleaner, but it was beer. He glanced at the ancient Rheingold clock behind the bar and watched the minute hand swing onto the twelve. Four o'clock. "What channel we want?"

"Eight."

"Stay put."

Jake got up and went to the bar. He waggled his empty glass at Ernie.

"Another one of these, and put on Channel eight."

Ernie nodded, refilled the glass, then pointed the remote at the screen. Cries of outrage arose from the bar and the surrounding room as the game disappeared.

"Fuck y'sall," Ernie said.

The Rheingold clock must have been slow because the show on 8 was already off and running.

"*Oprah?*" Jake said as he returned to the table. "You didn't tell me you wanted *Oprah.* We could have a riot in here."

"As long as he don't change the channel before you see the guy."

"He won't. Unless someone tops the twenty I gave him when I came in."

The guy, the guest, was a sight. A vaguely familiar apple-shaped head on a Humpty-Dumpty body. And artificial turf—a curly rug on his winesap head. Not a bad rug—you had to take two, maybe three looks to tell for sure those curls were not homegrown—but not a great one. Not Sinatra quality.

"I give up," Jake said. "Who is it?"

"That, my friend, is Whiny. Known to the rest of the country as United States senator Stanley Weingarten."

Jake refrained from telling Fredo that they weren't friends. He was thinking. A senator. They wanted him to hit a senator.

Then the guy started talking. What a voice. Like fingernails on the mother of all blackboards. When Fredo had called him Whiny, Jake had assumed it was because of his name. Listening to him now, he knew there was another reason.

And didn't he ever stop for air? Oprah had asked him one question and he was off to the races.

". . . and I know that we've got to find better, more efficient ways to fight crime, but good Lord, we don't want to turn the country into a police state."

Oprah jumped in when Whiny finally took a breath. "I understand you're against the new wiretapping bill. Don't we need to know what drug dealers and organized crime are talking about and planning?"

Weingarten's voice jumped an octave. "Of course we do! But to allow the FBI such broad powers is to practically make them a law unto themselves. Fight crime, yes, but not at the cost of free speech and privacy." He sighed dramatically. "But you know, I'm beginning to wonder if fighting the good fight is worth it."

Oprah looked startled. "I can't believe I just heard you say that. This has been Stanley Weingarten's fight for the last fourteen years!"

"I find it a little hard to believe myself," Whiny said. "But maybe that's what the country wants. Sometimes I think maybe I'm a dinosaur. Maybe I should get out of the way and let the Justice Department do anything it damn well pleases. And then later on I can shake my head sadly and say I told you so."

"Don't count on that, asshole," Fredo muttered, then turned to Jake. "Seen enough?"

Jake nodded and shouted to the bar. "Thanks, Ernie. That's all we can stand. Put the game back on."

Cheers from around the room.

"So what's the beef?" Jake said.

"Mr. C says Whiny's gotta retire from politics, if you know what I'm saying."

Mr. C was Bruno Caposa, head of the Lucanza family for the last twenty years, and Fredo's uncle. Which explained why Fredo, whose mean streak tended to overpower his intelligence, had made it to capo in Mr. C's organization.

"I gathered that. Why?"

"How come you want to know? You never wanted to know before."

True. Jake had done a number of jobs for Mr. C over the years, jobs the Big Guy had wanted done clean, with no connection to his organization. After what had happened to Gotti, Mr. C was putting even more distance between himself and the wet work. Fredo had arranged most of the jobs and Jake had never asked why. Because he'd never cared why. Usually one bad guy hired him to hit another bad guy, and the cops and DAs made outraged noises in public but behind closed doors they high-fived each other and crossed another jerk off the list.

This was different.

Jake said, "This time I do want to know why. We're not talking about some two-bit wise guy here, or even another boss. We're talking about a U.S. senator, somebody lots of people voted into office, somebody who'll turn on a world of heat when he goes down. Not just local and state heat, but federal heat—global warming, Fredo—so I want to know the story from day one."

"All right," Fredo said. "I'll nutshell it for you. Coupla years after Whiny gets elected for his first term, a bunch of hard-nosed Southerners start pushing for this crime bill. It happens regularly, but this one was real scary. It had all sorts of provisions that were going to cramp our style something fierce. I tell you, we was all sweating bullets, if you know what I'm saying. I mean, we'd already took a bad hit with this legalized gambling shit."

Jake couldn't help but smile. "Save that for the gambling commission. Don't try to run it on me."

"Okay, sure. We've got our hands in the casinos, but it ain't like the good old days. And I mean, sure, we've still got sports betting and all, but how long before they legalize that? We still got some numbers, but state lotteries have taken a big chunk out of that. I mean, we can't offer a multimillion-dollar hit. So what are we left with? Drugs and girls. And I tell you, Jake, since this AIDS shit come along, we ain't doing too good with the girls either."

"You're breaking my heart, Fredo."

"Yeah, well, it's dog-eat-dog out there, Jake. But anyway, this brand-new Senator Weingarten sends word through channels that he's looking to talk to some highly placed people, if you know what I'm saying. Things go back and forth—dat-da-dat—and eventually a very quiet meet is set up with some of the bosses. Whiny tells them he's planning this fierce opposition to any and all anticrime bills. Trouble is, with all the mailings and traveling expenses and TV airtime he'll have to buy, it's gonna be expensive, and he doesn't have the funds to wage the campaign in a manner that will guarantee its success. Would they care to contribute to the Weingarten war chest?"

Jake nodded appreciatively. Weingarten was no dummy. He didn't go in and threaten, didn't pull some dumb pay-up-or-else scam. That would have been blackmail, and that would have got him nothing but trouble. Instead he'd said, I'm going to orchestrate a major opposition to legislation that happens to be dangerous to you, and I need help to do it right. So, how would you pillars of the community care to help? The Big Boys could almost feel like public-minded citizens when they forked over.

"I bet they went for it big."

"You know it," Fredo said. "Practically fell over each other to contribute. My uncle tells me he knows how Whiny keeps getting reelected: The guy could sell matches to a guy on fire. And he would, too. Anyway, the deal is struck and Whiny does his thing, and he's beautiful, man. He gets the ACLU involved, all the free-speech groups, mass mailings around the country telling people to write their congressmen, and he goes to the telcos, who get their lobbyists to start buttonholing politicos and giving them an earful whenever they can."

Jake gave a low whistle. "The ACLU, the telephone companies, and you guys. There's an unholy trinity."

"But it worked. The combination of inside pressure and outside pressure killed the bill."

"And you've kept the good senator on retainer ever since?"

"You got it. He not only plays on our team, he tells us about other politicos who've got itchy palms, and let me tell you, there's a shitload of them down there. But Whiny takes the lion's share. Man, I'd love to get into his Swiss account. I'd retire."

"And now he's holding you up for more?"

"Let's just say, he's being very unreasonable. He wants more, we're willing to give him more, but not right now. I mean, the families are a bit fucked-up right now. Castellano went down, Gotti got sent up, the Luchese family is just barely holding together. My family's the only one around that's still in one piece. My uncle's told Whiny he'll get what he wants but he'll just have to be patient, wait till things settle down. What's Whiny do? He starts pulling this shit." Fredo jerked a thumb at the TV. "Starts talking about how *tired* he is of the fight, how maybe he should withdraw his opposition to what he's beginning to see as 'the will of the people.' The law-and-order politicos hear that and they're already making noises. The fat son of a bitch."

Right, Jake thought. Whiny bows out and the opposition loses its conductor. The Boys could be in big trouble.

"What's retiring him going to do?" Jake asked. He had an idea but wanted to hear what Fredo had to say.

"It shuts him up, for one thing. And it makes him like a . . . whatayacallit . . . one of those Christian guys they threw to the lions in the old days."

"A martyr."

"Right. Whiny the fuckin' martyr. And we blame it on some gun nut."

"Why a gun nut?"

"Why not? Everybody starts talking about stricter gun control instead of the stuff that can really hurt us. Man, I *love* gun control. Too many citizens with guns out here, know what I mean? *We* should be the only guys with the guns."

Jake nodded. Properly manipulated, a martyred Senator Weingarten could be an even more potent weapon than he'd been while alive.

Fredo leaned closer. "But he's got to go down right, know what I'm sayin'?"

Jake stiffened. "I hope you're not saying you pick the time and place, because if you are, it's no deal."

"No, listen, Jake. Whiny's speaking at a big free-speech rally in the city the end of next month. Mr. C says it's gotta be then. And he's willing to make it worth your while."

Sarge's Rule Number Two: Never let anyone else choose the time and place of a hit. Never.

"No way," Jake said.

2

SARGE (I)

His name was Herbert Nacht but he wanted to be called Sarge. Insisted on it. He didn't wear fatigues or combat boots, but one look at him and you knew he'd done time in one of the services. Heavyset, thick neck, red crew-cut hair, and bright blue eyes.

Sarge.

Jake was fourteen when social services placed him with the Nachts, his fourth foster home in as many years. The Nachts were both in their early forties, but where Sarge was big and bluff, with an easy smile, Mrs. Nacht was reserved, perhaps even distant, but never unkind. Mostly she sat around the house, smoking her unfiltered cigarettes. And coughing.

The Nachts lived in a three-bedroom riverfront ranch in Atlantic County, New Jersey. They were two of a handful of year-round residents. Most of the other homes were used in the summer only and remained dark and empty from Labor Day to Memorial Day. A quiet neighborhood.

Most of his previous foster fathers—a seemingly endless single-file parade, trailing backward through the infinity of his childhood—had barely acknowledged his existence, so it came as a shock to Jake when Sarge actually spoke to him like another human being, and even devoted some time to him.

Most of that time was spent teaching him to shoot.

Jake had only been with the Nachts a week when Sarge first took him out. When Sarge came out of his bedroom toting a rifle in a nylon traveling bag, Jake had thought they were going hunting. When Sarge handed Jake a smaller, more compact case, he was sure of it.

"Here, son. You take this one. But be careful with it. You don't want to break it."

Son . . . instantly Jake warmed at the sound of the word. All the other foster fathers had called him "boy" or "kid."

Sarge drove him out into the woods, into the two thousand square miles of sparsely populated forest known as the New Jersey Pine Barrens. They drove a long time.

"This looks like as good a place as any," Sarge said as he stopped his old army jeep.

Jake shrugged. This spot in the road looked no different than a million others they'd passed in the last hour or so.

Sarge stepped out and did a slow turn, hands on hips. "A million acres of nothing, Jake. Or almost nothing."

Jake got out on the other side and looked around. Pines everywhere—ahead, behind, crowded up close to the road they'd been traveling, leaning over them like bystanders at an accident. Not big towering pines; no majesty to these scruffy, scraggly things maybe twenty or thirty feet high with bent and twisted branches and patchy needles. They devoured the two sandy ruts that passed for a road around here as it curved off in either direction. If there were hills or valleys or lakes or streams around, Jake couldn't see them. Just the pines. Pitch pines, Sarge called them.

Jake called them creepy. The whole place gave him the creeps. Especially the silence.

"Let's head over there." Sarge led the way, carrying his rifle by the handle on the case. "Whatever you do," he said over his shoulder, "stick with me. Do not wander off."

"Why not?" Jake hid a smile. Would the Jersey Devil get him?

"You could get lost. Every year hunters enter the pines and are never seen again. And I don't mean never seen alive, I mean never seen again, period."

The creepy feeling in Jake graduated to uneasiness.

"What happens to them?"

"Who knows? Get lost, most likely. And these are experienced hunters and trackers. I tell you, son, you lose your bearings in here and you can wander for days without seeing another human being. As a matter of fact, there's areas in the Pines that human beings have never laid eyes on. As for those hunters, they probably starve to death."

Jake inched closer to Sarge as he followed him. But not too close. The more he thought about this situation, the less he liked it. Anything could happen to him out here—*anything*. And who'd know? The state agency was supposed to screen all the foster homes but sometimes they screwed up. He'd heard horror stories about kids who'd been buggered by foster fathers. Jake fingered the bulge of the pocketknife in his jeans. That wasn't going to happen to him.

He'd been pretty lucky so far, he guessed. Nobody'd beat him or groped him in all the homes he'd been in—he'd lost count of how many there'd been. As far back as he could remember he'd been in foster homes. Nobody seemed to know who his parents were and Jake had stopped caring a long time ago. At least nobody'd put him to work on a farm or in a sweatshop or the like. He didn't want trouble and he didn't cause it; he'd learned not to expect love or kindness so he didn't miss it when he didn't find it. He learned not to feel much of anything for anyone, and above all not to get attached to anyone because sooner or later—sooner, most likely, if past experience meant anything—they'd be out of his life and he'd be shunted somewhere else. So he kept to himself. All he wanted was a roof over his head, a place to sleep, and enough food to keep him going until he was sixteen and could strike out on his own and get off this foster-home merry-go-round.

Adoption? Forget it. Walking into a *Leave It to Beaver* or *Donna Reed Show* household and being taken under the wings of the Cleavers or the Stones and being given their last name and coming home to smiles and home-cooked meals and being tucked into bed at night with a kiss on the forehead—what a joke. That dream had been dead so long he barely remembered it had ever existed. Hard to believe he'd been such a little jerk to believe it might come true someday, and to hold on to it for so long despite shifts from one foster home to another. Besides, he was fourteen now. Nobody adopted eight-year-olds, let alone fourteen-year-olds.

Sarge stopped at the edge of a stream with water the color of iced tea.

"Don't let the color put you off if you get thirsty," Sarge said. "That's cedar water. You won't find anything purer."

He took Jake's case and removed a stubby telescope. He set it up on a short tripod and swiveled it around until he found what he wanted. Then he motioned Jake over.

"This here's a spotter scope. Take a look."

Jake peered through the lens and pulled back as the branch from a tree hundreds of yards upstream seemed to jump at his face.

"Whoa!"

"Yeah. That's a dandy, ain't it? Now check out the crosshairs, son. What's in them?"

Jake squinted into the scope. "A pinecone."

"Right. Now keep your eye on it."

Jake tried, but he couldn't resist keeping a wary eye on Sarge as he slipped the rifle from its traveling case, dropped into a cross-legged position, adjusted the telescopic sight on the gun, twisted the sling around his arm, and took aim.

Jake knew it was coming as he refocused on the pinecone, but still he jumped when the shot cracked the silence. Through the lens he saw the cone explode.

"Wow!" The rest of his vocabulary—except for the four-letter words that he was afraid to say around Sarge—had vanished like smoke. Only one word left. *"Wow!"*

Sarge grinned at him. "Courtesy of the United States Marine Corps. Want to see me prune the branch it was on?"

As Sarge turned back to his rifle, Jake squinted again into the scope. Another crack and the end of the branch pinwheeled away.

"That's so great!" Jake said. "Can you teach me to do that?"

Sarge's grin broadened. "I was hoping you'd say that."

The next morning, Sarge took Jake into an oversized closet, almost like a windowless room off the big bedroom, and showed him his rifle collection. He stood Jake before a glass case on the wall.

"See that baby?" he said, pointing at the rifle within. "That's a Garand M1C with a Lyman Alaskan two-point-two hunting scope. Back in 1942 the marines taught me how to shoot with that, and hit anything I could see through the scope. Not the greatest rifle in the world, but pretty damn effective, let me tell you. I did good work with that."

"You shot people?" Jake said. He'd never met anyone who'd actually killed another person. "How . . . how many did you—?"

"Never you mind about that," Sarge said. "This ain't no time for war stories."

He lifted a slim-barreled rifle with a glossy stock from the bottom of one of the wall racks, hefted it, then thrust it toward Jake.

"Here. This one's yours to use."

Jake hesitated, thinking Sarge was putting him on. But when he saw that the man wasn't kidding, he took the rifle into his hands like a priest receiving a chalice.

"A gun? For me?"

"Not a gun, Jake. Never call a rifle a gun, least not in my hearing. It's a rifle or it's a weapon, but it's never a gun. A pistol can be a gun, but never a rifle. Got that? This one's a Ruger 77 bolt-action .22 chambered for long rifles. You'll learn to shoot it, you'll learn to assemble and disassemble it blindfolded, you'll learn to clean it. And you will clean it. Every time you use it. You'll treat it as your own. You'll be responsible for it. If you aren't good to it, you're outta here. Get it?"

Jake nodded reverently as he balanced the weight of the rifle in his hands, felt the lightly oiled finish of the smooth stock, watched the light from the overhead fluorescent stretch up and down along the gleaming blue-black finish of the barrel.

This one's yours to use.

I've died and gone to heaven, he thought.

"When can I shoot it?" he asked without looking up, having eyes only for the rifle.

When Sarge didn't answer right away, Jake dragged his gaze off the Ruger and looked up. Sarge was staring at him with a faraway look, as if seeing a younger version of himself and remembering his own first rifle. Finally, he grinned.

"We start today. Slip your weapon into one of those carrying cases in the corner and we're off."

Another jaunt into the pines, but this one was shorter. Sarge stopped the jeep at the edge of a small clearing and pointed to a fallen tree.

"There's a good spot."

He pulled a blanket from behind the front seat and led Jake into the clearing, where he spread the blanket on the sandy ground.

"What's this for?" Jake said.

"To catch your brass."

"Brass?"

"Your empty shells. One of my rules is never leave your brass behind. Never."

That was the first of many rules Sarge would hand down. Jake made a point of memorizing each one.

Sarge sat him down and showed him how to load the rifle, how to wind the sling around his left arm military style to help steady the rifle in his hands, how to line up the target in the open sights—

Sarge promised him a telescopic sight when he was ready for it—and how to squeeze the trigger instead of pulling it.

For his first shots Sarge had Jake rest the stock of the rifle on the fallen trunk.

"The first thing I want you to do is get to learn how the sights work. Later on we'll work on the different firing positions and steadying your hands. But for now, just pick out a pinecone on that tree over there and take a shot."

Jake could feel his hands trembling. His sweaty palms slipped along the stock. This was the moment he'd been waiting for through all the talk, all those practice shots on an empty chamber. He was loaded up now. This one was for real. He picked out a cone, the biggest one he could find on the nearest tree, lined it up in the sights the way Sarge had told him, and pulled the trigger.

Missed.

Damn.

He tensed, waiting for Sarge to start yelling at him. But the voice at his side was unperturbed.

"What're you waiting for, son? Try again."

Jake chambered another round, aimed again, pulled the trigger again, and missed again.

Double damn.

But still no shouting from Sarge.

"You're pulling the trigger instead of squeezing it like I told you. *Squeeze* it. Squeeze it so slowly that the shot comes as much of a surprise to you as it does to me."

Jake put his cheek back against the stock, sighted on the cone, and *squeezed* the trigger as gently as he could, squeezed with such excruciating slowness that he began to think it would never fire, and then suddenly there was a crack and the pinecone spun away out of sight.

"I did it!" Jake whispered. "I got it!"

Sarge slapped him on the back. "Okay. You killed your first

pinecone. Now let's get some more. Lots more. Don't be shy. One thing we sure as hell got no shortage of out here is pinecones."

Sarge took Jake shooting every day he could, afternoons after school and early morning on weekends and during the summer. The only exceptions were rainy days and those occasions when Sarge had to go away on business. Jake didn't know what that business was; in fact, Sarge was home far, far more of the time than he was away. But still, even when he was away for only a day or two, Jake counted the hours to his return.

Shooting wasn't all he learned. On rainy days he'd have to practice breaking down and cleaning his .22. After he'd mastered that, Sarge made him learn to disassemble and reassemble every rifle in his gun room. Rainy days were also a time for making reloads. Sarge showed him how to reuse old brass, how to customize the charge in each cartridge and tailor the rounds for different uses.

And along the way, Jake became a crack shot. So good, in fact, that shooting at pinecones began to get old. And that got Jake into some trouble.

It happened when they were out in the pines at a new clearing on a chilly after-school afternoon. Jake was still braced in the sitting position, the strap twined around his left arm, his elbows resting on his knees, as Sarge took a break from picking out the cones he wanted Jake to hit. Suddenly something small and gray with a bushy tail popped into view. A squirrel. Winter was coming and it probably thought it had struck gold with all the shattered pinecones littering the ground. Jake watched it duck behind a bush, then saw it hop onto a log and start nibbling at something clutched in its paws. Without a word he swung the barrel left, quick-sighted, and popped off a shot. The squirrel tumbled off the log.

"Got him!"

"Got who?" Sarge said, looking up.

"A squirrel." Jake was fairly bursting with pride. "He was over there on that log. I just popped him."

"You shot a squirrel?"

Something in Sarge's eyes, in his voice, took the edge off Jake's exhilaration.

"Yeah. Quick-shot him. Like you've been showing me."

Sarge held out his hand. "Show me."

"What do you mean?"

"Give me the rifle and go get him. Show me this squirrel you think you killed."

Jake passed the rifle over and ran to the log.

The squirrel lay on its back on the other side. Its left hindquarter had been blown off by the .22 LR. The stump was still oozing. Blood was puddled around its limp tail. It was dead, but its bright black jelly-bean eyes stared up at him. Suddenly, Jake's pride didn't seem quite so fierce as it had a moment ago, but he'd been right. He'd hit it. He took a breath, picked the squirrel up by its blood-soaked tail, and brought it back to Sarge.

"Told you I got it," he said, holding up the prize.

"That you did," Sarge said, but he wasn't smiling. "Now tell me why you shot it."

"Well, I saw it and I wanted to see if I could get it before it ran off."

"Well, you got it all right," Sarge said. "But you do surprise me, Jake. I never took you for a squirrel eater."

"Squirrel eater? What are you talking about?"

"Out here in the woods, the only time we kill something is if we're gonna eat it."

"I'm no squirrel eater."

"You are now, son." Sarge took the dead squirrel from Jake and dropped it into one of the plastic bags he used to store their used brass. "You are now."

Despite Jake's protestations, Sarge made Jake dress the squirrel, stood over him and talked him through the gutting and skinning. And all the while those beady black eyes kept staring up at him, making him feel sick inside. Finally Sarge took over and stripped the bloody meat from the squirrel's flanks and remaining leg. He brought that in to Mrs. Nacht while Jake washed the blood off his hands and tried to scrape it from beneath his fingernails. And tried not to think about the coming meal.

For dinner there was niblet corn, green beans, mashed potatoes, and meat—steak for Sarge and Mrs. Nacht, and . . . something else for Jake. Ragged chunks of browned meat.

"I'm not eating this," he said.

"You are eating it," Sarge said. His voice had a flinty edge to it that Jake had never heard before. "You kill an animal, you eat it—that's the rule around here."

Jake stared at the plate and all he could see were those two black eyes staring at him. He glanced at Mrs. Nacht for maybe a little help but she was concentrating on her own plate, slicing her steak as a cigarette burned in the ashtray by her elbow.

"I *can't!*"

"You'll eat it or you're outta here. You're the fourth boy I've had through here in two years and the first one to show any talent, but damn it I'll kick your ass back to the state first thing tomorrow morning if you don't clean that plate."

For the first time in longer than he could remember Jake thought he might cry. But he swallowed the sob, picked up his fork, jabbed it into a piece of the meat, and shoved it into his mouth. He tried to swallow without chewing but it was too big. He had to bite into it, grind it down. It was chewy and stringy and had no particular flavor. It was just *there.* Without swallowing he shoved another piece into his mouth, then another, and another and another until all the fried squirrel flesh was packed between his jaws and he was chewing and chewing the gristle and fat and meat with his eyes closed and finally there was nothing left to do but swallow but it was so big and he wanted to gag but he didn't dare so he forced it down in one long greasy swallow.

Then he sat there breathing hard, sweating.

"There," Sarge said with a slow smile taking shape. "I knew

you could do it. Look on the bright side. It could have been a skunk."

That did it. Jake's stomach lurched and he was running from the table. The bathroom was too far so he fled through the back door and heaved up the squirrel meat over the back porch railing. It tasted worse coming up than it had going down so he kept on retching until his sides ached and his gut burned and there was nothing left to come up. As he hung there gasping, he heard Sarge come out on the porch and stand behind him.

"I hope you learned something today," Sarge said softly.

Jake said nothing, didn't even turn around.

"Shooting's fun," Sarge said. "Lots of fun. But killing's serious. That rifle gives you power—the power of life or death over any living thing in your sights. You don't take that power lightly. Any time you kill something, you have a reason for doing it. Are we clear on that, Jake?"

Jake nodded, but still did not turn around.

He heard Sarge step closer, felt a gentle hand on his shoulder.

"You got talent, Jake. You're a natural. I didn't tell you, but that was a great quick-shot kill on that squirrel. With practice and dedication, you could become one of the best shots I've ever seen. But you've gotta follow the rules. And that's a rule you must never forget: Don't kill just for the heck of it. Ever. If you can remember that, I'll work with you till we're both ready to drop. What do you say?"

Finally Jake turned and faced Sarge. He saw that the man had his hand extended.

"Deal?" Sarge said.

Jake took the hand and they shook.

"Deal," Jake croaked—the only word he could manage. He was filled with emotions he had never known before. He realized he loved this man called Sarge.

He had finally found a father.

3

BERNIE

Jake's "No way" to Fredo eventually became "Okay" to Mr. C, a man whose offers could not be lightly refused, and three weeks after the meeting in Leonardo's Jake was tooling north on the Garden State Parkway, heading for Manhattan.

He listened to the weather as he drove. A huge high-pressure system was swinging down from Canada. A clear, bright weekend with lower-than-usual humidity lay ahead. In fact, this Sunday was shaping up to be one of the ten best days of the year.

He smiled. If the weatherman was right, the day after tomorrow was going to be a beautiful day for a hit.

It had taken awhile—weeks, in fact—but Mr. C finally had come to terms with him. Jake would do the senator at a free-speech rally as requested but it was going to cost Mr. C a flat million—half up front, half after the senator was officially pronounced DOA.

Whiny wasn't the only guy with a Swiss account.

And Jake knew he was going to need his account. He wanted to be out of the country when all the heat came down. That was why he'd held out for seven figures.

Of course, plenty of the Boys would have done it cheaper—tried to do it, anyway. But they'd have screwed it up. Mob

CECIL COUNTY
PUBLIC LIBRARY
301 Newark Ave.
Elkton, MD 21921

soldiers were fine for street shootings of informants and uppity rivals and run-of-the-mill deadbeats, great for meat-hook tortures and dumping bodies in trunks or rivers, but when it came to finesse, they couldn't cut it. The Boys weren't *snipers.* And ever since Gotti went down on murder, the surviving bosses had become very touchy about that little pastime. The Feds weren't dicking around with tax evasion and extortion or racketeering charges anymore, they were devoting their investigative muscle to murders.

Nothing funny about a murder-one conviction.

Which was fine by Jake. As a result, he'd had plenty of work these past few years.

Still, while a cool million for Whiny went a long way toward convincing him he could learn to live with his misgivings about this particular hit, nothing could entirely reassure him. He was breaking one of Sarge's cardinal rules: Never let anyone—neither the client nor the target—dictate the conditions of a shoot; always choose your own time and place.

Following that rule faithfully was what had kept him in business, he was convinced. Timing the hit to this free-speech rally was like being locked into a straitjacket. Worse, Mr. C wanted it done as soon as he started speaking—probably he'd be watching and didn't want to listen to any more of Whiny than he had to.

Jake could understand why Mr. C wanted a very public killing. Not even the densest citizen could miss the tragic irony: the defender of free speech shot down while speaking, murdered by some rifle-toting gun nut as he pushed for gun control instead of speech control. To hell with the wiretaps and electronic bugging! Stop the guns! A total gun ban is the answer!

More gun-control legislation would pass in the following month than in the past decade.

Mr. C will be getting a lot for his million, Jake thought.

He took a deep breath and let it out. By Sunday afternoon at this time it would all be over; and by Sunday night he'd be six miles above the Atlantic, Heathrow bound.

But he had a lot to do before then. He'd found his perch for the hit—that was paramount. If he hadn't been able to find a good one, he'd have let the million slide, because what good was a million—even ten million—if you couldn't insure your escape? A final condition he'd agreed to was to leave the perch—a hotel room—looking like it had been rented to a gun nut. Fredo had supplied him with some Saturday night specials, an AK-47, and even a copy of *Shotgun News.* Jake had agreed to leave his own rifle as well. Of course, he'd planned to anyway. Sarge had taught him that.

Sarge, Sarge. The very act of driving north toward New York City would always make him think of Sarge. And those thoughts now made him shudder.

Instead of heading directly into the city, Jake took a quick detour to Bernie Marsh's office building in Paterson.

"Hey, Jake," Bernie said, rising behind his desk and smiling nervously as Jake stepped through his office door. "Something wrong?"

"Why should anything be wrong?"

"Because I . . . well, I didn't expect to see you again so soon, you know?" Bernie's words rattled out at top speed and his palm was moist as they shook hands. "Hey, Jake, what I mean—it's just that you made your usual stop in June and I figured I wouldn't see you again till December."

"I want to set up a little vacation time, if that's all right by you."

"Sure! Sure!" Bernie laughed. The sound had a hysterical tinge. "Is that all? Take all you want! You've got plenty coming! I mean, you're my best employee. Never misses a day, never complains, never sick, never takes vacation!" He laughed again. "I wish I had a hundred like you!"

"I should be gone for a month. Starting now. So hold my checks. I'll call you when I get back."

The tension seemed to whoosh out of Bernie as he sat down. "Sure thing, Jake. Have a great time."

Jake made sure to stop and say a few words to Bernie's secretary, Marge, on the way out. Never hurt to cement your status as a longtime employee.

Jake Nacht was indeed a longtime employee of Marsh Management, Inc. Almost fifteen years now. Since shortly after Bernie had come to him looking for a way to retire his partner, Gus Abelard.

Gus had got into nose candy in a bad way. So bad that he'd embezzled the partnership account dry and was looking for a way to trade his shares to his supplier in return for a big score of blow. Bernie had tried everything, but Gus was completely out of control. They were starting to lose clients. The partnership—then called Abelard-Marsh Enterprises—was in the real estate management business. Once people started losing confidence in your stability and reliability, you were done. They never came back. And that was beginning to happen to Abelard-Marsh because of Gus.

So Gus had to go.

Jake had followed Gus until he spotted him in the middle of a street-corner buy in downtown Paterson. Jake did him drive-by style with a Beretta that he later dumped in the Paterson River. As a public service, he also took out the two pushers with Gus. That made it look like a drug-war hit. Never much of an investigation. No witnesses. No one even heard the shots. No one in that corner of town never sees or hears nothing nohow. And Gus was listed as an innocent bystander.

Bernie paid up on time, and that should have been that, but then Jake had an idea. When he first approached Bernie with it, the guy thought it was a shakedown. But when he saw Jake was on the level, he went along.

So for the past dozen or so years, Jake had been giving Bernie thirty large a year in semiannual installments. In return, Jake Nacht was listed as an employee of Marsh Management, Inc. A night watchman, assigned solo duty to one of the abandoned warehouses or factories on the Marsh Management list of properties, receiving $26,000 in salary and another $4,000 in medical and dental benefits. The whole deal was pretty much a wash. Jake got his money back—less deductions—in salary and benefits, and Bernie actually came out ahead: he took a $30,000 deduction on his corporate taxes.

But the real dividend, the whole reason he'd set this up with Bernie, was that it made Jake Nacht a solid citizen, a blue-collar vertebra in the backbone of the nation's workforce. And should officialdom ever come snooping, Jake Nacht was on the rolls as a taxpayer with a visible and very legitimate source of income. Someday that simple fact might mean the difference between freedom and the joint. So though he resented every dime in withholding he had to send off to Trenton and Washington, Jake consoled himself by likening the taxes to disability insurance premiums—you paid them and hoped you never had to collect on the policy.

But he was leaving nothing to chance on this hit. He was buying a few extra insurance policies—just in case.

When he got to the city, Jake found a slot in the park-and-lock lot down the street and walked his suitcase into the lobby of the Belvedere Hotel.

He might have bailed out of the hit if he hadn't found a place like the Belvedere. Turned out it was the oldest hotel in the area of the rally. Old hotels were the best. The older the better, in fact. The old ones had sash windows. Cutting a hole in a plate-glass window of one of the newer hotels got a bit dicey; it created a defect in the mirrorlike facade, like a fever sore on a beautiful woman's face. Defects attracted attention.

The Belvedere had casement windows.

Perfect.

He checked in as Jake Nacht, using Jake Nacht's Visa card, with a planned departure on Sunday morning.

"I'm a light and a late sleeper," he told the woman at the

registration desk. "If possible, I'd like a quiet floor, as far from street noise as possible, and a room that doesn't get the morning sun."

She smiled. "I'll see what I can do." She tapped various combinations into her keyboard, studied her screen a minute, then nodded. "I can give you something on our top floor on the north side. That should fit the bill perfectly."

"If you say so."

He hadn't expected any problem. The Belvedere was not a first-rank hotel; more in the faded-glory class. Even the big names were half-empty on August weekends. Most of the city seemed to close up early and clear out on Friday afternoons.

The bellhop led him to room 1017. Jake tipped him two bucks—not a great tip, not a bad tip, just an ordinary, mediocre, immediately forgotten tip. As soon as he was alone, he checked the windows to make sure the sashes opened. They were stiff but he forced one up. He stuck his head outside for a look. The DEA building was out of sight—around the corner to his left and downtown from here. That was okay. This wasn't the perch.

The tenth floor looked down at the scattered strollers below. Mr. C had wanted Whiny drilled from a sixth-floor window, like JFK. Maybe he thought that would induce Oliver Stone to make a movie about the Weingarten assassination. But Jake drew the line at letting someone else choose the perch.

He studied the fire escape route map fastened to the inside of the door, locating his present room, then trailing his finger along the hall and just around the corner to the unit he *really* wanted. The two rooms were a little closer together than he liked, but not too bad. Just as long as he wasn't right next door.

He'd move into the other unit tomorrow.

But for now it was time to kick back, have a couple of drinks, maybe watch a movie on TV. Anything but sleep. Because lately, as happened every so often, he'd been dreaming about Sarge.

4

SARGE (II)

After the squirrel incident, Jake graduated to moving targets.

Moving pinecones.

Sarge would tie a string to a tree limb, attach a pinecone to the string, and set it swinging. He taught Jake to lead his target—to match the speed of the bullet against the forward movement of the target and aim ahead of it so that bullet and target arrived in the same place at the same time.

After Sarge explained the principle, Jake quickly began putting it to work.

The first cones were on a long string, swinging in wide, slow arcs. Within half a dozen tries Jake was hitting them regularly. Sarge moved him back. And back. And still Jake was knocking the hell out of those cones. So Sarge shortened the string, diminishing the arcs, increasing the speed of the cones. Jake needed a few shots to adjust; then he was knocking those to pieces as fast as Sarge could set them in motion.

"Enough!" Sarge said. "You're wearing me out." He shook his head, grinning as he punched Jake lightly on the shoulder. "You're a natural, son. What an eye. I've never seen anybody catch on that fast."

Jake soaked up the praise like a dry sponge. He could not remember ever wanting to please another person like he wanted to please Sarge.

"Just a few more?"

"Nah. You're too good for this nickel-and-dime stuff. We've got to move you up to shotguns and clay pigeons."

"All right!"

"But remember," Sarge said with a sidelong look. "I said clay pigeons. No real ones."

"Don't worry, Sarge. I'm no pigeon eater either."

As they laughed together, Jake realized that he finally knew what people meant when they said it was good to be alive.

The shotgun was a whole different story. The 12-gauge kicked and boomed and threw his aim off, but that was compensated by the fact that instead of a single bullet he was firing clusters of a dozen or more lead pellets. The skeets moved a hell of a lot faster than the pinecones too, but Jake started connecting with them soon enough once Sarge told him to continue the swing of his shotgun barrel after he'd pulled the trigger.

"Eight in a row!" Sarge said, shaking his head. "Shit, I'm not wasting no more clay on you. Next week, for your fifteenth birthday, I'm taking you out into the real world. That'll be one of your presents: We'll hunt us up some real-world targets."

"Like what?" Jake asked, flush with excitement and pride.

"Cars."

Jake spent days wondering about Sarge's remark about cars. Were they going to a junkyard and plunk away at rusted-out hulks? Sarge wouldn't say. When Jake pressed him for the fourth night in a row, Sarge gave his standard answer, but added something else:

"You'll see when the time comes. But in the meantime, I'm

going to let you stay up late tonight. I just checked the *TV Guide* and it says my favorite movie is on Channel five tonight."

"What's it called?"

"The Most Dangerous Game."

"Never heard of it," Jake said. But that didn't matter. If it was Sarge's favorite movie, how could it be bad?

"Don't worry. You'll like it. It's an oldie but a goodie."

Even if he didn't like it, just staying up late with Sarge would be fun. And it was sure better than watching all those news shows about the war in Vietnam. Whenever the war was on, Sarge got lost in the TV.

That night, after the eleven o'clock news, Mrs. Nacht heated up a container of Jiffy Pop and left Jake and Sarge to watch the movie. Sarge hadn't been kidding when he'd called it an oldie. And Jake wasn't so sure it was such a goodie. For one thing, it wasn't in color. And it was very dark and grainy.

"See that girl?" Sarge said, pointing at the screen. "That's Fay Wray, the same one King Kong went nuts over."

Jake didn't recognize her, even though he must have seen *King Kong* a dozen times. Not that it mattered. This movie was definitely weird. All about this mighty hunter type who gets people to come to his jungle island and then hunts them down. Sarge spoke only when the commercials came on, and there were plenty of those, but when the movie was playing he stared at that screen like he was hypnotized or something.

"Well?" Sarge said, switching on the lights and turning to Jake as "The End" lit on the screen. "What you think of it? Wasn't it great?"

"Yeah!" Jake said, trying his best to sound enthusiastic. "That was really neat."

"Neat ain't half of it," Sarge said, glancing back at the screen. "Greatest movie ever made. The title says it all. The most dangerous game: another man."

The weird light in Sarge's eyes gave Jake a queasy, crawly feeling inside.

The next day, Sarge picked him up after school in the jeep and took him through a woods he had never seen before. This wasn't like the pines, and yet it was. Plenty of pitch pines about, but lots more oaks and elms and maples, the chill fall air turning their leaves orange and gold and laying a crackling carpet of brown ones underfoot.

Sarge stopped at the base of a rise and led Jake and his .22 upward through the thick underbrush. Jake heard the sound of traffic faintly from the other side as they neared the top. Sarge motioned him into a crouch, and they crawled the rest of the way to the crest.

The grassy slope fell gently away before him. At its base Jake recognized the two-lane blacktop of the southbound Garden State Parkway.

Suddenly his guts were in a knot. He thought about what Sarge had said about that movie, *The Most Dangerous Game,* how his eyes had seemed to glow when he'd talked about hunting another man.

"I . . ." Jake began, and noticed his teeth were chattering. "I don't think I want to do this."

"Do what?"

"Shoot somebody."

"Shoot some—! Are you crazy, boy? Whatever—wherever did you get that loony idea?"

"Well—"

"That's the craziest thing I ever heard of!"

"Well, you said we were gonna shoot at cars."

"Right. And cars ain't people!"

"But people drive cars."

Sarge laughed. "Okay, okay. I can see where you got confused. No, we ain't gonna shoot no people. We're gonna shoot some tires—do a little mischief, that's all."

Jake allowed himself to relax . . . a little. Shoot out a tire on a moving car—that could be dangerous. That could kill somebody dead as a bullet.

"Gonna have to be patient, though," Sarge said. "Got to pick your car carefully. Can't be going too fast or they might wrap themself around a tree. Can't be traveling in a pack or they could swerve into somebody else and cause a pileup. Remember, we're not looking to hurt anybody, just pop a couple of tires."

Jake wished he were back aiming at pinecones and clay pigeons. This was scary.

"I don't know, Sarge . . ."

"Show me you can do it," Sarge said, that edge creeping into his voice. "Just show me you can do it, Jake."

But somehow the words echoed in Jake's head as "Show me you *will* do it."

"Someone like that," Sarge said, his voice lightening up as he pointed to a pickup truck rattling by. "Hit that rear tire there and you'll give that guy twenty or thirty minutes of much-needed exercise. Or better yet," he said, pointing to a Cadillac cruising past, "make a rich guy get his hands dirty."

That didn't sound so bad. More like mischief than actually shooting at anybody.

And the last thing he wanted to do was displease Sarge.

Jake wrapped the strap around his left arm, snuggled against the stock in the prone firing position Sarge had taught him, and waited.

Finally he saw the perfect prey: a Volkswagen van with a big peace symbol painted on the side.

"Oh, get this one," Sarge said. "You've gotta get this hippie."

Jake took aim on the blacktop just inside the white line along the shoulder, gave the rear tire a two-foot lead, then fired.

If the tire popped, Jake didn't hear it, but he did see it collapse into a flabby mass of rubber whirling around the hubcap. The van shimmied and pulled off onto the shoulder.

Sarge whooped and slapped him on the back.

"Got it!"

But Jake wasn't through. With sudden exhilaration surging through him like electric current, he took a bead on another rear tire coming along. This one belonged to a black Mercedes with gold trim. A big-shot car, cruising the right lane, the windows rolled up tight against the chill.

Another shot, another useless tire. The Mercedes skidded to a halt behind the van.

Sarge put a hand on his arm.

"Whoa! That's enough. Two's plenty. We're not looking to attract too much attention here."

They huddled together in the brush for a few more seconds, watching the longhaired driver of the van and the three-piece suit from the Mercedes get out of their respective rides and stare at their useless tires.

"I'll bet they'll have plenty to talk about," Sarge said as he started to slide backward. "Let's get outta here."

Jake followed him, rising to a crouch, then straightening up when they were out of sight of the parkway. As he ran down the hill toward the jeep, Jake began to laugh. He wasn't sure why. Maybe it was a release of the almost unbearable tension that had been building within him these past few days; maybe it was the thrill of being able to be a bad boy with an adult's approval; or the knowledge that he had just gotten away with something dangerous and illegal; or the feeling that he was now an outlaw of sorts; or the tighter bond he sensed he'd formed with Sarge. Maybe it was all of those things. Whatever it was, he had to laugh to show the world how wonderful he felt.

Sarge didn't drive directly home. He followed a path back into the pines. When they were well away from the parkway he tossed a brown paper bag into Jake's lap.

"This is your birthday present."

Jake pulled the bag open and reached inside. His hand shook. He couldn't remember the last time someone had given him a birthday present, if ever. No one was sure exactly when his birthday was anyway. The date had been guesstimated at the time he'd been found as a squalling infant in a trash can in Camden in mid-November of 1955.

He pulled out a rectangular wooden box and fumbled the catch open. Inside was a telescopic sight.

"For me, Sarge?"

"Yeah. It's a Redfield 3-9x variable power scope. I figure you're ready to move up to centerfire rounds and longer distances."

Jake wanted to hug him but didn't think Sarge would appreciate that, especially while he was driving.

"There's more in there," Sarge said.

Jake dug into the bottom of the bag and came up with a large, irregular object wrapped in oilcloth. He unwrapped it and found the strangest-looking pistol he'd ever seen. It was boxy, with a four-inch barrel and a wide, funny-looking grip. Jake was speechless.

"That's a collector's item, Jake," Sarge said. "A Mauser Bolo with a broomhandle grip. The real thing. Took it off a dead German officer myself back in the war."

Jake cradled the treasure in his hands as if the jostling of the jeep might break it. A question leaped into his mind and he had to ask it.

"Did you . . . kill him, Sarge?"

Sarge nodded, looking straight ahead. "Yep."

"You kill lots of Germans?"

Another nod. "Better'n two hundred I'd say. I stopped counting at around fifty. Used to notch my stock every time I bagged one, but it got ridiculous after a while. I mean, pretty soon I wasn't going to have a stock left."

"Two *hundred?*" Jake said.

"One by one. I was the best goddamn sniper the Corps ever saw. And that's no brag. That's a fact."

"You were a *sniper?*"

"You say that like it's a dirty word."

Jake wasn't sure how he felt. Somehow sniper didn't jibe with his preconceptions about Sarge's role in the war. He'd always imagined him charging up a hill in the face of deadly machine-gun fire, like Audie Murphy or John Wayne. A sniper seemed . . . sneaky.

"I . . . didn't . . . I . . ."

"It *is* a dirty word in some circles. Especially in officer circles. Officers like to stay back and send the footsloggers into the action to get chewed up by the enemy; when their side wins, they take the credit; when it loses, it was the footsloggers' fault. The sniper changes that. The sniper disrupts their plans by singling out the officers and killing them. 'That's not cricket,' they say. It disrupts the chain of command and leaves their cannon fodder directionless. And what's worse, it puts officers in danger, for Christ's sake! Nobody's supposed to shoot at *them!* I tell you, Jake, one well-trained sniper with sight access to key enemy personnel can turn a whole campaign around. I know. I've done it."

Jake had to smile as a wild thought struck him. "Did you follow your rule back then?"

"Which rule's that?" Sarge said.

"Always eat what you kill."

Sarge laughed so hard he almost drove off the road.

Jake trained through the winter with his telescopic sight on one of Sarge's Remington 700s. This was a much heavier weapon, firing enormously more powerful .308 rounds. The forestock was fitted with a bipod for stability. There was a lot to learn: choosing the right load for the distance, correcting for elevation and wind. The first day out, Sarge clamped the rifle in a barrel vise and taught him how to bore sight and zero in his scope for various distances. Yet despite the reams of information being tossed at Jake, everything Sarge said seemed to make instant sense. Whatever he heard was absorbed by his brain and disseminated to his limbs with no apparent effort on Jake's part. Almost as if he'd known it all along and Sarge was just giving him a refresher course.

By the spring Jake was able to hit anything he could quarter in the crosshairs of his scope.

"Are we ever going hunting?" Jake said one day as they were finishing up a practice shoot. He was becoming restless with all this practice. He wanted to shoot something other than pinecones. Something that *mattered.*

"Hunting for what?" Sarge turned to stare at him. The close scrutiny made Jake a little uncomfortable.

"I don't know. A deer or something. Something that moves."

Sarge smiled. "Something that tastes good?"

"Yeah. Something that tastes good and *moves.*"

"No challenge in pinecones, huh?"

"Not much."

Sarge shrugged. "All right. You want to go out hunting, we'll go. If you think lying in wait for some dumb animal with no defenses other than speed and instincts, then sighting down on it from so far away that it can't smell or hear you, and then snuffing out its life by squeezing the trigger on a superb killing instrument like this Remington is what you call a challenge, or what some people call a 'sport,' then we'll go. You just say when."

Suddenly the idea wasn't as attractive as it had been a moment ago.

"Yeah. Okay, Sarge. I'll let you know."

Sarge began making day trips and night trips during those scope-training months. First he said they were for "business" and then he began saying they were for "research." Then one afternoon Jake came out of school and found Sarge waiting at the curb in his car.

"Want to go hunting?"

"Yeah!" Jake said, and hopped in the passenger seat. "When?"

"Right now."

But they didn't drive into the pines. Instead, they took the parkway north. Jake noticed, too, that Sarge wasn't wearing hunting clothes.

"Where we going?" he asked.

"New York City."

"What are we gonna hunt there?"

"You'll see."

They switched to the turnpike and entered the city through the Holland Tunnel. Jake had been to Manhattan before on school field trips but he'd never been to Chinatown. As Sarge inched along Canal Street, Jake stared, fascinated, through the window, drinking in the alien neon ideograms on the signs, the roasted ducks—heads, feet, bills, and all—hanging in the food market windows, the Asians packed shoulder to shoulder along the narrow sidewalks. Then they turned uptown, crawled through Little Italy and other, nameless neighborhoods, turning this way and that until Sarge found a parking spot on a darkening street.

"Put these on," he said, and handed Jake a pair of black leather gloves.

"It's not that cold."

"Wear them anyway." Sarge began wriggling his hands into a pair of his own.

Jake did as he was told. The leather was thin and tight, almost like a second skin.

"Let's go," Sarge said.

He hopped out of the car and removed a large canvas duffel bag from the trunk. Jake had a thousand questions but bit them back. Sarge's face was tight, tense. Jake's instincts told him Sarge wasn't in a talking mood. They walked four or five blocks through the dusk, crossing streets and rounding corners until they came to a darkened warehouse. Sarge had a key. He unlocked a side door and Jake followed him inside, then up the seemingly endless flights of stairs to the roof.

A chill wind shuttled across the rippled roof, bringing Jake the sharp scent of tar, but he barely noticed. He stood still and gaped at the nighttime splendor of the Manhattan skyline looming over him. Lights, millions of lights, riding the flanks of steel and granite spires into the night sky.

"Over here, Jake."

Snapping out of his reverie, he scurried over to where Sarge knelt by the edge of the roof, unzipping the duffel bag.

As Jake squatted beside him, Sarge pulled handfuls of sweatsuits and socks and sneakers from the bag and dropped them on the roof. Then he gently removed an oblong object wrapped in a flower-print sheet. He stuffed the gym clothes back into the duffel, then unfolded the sheet.

A rifle lay inside, a model Jake hadn't seen before. It had a scope similar to Jake's and a bipod folded against the forestock.

Foreboding stole over Jake. "What . . . ?"

"It's an AR-10, son, with a Leatherwood-modified Redfield scope. Semiautomatic, chambered for thirty-aught-six."

"But what . . . ?"

"Somebody's gonna die tonight, Jake." He paused while that sank into Jake's numbing brain. "Y'see, I never stopped being a sniper."

Jake leaned his back against the wall and closed his eyes while Sarge unfolded the AR-10's bipod legs and positioned it near the roof ledge. His stomach knotted so fiercely he could barely draw a breath. It was a while before he could speak.

"Who?"

"A bad guy," Sarge said, sighting through his scope. "Seems he's been cheating some other bad guys—skimming their numbers take—and so the other bad guys want him dead."

"And they hired you?"

Sarge looked up from the scope. His expression was unreadable in the shadows.

"Right, son. It's what I do. Take money from one bad guy to kill another bad guy. I look on it as a public service. One less diseased rat in the trash heap. Is that a problem for you?"

"No," Jake said. "No problem."

But that wasn't completely true. In fact, that was hardly true. Jake hadn't been able to imagine having a problem with anything Sarge did. Anything. But this was so far beyond anything he'd imagined. This was going to take some getting used to. But he knew he could get used to it.

Because it was Sarge.

If Sarge said the guy he was going to kill was a bad guy who needed killing, then it had to be so.

"Good," Sarge said. "Take a look through the scope."

Jake approached the rifle hesitantly. It was angled slightly downward and pointed uptown. Sarge wasn't going to make him pull the trigger, was he? Jake figured he'd do just about anything for Sarge, but he didn't know about that.

He fitted his eye to the scope without touching any other part of the rifle. The reticle was centered on the lower pane of a narrow window on the fourth floor of an apartment building a block away, across a little park. The window was dark.

"There's no one there," Jake said.

"Not yet. But there will be. It's a bathroom."

Jake lifted his head away from the scope. "What's his name?"

"Doesn't matter," Sarge said. "It's easier to think of the target as just that: a target. It's not a person, it's just a target. This particular target has a heavy beard. Often shaves twice a day. *Always* shaves a second time if he's going out at night. And he thinks he's going out tonight. The bad guys who want him dead have invited him out to a dinner meeting at Positano's on Mulberry Street. He's not going to make it. So they'll all be sitting there, innocent as hell, waiting for their pal to show up when he gets blown away."

Jake began to shiver.

"Take a look through that scope again," Sarge said.

Jake obeyed. The bathroom was still dark.

"That window there," Sarge said, "might pose a problem. Because of the angle we're firing from, a bullet might be deflected by the glass, especially the hollow point or soft point that'll assure you of a one-shot kill."

Jake glanced up at him. "Really?" It was hard to imagine a pane of glass deflecting a bullet.

"Yeah. Really. I've seen it happen. But there's a way to take care of that."

He held out his hand. Jake saw starlight gleaming off metal objects in his gloved palm. Jake took one and held it up. It was a rifle round.

"That's a thirty-aught-six FMJ with—"

"FMJ?" Jake asked.

"Full metal jacket. The kind approved by the conventions of war. Can you imagine that? They've actually got rules for killing. But let me show you a trick." Sarge put the round aside. "That's for our first shot. We don't care if it hits our target, all we care to do with that is shatter the window."

Sarge's use of "we" and "our" did not pass unnoticed. It made Jake uneasy but it also linked him to the man, as if they were sharing something.

Sarge pulled a jackknife from his breast pocket and flicked it open. "But we're gonna fix the next two."

Jake watched closely as Sarge carved the copper off the tip of the bullet and exposed the lead beneath.

"What this does," he said, "is allow the bullet to expand once it hits the target. Then it acts like a soft point—little hole going in, big hole coming out. We used to do this in the war. Snipers on both sides did. But you had to be damn sure you didn't get caught with any in your magazine. They found these on you and you got shot on the spot—with your own ammo."

He carved the point off a second round.

"And you've got to be careful not to cut away too much of the jacket. Do that and when you fire it the lead will rip through the open end of the jacket and leave it behind in the bore. Then you're jammed good."

He loaded the two doctored rounds into the AR-10's clip, topped them with the untouched round, then inserted the clip into the underbelly of the rifle and slid the bolt back and forward.

"There. We're ready." He looked over the rim of the roof

toward the apartment building. "And it looks like our target is home."

Jake backed away as Sarge shouldered the AR-10 and nuzzled his cheek against the stock. He slipped his hands over his ears but didn't close his eyes. He watched Sarge, entranced by the man's utter concentration. He and his weapon seemed to fuse into a single being. Jake waited. And waited. And just when it seemed as if Sarge was never going to fire, he squeezed off three shots in rapid succession, maybe in the space of a second. Then he was up and grabbing Jake's shoulder.

"Time to go."

He picked up the duffel bag and guided Jake toward the roof door.

"But the rifle," Jake said. "The brass."

"This is one time we leave the brass. *And* the rifle. The sheet too. They're not traceable. There's not a weapon in the world worth enough to risk getting caught with after a hit."

They pelted down the flights or stairs but when they hit the street again, Sarge placed a restraining palm flat against his chest.

"Okay, take it easy now. As far as anyone's concerned, we're just a father and son strolling along, looking for a place to grab a bite before we head back to Jersey."

They ambled back to the car, tossed the duffel into the trunk, and took their seats. Jake began to shake uncontrollably. He wanted to laugh and he wanted to cry and he wanted to throw up. But one thought raced over and over through his mind: *We did it! . . . We did it! . . . We did it!*

And it had been so quick, so clean, so . . . *easy.*

"How're you doing, Jake?" Sarge said as the car pulled away from the curb. "You okay?"

"I don't know." Jake couldn't stop the shakes. "I'm cold. And I think I'm scared."

"That's good. I'd be worried about you if you weren't scared. Scared's a good thing to be feeling right now."

"Did you get—I mean, hit the target?"

Sarge nodded a couple of times. He seemed neither happy nor sad.

"Yeah. Twice. Big deal. He couldn't shoot back. He never knew what hit him. He was just standing there before the mirror, shaving. A goddamn sitting duck. I mean, what kind of challenge is that? Nothing to it."

Jake started to picture what that bathroom looked like right now but decided he'd better not. His stomach was already queasy.

"You did good up there, Jake. I figured you had the right stuff, but you can never be sure about a man until you get him in the field. And you did fine."

A man . . . Sarge had called him a man.

"What if I hadn't done good?"

"Then I'd have called off the hit. Made some excuse to the guys waiting at the restaurant and come back some other night. But I didn't have to. I'm proud of you."

Jake's nausea faded away.

Sarge grabbed Jake's shoulder and gave it a gentle squeeze. "As a matter of fact, first thing tomorrow I'm going to start the paperwork to adopt you. You're the son I've been looking for. That is, if it's all right with you."

All right? Of course it was all right! But Jake was unable to tell Sarge that. At least at the moment. He'd begun to cry.

5

THE PERCH

Early Sunday morning, Jake reentered the lobby of the New York Belvedere as someone else. That someone else was a sight to behold: He had a thick black mustache and longish black hair that fell over his ears and forehead; he wore a dark blue knitted watch cap, blue-blocker sunglasses, and a bulky white turtleneck sweater; he had a suitcase in one hand and a golf bag slung over his other shoulder. And despite the August heat he wore tight leather driving gloves.

"Elliot Guyer," he said, tapping a bogus American Express card on the counter at the registration desk. "Got my room ready?"

The clerk asked for the spelling of his name, then went to the computer to check the reservation file. Jake had made the Guyer reservation shortly after his own. The Guyer name wasn't his own invention; it was on the bogus plastic he'd bought off one of Fredo's boys for this job. This would be the only time he'd use it.

"Yes, Mr. Guyer," the clerk said, smiling. "We have your reservation."

"I got more than a reservation, pal," Jake said. "I got a specific room reserved. Number ten-seventeen."

"I'm sorry, sir. I don't see any—"

Jake slapped his palm on the counter. "Check it out, man!

Whenever I come to the city I stay on the top floor, and I stay on the west side because I like a little light in the afternoon, and I was told room ten-seventeen was reserved for me." He raised his voice. "And I want ten-seventeen—not ten-sixteen and not ten-eighteen—ten . . . seven . . . teen! Is that clear?"

Provided he ended up with the room, Jake didn't mind the mix-up. Gave him a chance to make a scene. By the time he was through here, everyone on the Belvedere's morning shift would remember the loudmouth with the golf bag.

"Oh, yes," said the clerk. "Here it is. Room ten-seventeen. There's a note here to hold it for you."

"Damn straight," Jake said. "Guaranteed it with my credit card last week."

"That you did, sir."

The rest of the registration process was completed without a hitch and the deskman rang for the bellhop. A rail-thin black guy appeared and picked up Jake's suitcase. But when he held his hand out for the golf bag, Jake waved him off.

"No way, man. These are Pings. Nobody touches these suckers but me."

When they got to 1017, Jake tipped the bellhop a quarter. The guy stared at the coin in his hand for a moment, then started bowing.

"A quarter! Oh, thank you, sir! *Thank* you! A whole quarter! I'll call the wife and kids right now! Wait till they hear! A whole *quarter!*"

Jake closed the door and smiled. One more person guaranteed to remember the bastard in 1017.

He went to the window and raised the sash. Two blocks downtown and across the street he saw workers putting the finishing touches on the speaker's platform.

Excellent.

He closed the curtain and rubbed his belly. He'd already had breakfast as Jake Nacht two doors up the hall in room 1021 but he was still hungry. Nerves.

Because this wasn't going to be an ordinary hit. This was going to be an assassination.

Jake had known that when he took the job, but it was reinforced in no uncertain terms when he turned on the TV and saw United States senator Stanley Weingarten's face staring back at him. He was on something called the *Face the Nation.*

Jake sat down and tried to watch the show.

It wasn't easy. Hard to believe people actually sat around on Sunday mornings and ate up this drivel. Talking heads. *Empty* talking heads. And the emptiest head of the three was the guest, Whiny Weingarten.

The target.

As Jake began unpacking his rifle from the golf bag, he forced himself to listen. The way Whiny was running off at the mouth you'd think he knew he was making his last TV appearance today. His last *live* appearance, anyway. He rattled on like he wanted to get everything said at once.

And he made every lie sound so damn sincere.

Jake worked the freshly lubed bolt back and forth. He'd almost be willing to ice this phony bastard for free.

Almost.

Another of Sarge's rules: Don't get involved. Never let yourself feel anything for the target. Like or dislike, either way could mean trouble. The problem with like was obvious—you might start thinking of your target as something more than a target. A target had to stay just that: a target. And dislike could undermine you by getting your juices flowing and tripping you off on some elaborate embellishments; instead of concentrating on getting the target dead, you try to do him in some way that leaves him humiliated as well.

But something about United States senator Whiny Weingarten made Jake want to find a way to ice him when his pants were down. Watching the fat phony sit there and ooze sincerity and exhausted idealism as he jawed about "giving up the good fight" made Jake's gorge rise.

Unable to take any more, he switched off the set and began preparing the room.

Everything was pretty much in place by the time a small crowd began to gather in front of the podium. The door to the perch room was locked and chain-bolted, with a chair angled under the inside knob, and a Do Not Disturb sign hanging on the outside. The gun-nut paraphernalia was spread out on the table. The Guyer AmEx card and the 1017 key were there too. The key to 1021 was snug in his pocket so he'd be sure to have it on him when he bailed out of here.

Room 1021 was his escape hatch.

After a hit, every instinct told you to run, to put distance—as much as possible as fast as possible—between you and the perch. If you were out in the open or even down on the street, that was a good instinct.

But not in a hotel. If the cops finger the hotel as the source of the shots, they'll be all over it in minutes. Sure, you could get lucky. They could go off in the wrong direction, leaving you to cruise down in the elevator, waltz through the lobby, have the doorman call you a cab, and be halfway home before they found the right building. But Jake didn't believe in luck. Good luck was the result of careful planning. Bad luck resulted from leaving something to chance. And the way Jake saw it, the worst thing that could happen was to make your hit, head for the exit, and find the place surrounded by cops. There you are, wandering the hotel halls without a room you can call your own. When the cops ask you your business here, what do you say? If you tell them you're a guest, they'll want to see your room key. If you say you're visiting, they'll want to know who. And when you come up empty on both . . .

You are Sylvester with Tweety feathers on your mouth—suspect number one.

But if you've got another room, registered under a separate

name, you can step out into the hall and demand to know what all the ruckus is about.

Pulling off the phony mustache, Jake flushed it down the toilet, then tossed the black wig out the window and watched it flutter down toward the street. The shades, watch cap, and Irish knit sweater he had already dropped in a corner. He hadn't bothered to change the jeans—everybody wore jeans—and of course the gloves were still on his hands; he'd drop those in the hall as soon as he left the room. And then he'd be a clean-shaven, sandy-haired man in a checkered shirt who bore no resemblance whatsoever to that bastard who'd rented 1017.

Jake stepped to the window and adjusted the focus on his scope. Beautiful morning for a hit. Damn near perfect, in fact. High, bright sun, rising behind him, just clearing the buildings to shine now directly on the podium. He'd have no trouble locking in on the target. And because of the ten-story downward path of the bullet, the elevation adjustment would be negligible.

He glanced at the flag atop a nearby federal building, one that would no doubt be flying at half-mast this time tomorrow. It hung limp on its pole. Excellent. A typical August day in New York, with no need for windage adjustment.

Jake had left the window open and the curtains drawn to within inches of each other. He kept the muzzle a good six inches back from the gap as he sighted through to the street below. He'd brought a Steyr-Manlicher SSG-PII for the job—bolt action, chambered for .308. Usually he liked a .223 but this hit was going to run a good four hundred meters. The .223 wasn't reliable enough over three hundred. The SSG-PII had a green plastic stock and a long, heavy, sightless barrel for greater muzzle velocity and accuracy. The scope was a steel-tube 6-power Kahler ZF 69 which Jake had zeroed in to one-half MOA. A beautiful weapon. A shame he'd have to leave it behind. But that was something else he'd learned from Sarge.

Jake rested the rifle's bipod on the table he'd moved up against the windowsill; the stock was rock steady against his cheek as he centered the scope's crosshairs on the mayor's nose.

Okay. The perch was ready. All he had to do now was wait for the opening remarks to run their course and for Tweety to step up to the podium.

As it always did just before a hit, Jake's thoughts veered toward his last day with Sarge.

He hated remembering that day.

6

SARGE (III)

Throughout the summer of Jake's sixteenth year, Sarge trained him in the fine points of precision fire with the AR-10 semiautomatic. He'd sit beside him with a spotter scope and spur Jake on. He was relentless, ceaselessly urging Jake to push his weapon to its limits of accuracy, and then go beyond those to find his own.

"You're almost there, Jake," he'd say. "I want you down to one MOA. I know you can do it."

Jake would nod and keep firing. One MOA—one minute of action—came down to shooting a one-inch group at one hundred yards. Jake would have thought such a feat impossible if he hadn't seen Sarge do it again and again.

So Jake kept after it. If Sarge thought he could do it, then maybe he could. What he didn't understand was the vague sense of urgency he was picking up from Sarge. Nothing he could pin down, but he couldn't escape the feeling that Sarge was training him for a purpose. And he didn't feel he could ask. Sarge would let him in on things in his own good time.

Despite all the practice, Jake never tired of shooting. In fact, when Sarge wasn't pushing his skills with the rifle, Jake was out on his own, practicing with the Mauser Sarge had given him for his last birthday. He loved that pistol, loved the look and feel of it, and loved the fact that it was a gift from Sarge. He took it with him whenever they journeyed into the pines.

But throughout the summer it was not his progress toward Sarge's elusive 1 MOA that haunted him, but the slow progress of the adoption proceedings. The interviews, the home inspections, the physical exams—they never seemed to end. Jake had never imagined that anything so intangible could become so important. He couldn't remember wanting anything so much in his life.

Without warning, two days after Labor Day, the papers arrived in the mail. The adoption had gone through. Jake was no longer an orphan. It was now official: He was Jake Nacht.

Sarge took Jake and Mrs. Nacht—it would be a long time before he'd be able to call her Mom, if ever—into Philly for dinner at Pier 5. Sarge drank too much and Mrs. Nacht had to drive home. She wasn't too happy about it. She didn't seem too happy about anything, including the adoption, but she was hard to read. Not that it made a bit of difference how she felt. He was Sarge's son now. That was all that mattered. He didn't care who his mother was.

Two weeks later, Jake shot his first 1 MOA.

Sarge seemed happier than when the adoption papers had come in.

"Forget about school today," Sarge said at breakfast on the morning of Jake's sixteenth birthday. He was dressed in camouflage fatigues. This was the first time Jake had seen him in anything even vaguely military. "We're hitting the barrens."

"More practice?" Jake tried to sound up but he'd been hoping for something else.

"You kidding? On your birthday? Not a chance. Bring your Ruger and scope, and bring anything else that suits you, and we'll do some traveling."

That old .22? Jake had been working out with the AR-10 the past half year.

"What're we doing, Sarge?"

Sarge winked. "I'll tell you when we get there." As Jake started to turn, Sarge tossed him a package. "And put these on."

Jake tore open the package. It contained a set of camouflage fatigues, just like Sarge's.

The air was cool, the sun was high and bright in a crystalline sky, and Sarge had taken him deeper into the barrens than he'd ever been. He stopped the jeep in the middle of nowhere—*truly* the middle of nowhere—and fixed Jake with an icy stare.

"All right, Jake Nacht. Time for you to prove yourself."

"Prove?" What was Sarge getting at?

"Time to prove you're worthy of the name."

"I don't get it, Sarge."

"I gave you my name, son. You're Jake Nacht. Now you've got to prove you deserve to carry it."

"How?"

"By killing me."

A chill stole over Jake. "What are you talking about, Sarge?"

"Do I have to spell it out for you?" Sarge said. He seemed to be getting annoyed. "I've taught you everything I know. Now it's time to lay it on the line and prove what kind of student you've been. You and me, out here, to the death."

"You're kidding."

Sarge turned on him, teeth clenched, face reddening. "No, I ain't kidding, buddy boy. This is the real thing. *The Most Dangerous Game* in real life. I've been waiting a long time for you, Jake. You're the best I've seen since the war. You've come further in two years than most people can come in a lifetime. When you hit that one MOA I knew you were ready for me. So now it's time. The only thing against you is you ain't blooded. So I'm gonna be fair. I'm gonna take your puny little Ruger .22 LR and let you have the AR-10. It's semiautomatic, it's thirty-aught-six. That gives you the edge in speed and power. But I'm still gonna get you."

Jake was speechless. What was Sarge talking about?

"Awww," Sarge said. "Don't look so surprised and mystified. Why do you think I spent all that time with you? Because I wanted a son? Shit, no! I wanted a target—one who could shoot back. I'm sick of all these sitting ducks. I'd be back in the war now if they'd take me, but they won't. So I have to settle for the next best thing. I've spent two years training you, Jake. Now it's time for payback."

"You've got to be kidding!"

"Kidding? You think I'm fucking *kidding*?" He grabbed the Ruger .22 and pulled a box of shells from his vest pocket. He opened the box and tossed one of the bullets to Jake. "Here's what I'll be shooting at you."

Jake caught the bullet and stared at it: a .22 long rifle. This couldn't be real. It was all a dream, a nightmare. Had to be.

"Sarge . . . ?"

But Sarge was pulling another box of shells from another pocket and tossing the whole thing to Jake.

"And this is what you'll be shooting at me."

A box of 180-grain .30-06 Federal Hi-Shok soft points. These were heavy, killer rounds.

"You get the big, semiauto centerfire, I get the bolt-action rimfire. That gives you one hell of an advantage."

"Advantage? I don't want an advantage, Sarge."

"Well, you're gonna get one, and believe me you're gonna need it."

"What did I do, Sarge?" Jake heard his voice begin to quaver. He tried to steady it but he couldn't. This was tearing him apart. "Did I do something wrong? Just tell me and I'll undo it. I'll make it up to you."

"What'd you do?" Sarge shoved a round into the chamber of

the Ruger and rammed the bolt home. "You became a great shot. You became the most dangerous game. If you hadn't, this wouldn't be happening."

The jeep seemed to be shrinking around them, squeezing out all the air, even though the windows were open.

"But you adopted me. Why? Just to kill me?"

"Nah. I did that because the social workers sort of forget about a kid after he's adopted. And I did it for cover, just in case someone does come around asking about you. Imagine our dismay: Me and the Missus go ahead and adopt you, and how do you repay us? By running off and disappearing as soon as you're sixteen. What an ingrate."

Jake fought back tears. "I can't believe this."

"Believe it, kid." Sarge pointed the rifle at him. "Now get out."

"No. I won't do this."

Sarge fired the rifle and Jake recoiled, startled by the blast, by the heat of the muzzle flash so close, by the tug of the bullet ripping through a fold of his shirt a hairbreadth from his skin. He toppled out of the jeep, scattering the .30-06 shells around him. Sarge leaned across the passenger seat and slid the cased AR-10 out the door. It landed on Jake.

"You've got a twenty-shot magazine, Jake. I suggest you load it to capacity."

Jake scrambled to his feet, leaving the rifle on the ground. His mind raced. He had to find a way out of this, a way to snap Sarge back to his senses.

"Sarge, please. You're breaking one of your own rules."

Sarge stared at him. "Yeah? What?"

"You said, Anytime you kill something, you should have a good reason for doing it. I can't kill you, Sarge. I don't have any reason."

"Yes, you do," Sarge said. His eyes sparked fire as he glared at Jake. "Because it's the only way you're gonna see tomorrow. Now, I'm gonna drive a few miles back east, far enough so's it'll take me about an hour to walk back here. You be ready for me."

"I won't. I can't."

"You'd better. I come back and find you standing here where I left you, I'll pick you off like a pinecone. Got that? So do yourself a favor: Be ready for me. And shoot to kill. That's what I'll be doing."

He threw the jeep into gear, U-turned in a spray of sand, and roared out of sight.

Jake didn't know how long he stood there in the sandy clearing, sobbing, waiting for Sarge to come back and tell him it was all a joke. But there was nothing funny about any of this.

Maybe it was a test.

For a while he'd been convinced it was a test. Like God and Abraham. One of his foster mothers had been a real Bible thumper, making him read passages aloud every night before bed. He remembered the story of God telling Abraham he had to sacrifice his son Isaac. He also remembered Abraham's reply in the Dylan song—*You must be puttin' me on!*

That's gotta be it, Sarge, Jake thought. You're putting me on, aren't you. Like God and Abraham. And you want to play God so you can step in at the last minute and say you were only testing me.

Another sob racked his chest. Sarge was already Jake's God. He didn't have to test him.

But deep inside Jake knew damn well this wasn't a test. Sarge hadn't been kidding. There'd been a killer gleam in his eye as he'd looked at Jake from the jeep. He intended to hunt Jake down today. Jake had to face that hideous truth. And as he did, his grief gave way to another emotion.

He was still terrified, but now he was angry as well.

The last two years had been a lie. Nothing but a lousy, rotten, goddamn stinking lie. And he'd fallen for it.

Jake's rage swelled. He began pacing back and forth in the clearing, clenching and unclenching his fists. What a jerk he'd been.

What an idiot. The rotten bastard had played him like Santana played guitar.

Jake screamed wordlessly at the surrounding trees. He found a dead branch and began beating it against the ground and smashing it across the trunks of the pines until he'd reduced it to kindling, then found another and beat that until it shattered, all the while screaming at the top of his lungs. He kept it up until he was hoarse and gasping for breath.

He wanted to die.

But he wanted to kill Sarge first.

That bastard . . . Sarge wanted to have his own little most dangerous fucking game. All right, Jake would give him one.

But where?

The worst place would be right here where Sarge had left him. Sarge probably expected one of two things: Either Jake would wait for him here, or start running west, away from him, hoping Sarge would never catch up.

Well, Jake had learned a few things from Sarge, and one of them was never do the expected. He was going to heed that lesson.

Jake picked up the AR-10 and began loading the Hi-Shoks into the magazine. When it was full, he checked the Mauser and chambered a bullet. Then he shoved it back into his shirt and began trotting east. Toward the sun.

Toward Sarge.

A mile or so along the path he found another clearing, one with a yellowing maple tree at its western end. The leaves were turning but they hadn't fallen yet. The spindly pines were worthless as perches—their sparse needles provided no cover even if you were lucky enough to find one sturdy enough to support you without swaying like a drunk on a high wire. But the maple was perfect.

He climbed the trunk, found himself a saddlelike perch, and settled into it. He braced the AR-10 on a branch and sighted through the scope. Sarge would be coming down the rutted path that wound into the clearing. That was when Jake would take him. *Blam!* A single .30-06 into the eye. The Hi-Shok would take off the back of his head.

Serve the bastard right . . .

Jake began to tremble. He didn't know if he could do this. He knew Sarge could. No problem for Sarge. But Jake . . . to quarter Sarge in his sights and pull the trigger . . . he didn't know . . . didn't know . . .

As he lifted his head and leaned back from the rifle he heard a crack. He jumped and almost fell as a bullet tore through the leaves and branches to his left and whizzed past his face.

Sarge!

Jake lurched forward and jammed his eye to the scope of his rifle. He switched it to low power to get the widest field and scanned the area around the clearing to his left.

Where was he?

Sarge had followed his own rule and done the unexpected. He hadn't followed the path back. He must have come through the brush. But how had he spotted Jake up in this maple? The leaves were thick and Jake was wearing camouflage. Was Sarge that good?

Despite the cool breeze flowing around him, Jake was sweating. Even amid the encircling tangle of leaves and branches, he felt exposed. Naked. And blind. He couldn't see a damn thing moving out there, with or without the scope.

In desperation, he fired half a dozen rounds into the brush around the clearing, then crouched on his branch, watching, waiting for the echoes of the shots to clear from his ears.

Nothing. The birds that hadn't already flown off were silent. Even the insects were silent. Was it possible? Could he have got Sarge with a lucky shot?

Just then there was another crack and splinters of bark exploded from the trunk next to his face. Jake recoiled and lost his grip on the AR-10. As it slipped from his fingers he grabbed for it and missed. The move overbalanced him. His weight off center, he reached for a nearby branch to steady himself but it snapped in his hand and then with a terrified yelp he was falling from his perch, tumbling ass first, the small, leafy branches slapping his face, the larger ones catching his clothes and ripping his shirt as he twisted and turned, grabbing for anything that would hold his weight. A branch as thick as his thigh caught him across the back. He heard ribs crack and the world went gray as white-hot bolts of pain shot through his chest. He slipped off that branch and tumbled the rest of the way to the ground, landing next to the AR-10. The impact knocked the wind out of him and sent another shock wave of pain through his chest. Gasping for breath, he rolled to a sitting position, picked up the rifle, and emptied the magazine into the perimeter of the clearing. When the hammer fell on an empty chamber, he reached into his pocket for the box of shells but stopped before his fingers touched it.

Sarge was walking toward him from the edge of the clearing. Eyes bright, red hair burning like fire in the sunlight, mouth a tight line, he looked like death.

"I'm really disappointed in you, Jake," he said in a low voice. "You forgot everything I told you."

"Sarge—," Jake began, and had to stop. Every breath was a knife wound.

"What kind of wild shooting was that? And this tree—it's the most obvious spot in the area to set up a perch. Hell, I was sitting in the brush back there watching you climb it. Do the *unexpected,* damnit! Don't you listen? I spent two whole years training you so's you could give me some kind of fight and what do you do? You screw up!" He bared his teeth and thrust the butt end of the Ruger at Jake's face. "Christ, I'm so mad at you right now I've a mind to cave your skull in with the wrong end of this."

Jake could tell he meant every word of it. He was nothing to Sarge—nothing more than a homemade target who'd shoot back. And now he was going to kill his homemade target.

Jake couldn't repress a sob, and the sob sent another stab of pain through the left side his chest. He rolled on his side and reached under his shirt to splint the painful area. His hand brushed the broomhandle stock of the Mauser Sarge had given him. He clutched it.

"You make me sick, crybaby," Sarge said. "I shouldn't even waste a round on you. Should leave you out here to starve, though I wouldn't even do that to a dog." He retracted the bolt on the Ruger and chambered a fresh round. "But there's that one chance in a million someone might come along and find you. And then you'd be spilling your guts about me. So I guess it's good-bye, Jake. Don't worry. I'll make it quick. I ain't no sadist."

He began to raise the rifle.

He's really going to do it!

Jake fired the Mauser through his shirt. The first shot missed. Shock was just beginning to register in Sarge's eyes as Jake pulled the trigger again. The second shot caught Sarge in the right side of his chest and he jerked right; the third caught him in the left shoulder and that jerked him back square with Jake who pulled the pistol free and put the fourth, fifth, and sixth rounds into the center of Sarge's chest, each one driving Sarge back with outflung arms, the rifle dangling by its sling from his left hand. He sat down heavily on the sand and stared dumbly at Jake.

"You bastard!" Jake's lungs allowed him only a whisper. "You filthy, lying *bastard!*"

He put the seventh round into the middle of Sarge's face, snapping his head back into a halo of red and laying him out full length on the sand. Jake struggled to his feet and staggered the two steps that took him to Sarge's side. He stood over him and pumped the last three rounds into Sarge's head, and then the magazine was empty but he kept pulling the trigger, sobbing, crying, cursing.

And then he turned and found the maple trunk and leaned against it and cried for the last time in his life. Sarge was dead. And so was a part of Jake.

7

THE HIT

Jake nuzzled against the cool green plastic of the SSG's stock and fitted his eye to the rear of the scope. Ten stories below and two blocks downtown, at street level, the mayor's distinguished gray head floated into the field. Jake read the mayor's lips as they finished his introductory remarks and announced the ceremony's principal speaker, United States senator Stanley Weingarten. The mayor's smiling face backed out of the field and the target's winesap head bobbed in to replace it. Whiny's face was shiny with sweat; it gleamed so brightly in the sun Jake considered fitting a UV filter on the scope. Whiny's artificial turf was looking especially artificial today, what with the heat and humidity curling the natural hair around his ears and neckline but leaving the toupee stiff and straight.

"As soon as he starts talking—get him with the first sentence." That's what Fredo had said his uncle wanted. Okay. For a million, that's what he got.

Jake settled more snugly against the rifle. No sense in drawing this out. No sense in making those poor folks down there suffer in the heat listening to fatso any longer than necessary. He quartered Whiny's head in the crosshairs, fixing the zero point on his right temple.

Outside, on the street directly below, a truck backfired loudly.

Jake allowed himself a smile. Thank you, truck. Do that again. No one'll have the faintest idea where the shot came from.

He took a full breath, let it out, then began the trigger squeeze . . .

. . . slowly . . . slowly . . . any second now . . .

Something slammed against the room door with terrific force. Jake started. The rifle fired. Before he could check to see if he'd hit the target, a voice began shouting from the far side of the door.

"Police! Open up! We know you're in there! Open this door or we'll break it down!"

Again something slammed against the door. Jake didn't hesitate. He thrust his head out the window and looked around. The window was set back with a sill of twelve-inch granite block. A ledge, slimmer maybe by half, ran along the flank of the building. With mad pounding and muffled shouts reverberating through the room behind him, Jake climbed out on the sill and eased himself onto the ledge to the right. He faced the wall—*don't look down!*—and inched along toward his other room. *Just two windows and around the corner, you can make it.*

What the hell happened?

Cops. Someone had tipped them off. That was the only explanation. Who? How? Why?

The questions pursued him along the ledge to the end of the wall. He blocked them out as he approached the corner. Getting around the right-angle bend was going to be hairy. But he couldn't slow. As soon as they broke into his room and found it empty, they'd be at the window, looking for him. If he got around the corner . . . and if no one in the neighboring room spotted him going past their window . . .

If, if, if . . . a lot of ifs.

Jake snaked his left arm around the corner, then his left foot, then began to shuffle the rest of himself around. He had a bad moment at the halfway mark when the corner of the building was bisecting him and his weight was centered somewhere over the sidewalk. A gust of wind came out of nowhere and nudged him away from the wall. He almost shouted in fear, but gritted his teeth, flattened his cheek and palms against the granite, and kept moving.

When he made it to the north side of the building, he had an insane urge to take a breather. Why not? a deranged part of his mind seemed to say. You're out of sight of room 1017, and out of sight of the rally area as well. You deserve a break.

Like hell, Jake thought. He kept moving, holding his breath as he passed 1019's window. But the room looked empty. He shuffled on toward 1021. As he reached it he prayed he hadn't relocked the window after looking out last night. He didn't think he had, but he couldn't remember for sure. He almost laughed when the sash slid up. He dove through the opening and lay gasping and shaking on the floor of Jake Nacht's room.

Now he could take a break, but only for a few seconds. Only long enough to compose himself.

As he lay there on the carpet he wondered if he'd made the hit. He'd never missed before, but he hadn't seen Whiny go down. He had a lingering impression of furious, chaotic movement around the podium after the shot, so maybe he'd been on target. But had it been a kill? Damn! If those bastards had hit the door a second later there'd be no question about it.

He sat up, stripped off the black driving gloves, and tossed them out the window. Then he slammed the window and peered out at the surrounding buildings. Most of them were offices, dead and empty—this section of the city was a high-rise ghost town on a Sunday morning. Had anybody seen him? Probably not. It had seemed like a lifetime out there but he'd only been on the wall a little more than a minute. And since when did New Yorkers look out their windows? What was there to see besides other buildings?

Yet it was still possible someone had caught his human fly routine.

Jake shrugged. If so, there was nothing he could do about it now. He'd have to proceed under the assumption that no one had.

He turned and stepped to 1021's door. He didn't have to press his ear against it to hear all the commotion out in the hall.

Okay, he thought, straightening his shirt and brushing off his jeans. Time to play the outraged hotel guest. He unlatched the chain, opened the door, and stepped into the hall.

Three uniformed cops in bulletproof vests, pistols and shotguns at the ready, stood outside 1017. Jake gathered from the excited, angry voices echoing through the open door that there were more within. As he watched, a fiftyish guy in a blue blazer and gray slacks stormed out of the room waving a pistol. A detective's shield flapped from the breast pocket of the blazer. His face was lined and tan with a grim, jutting jaw. His full head of silver hair sported a fifty-dollar cut. He looked like an aging yuppie bulldog.

"Son of a *bitch!*" said the blazer. "Where'd he fucking *go?*"

"Maybe he wasn't even in there," said a uniformed sergeant following him.

"Gimme a fucking break, will you, Harry? You saw the way that door was barricaded. He was in there. He went out the window. And unless he parachuted, he's still in the building. Seal the place. I don't want anyone leaving this hotel until they've been checked by me. And I want every goddamn room searched, one by one, starting at the top floor and moving down to the basement."

Jake figured now was as good a time as any to deliver his line. He put on his best irate expression.

"What the hell's going on out here?"

The sergeant named Harry turned to him. "Police business, sir. Please get back in your room."

"Can't you hold it down?" Jake said.

The guy in the blazer spun on Jake, eyes narrowed, lips twisted in a snarl, looking like he was going to chew him out. Instead he froze, stared wide-eyed for a second, then raised his pistol.

"That's him!"

He fired.

Jake was already ducking back into the room. He heard the shot, felt an impact like a Louisville Slugger against the back of his head and neck, and that was it. Everything went away—the cops, the hotel . . . everything.

8

DEAD MEAT

Jake remembered a few fade-ins and fade-outs, light coming and going, and voices, lots of voices, but this was the first time he actually got his eyes open and focused. He was looking at a white ceiling. In pretty good shape as ceilings go; only a few cracks.

His head throbbed like the aftermath of a two-bottle bender. His tongue tasted like someone had mixed a yard of cement on it . . . two days ago.

He tried to turn his head to see where he was but couldn't. His neck was fixed in some sort of brace. He could feel it pressing against his chin and jaw. He explored his surroundings with eyes only.

He was in a bed. With side rails. A plastic bag of clear fluid was suspended on a pole to his right, a clear plastic tube running down toward—

A hospital. He was in a hospital bed. Why?

Then he remembered.

That's him!

The detective in the blazer.

That's him!

Recognizing him.

That's him!

Pointing the pistol.

That's him!

Firing.

No question about it. The guy had recognized him. He had known what Jake looked like. He hadn't been in 1017 looking for Elliot Guyer. He'd been looking for Jake Nacht.

How the hell was that possible? Only Mr. C and Fredo had known he'd be there. They'd hired him to kill Whiny. Why would they tip off the heat to stop him? Made no sense.

Had to be someone else. Who, damnit?

A voice . . . coming from his left. Out of the corner of his eye he could see someone standing near the head of the bed. Wearing a blue blazer. The silver-haired plainclothes detective bastard who shot him. He was on the phone, talking low. . . .

". . . Nah. He's gonna make it. . . . Yeah, he'll be able to talk. Won't be able to do much else, but he'll be able to do that. Whether he will talk, I can't say. You know him better'n I do. . . . Uh-uh. No can do. I've got him under guard here. You want that, you send one of your boys. If they can do it, fine. But I can't. No way."

Jake heard a door open beyond the blue blazer. The detective mumbled, "Gotta go," and hung up.

Jake closed his eyes.

"Detective Danziger," said a new voice, male, soft, assured. "Would you mind waiting outside while I examine Mr. Nacht?"

"I don't know, Doc—"

"He's not going anywhere, I assure you."

"Yeah, but if he wakes up and starts talking, I want to hear what he says."

"If he wakes up, you'll be the first to know."

"Okay. I'll be right outside the door."

Jake's thoughts ranged wildly in all directions behind his eyelids as the doctor puttered around the bed. Obviously, this cop Danziger was bent, and just as obviously somebody was worried about Jake spilling what he knew about the Weingarten hit. And that somebody was looking for a way to shut him up for good.

Jake had to get out of here. He opened his eyes. A guy in a white coat with pale skin and thin, receding hair was standing at the end of the bed with Jake's foot in his hand, rubbing something along the sole. An icy wave of shock and alarm rolled through him.

"How come I can't feel that?" Jake said.

The doctor dropped Jake's foot and stared at him. Then he smiled.

"Ah, Mr. Nacht. I see we're awake."

"Damn right, we're awake. And how come I didn't know you were doing that?" Jake tried to raise a hand but nothing happened. He tried to figure out *where* his hands were and realized he couldn't even be sure he *had* hands. "How come I can't feel anything?"

Panic nibbled at the corners of his brain.

"Now, now, Mr. Nacht. Be calm. I'm Dr. Graham, attending neurosurgeon here. You were shot in the neck. I removed the bullet fragments, repaired the soft tissues, and closed you up. But the bullet caused a high cervical fracture. At the moment, you are paralyzed."

Jake pushed back the panic and grasped at what looked like a straw.

"At the moment?"

"Yes. Trauma of that sort causes edema—swelling—of the spinal cord, and that causes paralysis. If the cord is intact, you will regain your sensory and motor function when the swelling subsides. If not . . ."

"You mean you don't know?"

"We're waiting for the results of the MR scan of your neck. We'll know the exact extent of the damage then. But either way, you've got other things to worry about."

"Great. Like what?"

"Like the attempted murder of Senator Weingarten."

Attempted murder? That meant he'd missed. Damn it to hell! What else could go wrong?

"Who's Senator Weingarten?" Jake said.

Dr. Graham gave him a startled look, then stepped out of Jake's field of vision and opened the door.

Jake's mind revved into high. He was trapped here now and even a best-case scenario said it was going to be a while before he walked out. So he had to stay alive until then. The only way he could assure that was to deny everything. He was Jake Nacht, security guard from Jersey, here in the city to maybe see a play and hang out. He'd barely heard of this Senator Weingarten and hadn't a reason in the world to want him dead. He was an innocent bystander, shot by some trigger-happy New York cop.

That could work, yes. He had a lily-white past and was one of Atlantic County, New Jersey's quietest, most law-abiding, taxpaying homeowners.

Sarge's home.

Suddenly, in the midst of his fear, Jake saw Sarge, the image battering its way into his mind: Blood sprouting on Sarge's chest and face, and he'd never let himself wonder what the bullets had felt like going in, but now he knew. For an instant, Jake was Sarge, falling back as the slugs pierced him like hot pokers. Then he was above, looking down at Sarge's still, bloody form. Jake tried to wrench free of the memory, but it clung, smothering everything else, filling the hospital room with the cold light of another day.

He'd left Sarge where he fell, staggering back along the path until he found the jeep. He had nowhere else to go so he drove back to the house. Mrs. Nacht was sitting in her usual chair by the window when he stumbled into the house.

"Is he coming back?" she'd said.

Jake could only shake his head.

She'd nodded grimly, then lit another cigarette.

She never offered to treat Jake's wounds or take him to a doctor, but she did keep on cooking meals and keeping house. After three days she reported Sarge missing. Told the state police he went out hunting and never came back. She never mentioned that Jake had been with him. And she never mentioned Sarge again after that.

As soon as Jake had been well enough, he left, found a job in the GM plant up in Edison. A few years later he got a registered letter informing him that Mrs. Nacht had died—of lung cancer, it turned out—and since Herbert Nacht had never been found, the Nacht house was Jake's.

At first he'd wanted nothing to do with the place or anything else connected with Sarge, but then he decided, Why not? It was a nice piece of property and it guaranteed him the last laugh on Sarge.

Shortly after he moved in, a guy came looking for Sarge. Had a job for him; hadn't been able to contact Sarge through the usual channels so he'd come looking. Jake gave it about two seconds' thought—his couple of years on the GM line had seemed like a lifetime—and said he was Sarge's son and he'd taken over the business. The guy had said nothing doing until Jake took him into the pines and gave him a little demonstration.

The guy gave Jake his first contract. The first of many.

But unlike Sarge, Jake had never married. No Mrs. Nacht II. Just periodic trips to AC and a night or a weekend with a pro named Caitlin, or whomever he happened to pick up—

Jake broke free of the memories as he realized why his mind had been able to hurl him back into the past at a moment like this: The house, Sarge's *house*. The cops would search it from top to bottom for evidence against him. Would they find anything? For a moment, Jake's mind spun with fear, and then he got control again. One of the first changes he'd made in the Nacht place was to get rid of Sarge's gun room. He'd buried his arsenal deep in the pines where no one would ever find it. So there were no weapons in the house except the S&W Chief Special he supposedly wore to work as a security guard. The police would expect to find that.

Otherwise, the place was clean as a convent.

To his left, Jake heard the doctor say, "He's awake, Detective."

Danziger hove into view. He opened his mouth to speak but Jake beat him to it.

"You're the man who shot me! Dr. Graham, this man tried to kill me! Call the police!"

"He *is* the police," Dr. Graham said. "This is Detective Danziger, NYPD."

"I don't want him here. He—"

"You've got no say in the matter, Nacht." Danziger pointed a finger in Jake's face. "You're under—"

"He's already tried to kill me once!" Jake said, pushing his voice up an octave. The effort made his head throb harder. "He shot me for no reason at all! Now he's going to try to finish the job!"

Danziger's face reddened. "Knock that off!"

Jake started screaming. "Help! Murder! Help! He's going to kill me! Help!"

His headache was blazing now, but Jake kept up the volume as Dr. Graham began pulling Danziger toward the door.

"I'm going to have to ask you to leave, Detective. You're upsetting my patient."

"Bullshit!" Danziger said. "He's—"

"*Please,* Detective. His condition is very critical at this point and your presence is having a detrimental effect. You've already shot and crippled him. What *else* do you want to do to him?"

Danziger growled, shot Jake one last glare, then stormed out. Jake quieted when he heard the door slam.

"Is he gone?" he asked fearfully.

"Yes. Yes, he's gone," Dr. Graham said, stepping to the bedside. "But I'm sure he'll be back." He glanced over his shoulder, then back at Jake. "You just made a very serious accusation."

Jake knew this would be the first of many tellings of this tale. He kept it neat.

"It's true. You've got to believe me, Doctor. I don't understand it. I stepped out of my hotel room because of all the noise in the hall. I saw all these policemen crowded around the room two doors down. I asked what the racket was about and that man just . . .

shot me. I don't understand it." He blinked a couple of times, wishing he could squeeze out a tear. "I just don't understand it."

Doubt and belief warred on Dr. Graham's open face. He patted Jake's shoulder—a shoulder that didn't exist as far as Jake was concerned.

"I'll be looking into this, you can be sure," he said. "In the meantime, don't worry. We'll do everything we can for you. Everything."

"I'm sure of that," Jake said. "Just don't let that killer near me."

Jake was left alone for a while. Nurses popped in and out frequently, gazed at him with wary but sympathetic eyes as they gave him sips of water and did whatever it is nurses do, then left him to himself.

Which was good. Because he had a lot of thinking to do.

He figured the best way to stay alive was to stick to the story he'd told Dr. Graham: I'm an innocent bystander, totally out of the loop, who fell victim to a trigger-happy cop.

That would send a not-to-worry message to the Boys confirming what they probably knew already: that Jake Nacht was a stand-up guy who wasn't going to point the finger anywhere but at the cops.

But that didn't get him any closer to figuring out who'd saved Whiny's ass. And why.

He'd have to start looking into that when he got out of here. He'd find out who sooner or later, and then he'd find out why. And then he'd see some heads roll. Big-time.

Dr. Graham came in, looking like the Grim Reaper.

"I don't like that look on your face, Doc."

"We have the MR report, Mr. Nacht. I'm afraid the news isn't good."

Jake's mouth went dry. "Don't drag it out."

"Very well." Dr. Graham swallowed. "A fragment of the bullet sliced through your spinal cord, causing a ninety percent severance."

"What's that mean?" A sick, cold dread wormed through Jake. He could guess the answer but he had to hear it from the doc.

"It means you're never going to walk or use your arms again, Mr. Nacht."

The doc went on talking, something about all the wonderful things they were doing for quadriplegics these days, about eventually being able, after lots of rehab, to move a few of his fingers, maybe enough to operate a computer keyboard. But the words receded, drowned out by the roaring in Jake's ears as he looked into the future and saw a guy who couldn't feed himself, couldn't roll over by himself, couldn't wipe his own butt . . . an endless future . . . and the man had Jake's face.

Jake bit back a scream.

The man in that nightmare future couldn't even kill himself.

The next morning a nurse leaned over him and said, "Your attorney's here. Do you want to see him?"

Jake surfaced slowly from the swamp of depression, forcing himself to replay the words, then focus on them. Attorney? He didn't have an attorney. Which meant whoever was out in the hall had something else in mind besides the law.

Good. They'd come to kill him. Yesterday he'd been worried that the people who'd set him up would attempt to sneak in and finish the job Danziger had botched. Since his last talk with Dr. Graham, Jake had been afraid they *wouldn't.* So now this had to be it. This so-called attorney no doubt had a silenced .22 in his briefcase.

"Let him in."

The guy was balding and fortyish, wearing wire-rimmed glasses and a three-piece suit.

"Thanks for seeing me, Mr. Nacht," he said, thrusting out his hand and then snatching it back when it became obvious that no one was going to shake it. "My name's Steven Krosny and I think we have a pretty good—"

"Cut the bullshit," Jake said.

Krosny's eyes widened behind his glasses. "I beg your pardon?"

"Spare me the chatter. Do the hit and get it over with. Just make it quick."

He closed his eyes and waited as Krosny opened his briefcase. The guy didn't have to be good to pump a few .22 hollowpoints into his skull at point-blank range. He just had to know how to point and pull a trigger. Jake wouldn't feel a thing. And then this nightmare would be over.

"Hit? I don't know what you're talking about, Mr. Nacht. I'm here to make you a very rich man."

Jake opened his eyes. "What?"

Krosny had a legal pad on his lap. "I've looked into the evidence in your case—I have friends in the DA's office—and there's no way you're going to trial. They have nothing on you, Mr. Nacht. They can't even put you before the grand jury because they have nothing to show. You, however, have been hideously wounded and permanently crippled. You and I are going to make the city pay for your devastating injuries. Pay dearly."

"You mean you're not here to whack me?"

"What is whack? Is this slang of some sort? I'm here to help you sue New York City for about a zillion dollars, Mr. Nacht."

"Christ, you're on the level! What do I care about money now?"

"Plenty, I should think. After all, you're going to need skilled nursing care for the rest of your life. That's going to cost. You're going to need . . ."

Jake closed his eyes and let Krosny rattle on. He wanted to die and it didn't look like anyone was going to help him out. Of course, he could start singing to the cops about Fredo and Mr. C. That would sure as hell buy him some lethal attention, but he didn't want to go out with a canary in his mouth. No matter how bad things were, he couldn't allow himself to be remembered that way.

No, he'd have to live for a while, let all the therapists do their thing on him, and work real hard with them in the hope that someday he'd be able to find a way to do one last hit—on himself.

PART 2

DYING

9

BED

When he needed rest from his anger, Jake practiced smelling his way around his room. That slight chlorine odor came from the bathroom. TidyBowl added a faint, sweet perfume—

What a waste, having a bathroom.

Jake realized he had just made a pun. Hilarious. He glanced down at the curving hump the catheter raised in the blanket. It looked like a mole's burrow.

The air conditioner whispered to life. Jake rolled his eyes toward the wall, concentrating until he detected the faint fruity smell of the paint. They must have put on a fresh coat shortly before he was brought in. Pastel blue—better than pink but what was wrong with white? Not that it mattered.

He became aware of his own smells—the catheter, sweat, the oil in his hair, a faint meaty smell on his breath. He was part of the room now, like the paint and the floor wax and the toilet. For how long? Thinking of what the doctor had told him, Jake felt the dread welling up again. The floor seemed to open beneath him, dropping him into a dizzying free fall. Closing his eyes, he fought off panic.

You've asked me to be honest, Mr. Nacht, and I do think it's best. With this type of injury, I've never seen a patient walk again. The new biofeedback therapy may well build up sensation and perhaps some movement in your hands. Though you might not think so now, that will make a huge difference in making you less dependent. And don't write off the chance of a medical breakthrough.

I have to get out of here, Jake thought. I'll work hard on the therapy, get my hands back. Then I'll get the legs, I don't care what the doctor says.

Thinking about his legs, Jake felt a measure of hope. Clearly they *could* move. He had seen one of them twitch yesterday but had decided it was his imagination. Then it happened again today, just a few minutes ago, his right leg jerking under the covers. He hadn't been trying to move it, and when he did try, nothing happened. But surely Dr. Graham would consider the twitches a hopeful sign.

I *will* walk out of here, Jake thought, and blow Fredo's brains out. If that ambulance chaser Krosny can get the city to fork over a few mil, I'll take it, but I'm not going to stay paralyzed. I'm not some poor jerk who lies in a bed with tubes running in and out of him, who can't even sit to take a leak, who has to be spoon-fed like a baby. Not me.

Finding a spark of fury, he nursed it along. He imagined Fredo's smug, stupid face in the crosshairs of his scope. He imagined his finger squeezing the trigger—

His right hand, lying on top of the white covers, drew his gaze. With a mixture of hope and fear, he stared at the trigger finger, willing it to move. It lay still. He concentrated fiercely, trying to find the pathway from his brain to the hand. What would his nerves look like running through his arm—white tunnels, maybe? Just find the right tunnel and flash through to the finger.

The smell of sweat deepened. The hand remained still.

Jake tore his gaze away from the hand and stared at the ceiling. Okay, the tunnels were temporarily blocked. But they would open up again. He'd get through. You'll see, Fredo.

Jake breathed deeply. Getting too emotional. Got to get back on a more even keel. Panic or rage, both blocked thought. And he had a *lot* of thinking to do—starting with exactly what had gone down in that hotel room.

Why had the cops cut it so fine? If Detective Danziger had been straight, it might figure—he'd spotted a gunman in the window, rushed his squad to the hotel and barely made it. But I don't let heat spot me in the window, Jake thought. Besides, he knew my face, *knew* I was the mechanic. Some of his squad must have been straight, or Danziger could have walked over and put three more into my back. But Danziger is as bent as a snake sucking its tail.

So was the bastard early or late?

If they meant to let me whack Whiny, then punch my ticket to keep me quiet, he was early. Another five seconds and whoever set me up would have gotten at least half of what they wanted. This way they got zip. Whiny isn't dead and they can't know I won't talk.

So suppose they didn't want me to whack Whiny. That makes Danziger late—almost too late.

And it doesn't figure. If all they wanted was to pop me, why set me up on Whiny, then come after me just a few hundred yards from TV cameras and a brigade of blues? Why not just send out four guys with Uzis some night, catch me in an alley?

So suppose they wanted to *almost* kill Whiny, scare him real bad.

That works, Jake thought grimly. Here they've got this U.S. senator in their pocket, then he starts to shake them down. Why cancel a resource like that if you can bully it back into line? So they set up the hit, stop it in the nick of time, and send a very strong message to Whiny. See what almost happened to you, Senator? Lucky we were there. Maybe next time we won't be.

Danziger was right on time, Jake thought.

And I'm the patsy.

The rage started to build in him again and with it the sting of betrayal. Through seventeen hits, Mr. C had always played straight with him. And then he'd decided to toss him away. Whether they'd meant to kill Weingarten or scare him, Jake Nacht was not supposed to leave that hotel room alive.

First I'll kill Fredo, Jake thought. Then Danziger. Let Mr. C think about it for a while. Then I'll kill him.

Right. But when?

The rage gave way to a terrible sense of impotence.

How many days have I been here? Jake wondered.

He counted back over the nights, the periods when the room went dark and the hall outside settled into a hush. Three nights. Three days and three nights. Seemed more like three weeks, time crawling like a fly on the back of his eyeball. Through all those days he must have tried thousands of times to move his finger. Just his finger.

Jake thought about the therapy the doctor had mentioned. Biofeedback, whatever that was. And learning to hold a stick in his mouth and punch the telephone or the computer. Learning to pitch his voice to turn the lights or TV on and off. Deep breathing to make sure his lungs didn't get congested.

No further mention of learning to move his fingers.

What if I never get better? Jake wondered. What if I can't kill Fredo? What if I'm going to lie here until I die, tubes going in, tubes going out? For fun I can watch television. I can eat—if somebody feeds me. And I can always sleep.

The panic surged back. Jake fought it, closing his eyes, taking long, slow breaths. He heard her walk into the room, able to tell her soft, graceful tread from the sounds the other nurses made. So what? He wouldn't even open his eyes.

Somehow, they came open anyway.

"Hello, Mr. Nacht."

She smiled down at him. Her brown hair hung around her shoulders. Her face was pretty in a youthful sort of way, the skin smooth and freckled, her smile very even, the teeth white and perfect. Her eyes were brown with flecks of gold.

Quite a piece of work. He wanted to touch her, but it had less to do with her than wanting merely to . . . touch.

"Call me Jake," he said.

"All right." She seemed pleased. "And I'm Angel—Angela Deschanel, actually, but everyone calls me Angel."

I can see why, Jake started to say, but then something in her face stopped him. Men probably said that to her all the time. The last thing he wanted in his pathetic state was to come on to her—probably the last thing she wanted, too. "Okay, Angel. Good to officially meet you at last."

She lifted his hand off the spread and shook it.

The gesture startled him. He saw his hand in hers, but could not feel it, couldn't even feel his arm going up and down. But in an odd way, it gave him a lift just to see himself moving.

"Dinnertime already?"

"No. I just thought you might like your face washed."

"Sure."

He followed her with his eyes, watching as she went into the bathroom and returned with a basin. She was beginning to make him curious. She came in several times a day, often for tasks like this. Odd, in a busy public hospital like Manhattan General. He'd never thought much about hospitals, but from what he'd heard, nurses were overworked and in short supply. Ernie still groused about his gallbladder operation whenever he wanted to gross an unfavored customer out of his bar—how he'd needed his bedpan emptied and punched his button over and over and it had taken the nurses half an hour to respond.

Angel ran the washcloth gently over his face. The water was just warm enough. The soap smelled clean, free of perfume. She dried him off gently. He sensed that she was looking at his face, really looking. Most of the nurses who came in here avoided looking at him now, maybe rationing their sympathy, their horror—whatever he made them feel—so they'd have something left for the next loser.

"Thanks," he said. "That feels better."

"Good."

"When are they moving me out?"

She cocked her head. "Moving you out?"

"I imagine beds are scarce in here."

"Sure, but no one's thinking of moving you out. We have to run more tests, make sure you're stabilized and well enough to move. Besides, you haven't even started your therapy."

"I wanted to ask you about that. When Dr. Graham went over the schedule with me, he mentioned working on moving my hands."

Angel nodded. "That's the new biofeedback therapy. When you're ready, we're going to give it a try." She hesitated, eying him. "You don't want to hope for too much too soon. Your MR scan—"

"Scans can be wrong, can't they?"

Angel hesitated again. "Sometimes. Have you been trying to move your hands?"

"Yes," he said.

"Do you have any feeling in your fingers?"

"No."

"Your spinal cord was cut almost through," Angel said.

"But don't cuts heal?"

"No. Not in the spinal cord of humans—at least not yet."

Jake decided to drop his little bombshell on her. "I've seen my leg move—twice."

"Yes. That's normal in a case like yours. It's an involuntary reflex. When the spinal cord is intact, the brain suppresses the reflex."

He felt punctured. He stared at her, horrified, his last tiny reservoir of hope draining away. He couldn't feel, couldn't make anything below his neck move when he wanted, and now she was telling him that the one piece of hope he'd clung to was nothing. He was a spastic. His body, cut off from his brain, was only mocking him, defining him with those involuntary movements: *jerk.*

"There are some promising studies with animals."

Jake worked at producing a smile. "Thanks for being straight with me."

"There's a lot you can do," Angel said. "They're coming up with new devices all the time—"

"Please." He felt a strangling pressure in his throat.

She gazed at him. "I know. It's hard. If you don't want to talk about it now, you don't have to. You'll feel better after a while, when you've had some time to adjust."

No, Jake thought. I'll feel worse.

Angel fussed with his blanket, folding the top edge over, smoothing it along his chest. "You've really been on the news, you know. If you'd let me turn on your TV, you'd have seen yourself on channel nine. Evidently the man who shot at Weingarten disappeared into thin air. The cops smashed into his room seconds after the shot and no one was there. There's a ledge outside the window, and that's the only place he could have gone. The cop who shot you—Danziger—said that's why he thought you were the gunman. He thought you'd gone out on the ledge and made it into the other room." Angel gave a skeptical laugh. "He made you sound like Spiderman. He's been suspended, you know."

"Good," Jake said tightly.

"The current theory is that the gunman hid in a plumbing crawl space in the bathroom. When Danziger shot you, the cops all ran out of the room into the hall. That would have given the real gunman a chance to slip out and escape. It's all theory, but they have an APB out on a man named Elliot Guyer, who rented the room. Evidently the IDs were bogus, but the desk clerk said he's got black hair and a mustache, and he's heavier than you."

"An APB?" Jake said, knowing exactly what she meant, but wondering how she knew.

"All points bulletin," she said.

"You're pretty handy with cop terminology." He knew he was spinning things out, but he didn't want her to leave. He couldn't stand to be alone right now, to see the leg twitch again.

"When I went to college," Angel said, "I wanted to be a cop. But no one would take me seriously."

"Because you're so beautiful."

Angel looked at him with suspicion. "I wouldn't put it quite that way. More because everyone thought I was too fragile and innocent. Do you have brothers or sisters, Jake?"

"No." Not that I know of, he amended silently.

"I have five—four sisters and a brother. I'm the youngest. Everyone in my family talks about how spoiled I was. They don't know what it was like, being the youngest. Everyone looks down on you. You are patronized continually. Angel's so cute, Angel's our little treasure. If they play a game with you, it's their game. If they take you somewhere, it's where they want to go. When they take the family picture, you're always kneeling down front. You never stand in the back row. My head was patted so many times I'm surprised it isn't flat on top."

Jake wondered if she knew how she sounded. You had a family, he thought. Seven other people with your blood in their veins. People who loved you, treasured you.

And yet, he could see her point.

"You wanted to be a cop so you could give people orders?"

She gave him a penetrating look; he did not smile and neither did she. "That's it exactly," she said. "I wouldn't have admitted that to most people."

He said, "Being a nurse must be pretty hard, too. Maybe harder than being a cop."

"It is."

Her gaze lingered thoughtfully on him. He wondered what it would be like to kiss her. He could still kiss, but who would want to kiss him? You could only do so much with your tongue. And once you did it, you wanted to do other things. Having to stop with a kiss would be like chewing without swallowing. Better not to start.

"Well, I'd best be off," Angel said. "But before I go, let me set you straight on something. You don't have to worry about being shipped out of here. The city is footing your whole bill. They've told us to spare no expense. That's why you've got a private room.

Evidently they're scared silly of that lawyer of yours. This is what the cops call a bad shoot. They're liable, and they know it. You'll probably get millions of dollars."

"Every cloud has a silver lining," Jake said, smiling to take the sting from the words.

Angel studied him again. "Can I ask *you* a question?"

"As long as it doesn't involve fractions. I'm lousy at math."

She smiled then sobered. "*Was* it you that tried to shoot the senator?"

Jake felt a warning tingle in the skin of his neck. Was this why Angel was being so nice to him? Had the DA wired her? "No," he said, feeling let down.

"I'm sorry. I know it was a terrible thing to suggest, but I . . . had to ask you."

"Why?"

"Because it was on my mind and I want to be straight with you."

Interesting, Jake thought. He felt his mood lifting again.

"I'll see you at dinner," Angel said, and walked out of his room.

He watched her as far as his eyes could travel.

She's not just being nice, he thought. She likes me.

I wonder if I could get her to like me enough to kill me.

10

THE WHORE

Jake gazed up at the darkened ceiling, stymied. How could he get Angel to fall in love with him? His brain, dim and silent as the hospital around him, offered no answer.

Rolling his eyes right, he looked at the clock. The red LED numerals said ten minutes to three.

Go to sleep, he thought. Something will come in the morning.

But he knew it wouldn't.

He'd made love to a lot of women. But making one fall *in* love with him was an art he'd never imagined needing. Ironic. He'd got straight A's in self-preservation, a subject where even the B+ students ended up in prison or dead. Plenty of people had reason to hate Jake Nacht; the friends and relatives of seventeen dead targets would add up to a big hunger for revenge. But none of those people knew who he was. He'd succeeded in staying anonymous, determined that hate would never cost him his life.

Now ignorance of love might cost him his death.

If only there was some other way besides Angel. Mr. C, for example. He could probably get Mr. C in for a visit—a nurse would make the call for him. When Mr. C came in, he could tell him he was going to sell him out to the cops. Jake felt a tremor of disgust. The thought of even pretending to rat to the cops made him sick to his stomach.

And Mr. C wouldn't buy it anyway.

If I really meant to send him up, Jake thought, the last thing I'd do was warn him. I'd sing and let him find out when the cops and DA showed up at his door. Mr. C would see that right away. He'd know I was really just asking him to kill me.

Jake felt a pang of nausea. Pathetic. Mr. C had set him up in the first place. The only thing that appalled him more than the idea of living like a quadruple amputee was the thought of baring his throat to the bastard who'd done it to him—and then being turned down. Because Mr. C *would* turn him down.

No way I can make him afraid of me, Jake thought, except for getting up and walking out of here. But that will never happen. I'll never be able to come gunning for him and, by now, he knows it. Knows I'd have a hell of a time ratting him out, too. Told me no details of his operations. Only thing I know is that he paid me—through bagmen—to hit people. And I can't even *prove* that, except by getting him to hit me. Which he can figure out for himself. Wouldn't take him two seconds to figure I'm trying to set *him* up, that I'd already talked to the cops and was dangling myself as bait to get him to put the noose around his own neck. Mr. C wouldn't send a hit man within a mile of this place if I begged him.

Jake's mind went back to the seventeen targets. Some stood out in memory more than others. Seventeen men, dead—from the neck down *and* up. Mostly the scum of the earth, but even scum had friends and family who might consider revenge. Except that now the anonymity he'd worked so hard to preserve was working against him. Even if he could get in touch with a relative and prove he'd made the hit, even if that relative was capable of killing, why do it when a much better revenge would be to let him suffer endlessly? No, they'd look down at him and laugh, and that he could not stand.

Jake felt a sudden, powerful urge to tear at his hair. His hands lay impotent on the sheets. Goddamn! Living had become a nightmare, more people than he could count thirsted for his blood, but his only hope of dying was love.

Did it have to be Angel? She liked him, but he had no idea how to make it more than that. Was there anyone else, someone from the past who might have loved him, so he would not have to start from scratch?

He searched back over the years, recalling his relationships with women. Plenty of whores. He needed to bed women, that was his wiring.

But love was another matter. You could learn to do without it. He had not wanted love of any kind. Not since Sarge. And he didn't want it now, but that was beside the point. Point was, had any of those woman loved *him?*

He remembered Caitlin. Caitlin might have loved him.

Or maybe she'd just been grateful.

Jake was suddenly aware of his heartbeat, a quickening thump against his ribs. *Grateful might be enough.* I did it for me as much as for her, he thought, but she doesn't know that, and it doesn't change the fact that she owes me.

If she even remembers I exist.

Shaking off the defeatist thought, Jake rolled his eyes toward the phone, wondering for a second why his hand wasn't reaching for it—

Paralyzed.

And the blackness swooped in, covering him from mouth to toe, pushing him down into the bed as the voice sang in his mind, *paralyzed . . . paralyzed. . . .*

Caitlin O'Shea lay in her bed, unable to sleep. The last john of the night was gone. Time to take care of herself, sleep, forget. But she could not sleep. She kept thinking about Jake.

She got up and went to the French doors, opening them. A soft breeze blew off the Atlantic, lifting the sheer curtains back against her breasts and thighs. Finding a thin film of sweat, they stuck, shroudlike. With a shudder, she brushed them off and stepped, naked, onto her balcony. She gazed at the dark ocean and the three-quarter moon dangling over it. A short string of lights—a freighter—chugged along the horizon. Below her, the boardwalk was almost empty. Atlantic City was winding down for the night, heading for sleep.

What about Jake? Was he asleep?

Going back inside, she flipped on her bed lamp and pulled the *Times* from under the bed—the paper from the day it had happened. The attempted assassination of Senator Weingarten owned the front page, encircling a photo of Weingarten cowering on the platform, shielded by a New York state trooper. Peripheral figures were blurry—people diving for cover. Looking at Weingarten's fearful eyes, she felt a mixture of contempt and uneasiness. Whiny liked her to tie him up and talk dirty to him. The same Whiny who stood in line to support the war on drugs—every demagogue's favorite—but didn't give a damn if she *snorted* a line right in front of him. He'd like it less if he knew there was no way she could stomach him without it. But she never let that show. She was a professional.

Whiny wasn't that different from everyone else. Contradiction was the norm in human beings. She knew that better than anyone. People thought they were consistent, but they weren't. They gave to "Jerry's kids" but passed the beggar on the street. Men who wouldn't cheat at poker would cheat on their wives. When it came to good and bad, most people were part of each. In all her life, she'd met only one who was all bad.

And Jake had killed him.

At least she was pretty sure he had.

Caitlin closed her eyes, remembering the night. He'd called himself Mark Porter. A big man, handsome in a slightly unreal way. Square jaw, brilliant green eyes, wavy blond hair that never seemed out of place. Built like a ballet dancer with thick thighs, arms ropy with muscle, a gleaming, hairless chest.

The first time, she'd found him quite attractive. And the first few sessions, he'd been all right, just the occasional little bad omen—pinching a nipple, biting her shoulder too hard, ramming into her with extra force.

No problem. A lot of johns liked it a little rough. But she was a class act, not some Times Square whore. With no pimp, she had to be extra careful. So, after he'd slapped her one night, she'd warned him: No rough stuff.

Caitlin remembered his cold smile.

The next time, he came in with a dozen roses. While she was putting them in a vase, he hit her from behind.

She woke up naked, her mouth taped shut, and her hands and feet tied to the bedposts. Mark Porter, or whatever his real name was, sat beside the bed, watching her.

Her head ached horribly. Nausea swept her. She forced it back with a fierce effort, terrified she would choke if she vomited into the tape. Fighting for calmness, she focused her mind. *How do I stop this?*

Porter leaned forward and smiled at her. He held up something for her to see. A knife with a small triangular blade, the type artists used to cut mats.

"Do you think I could kill you with this?" he said.

She tried to scream. The tape held it back, smothering it down to a muffled bleat. She yanked against the ropes. They held her tight, biting into her wrists.

"The blade is only an inch long," Porter said reflectively. "Of course, if I make a crosscut beneath your breastbone, the round handle will slide through and I can get to work on your heart. But don't worry, that won't be for quite a while."

She'd known at once he was serious; she was going to die.

Porter set the blade against her nipple. She could feel its razor sharpness. She screamed into the tape and bucked against the headboard.

The door to her bedroom swung open.

Astonishment swept Porter's face. He turned, rising, and she saw someone coming at him.

Jake!

Caitlin drew a deep rapturous breath through her nose. For a moment the room swam, darkening at the edges.

As if in a dream, she saw Porter lunge at Jake. Jake slipped to one side, catching his wrist, twisting it up behind his back. The knife clattered to the floor. Jake spun him around. Porter swung at him. Jake ducked and hit him in the nose with the palm of his hand. Porter dropped to his knees, holding his nose as blood leaked between his fingers.

Jake picked up the knife and cut the ropes on her wrists and ankles. She ripped off the gag as he turned back to Porter. Thank God Jake had shown up early. What a beautiful sight he was, standing over Porter, gazing down at him. The look on his face was strange, though. Not angry, not anything. He looked like he was watching a dull TV show and thinking about something else.

"I wasn't going to hurt her," Porter whined. "It was just a game."

"You lying fuck!" Caitlin cried. "You were going to kill me."

Rage filled her. She sprang from the bed and rushed Porter, kicking him, pounding him with her fists. He cowered, as if afraid to resist.

After a minute, she felt Jake's hands on her, pulling her off.

"Go sit on the bed," he said.

She did.

"Get up," Jake said to Porter.

"What are you going to do?" Porter said in a whipped voice. The change in him was amazing.

"Nothing. I'm just going to see you out."

Porter looked up at Jake for a moment. Gradually, the fear left his face, replaced by a sly calculation. "You're her pimp?" Porter said.

"You got it," Jake said agreeably. "And your time is up for tonight."

Porter stood, pulling on his clothes. She could see his confidence returning. Confusion filled her. Was Jake just going to let him go?

Porter walked over to her and Jake let him. "This isn't over, bitch," he whispered.

But it was. Jake walked out with him and she never saw Porter again. Jake didn't come back that night. Later, she asked him what he'd done to Porter. All Jake would say was, "We had a talk. He won't be back."

Caitlin shivered. She picked up the newspaper again and paged to Jake's photo—the one from his security-guard badge. The single column of print beneath it was a sidebar to the main story. It told how Mr. Jake Nacht, an innocent bystander staying at the same hotel as the assassin, had been mistakenly shot by an overzealous police detective.

Caitlin looked at the face in the picture. Nothing about it to draw attention. The eyes were mild, the mouth relaxed. His thick blond hair, looking gray in the black-and-white photo, was neatly combed. He wore a plain uniform shirt. Looked just like a security man, placid, a little dull.

The photo lied. In person, you saw Jake's edge, the intelligence in his eyes, the underlying power of the man, quiet and controlled, that made him so attractive in a scary way.

"It *was* you, wasn't it," she whispered, still gazing at the photo. "You killed Porter and you tried to kill Whiny. They shot you, and then you fooled them into thinking it was the wrong man."

She put the paper down, thinking about Jake lying in the hospital bed, paralyzed for life. Did he have anyone to come see him at the hospital? He'd never talked about a family. He wasn't married—at least that was what he'd told her.

I spent a lot of time with you, she thought. And I barely knew you. She felt a surprising pressure of tears. You saved my life, Jake. And I haven't even been to see you.

A sudden resolve filled her. The hospital was only a couple hours' drive from here. It was long past visiting hours, but she could get around that. She could put on the nurse's uniform that she used with the johns who liked "hospital" sex. Jake was probably sleeping, but it wouldn't hurt to wake him up. He must have a lot of time to sleep nowadays.

Jake smelled her perfume—Poison. He'd bought her a bottle once at Saks. He felt a sense of wonder, turning as she stepped to the bedside. In the dark, he could not make out her face, but he knew it was her.

"You must be psychic," he said. "I've been thinking about you."

"Really?" she said softly.

"Step back into the light from the hall," he said.

She did, and he saw that she was wearing a nurse's uniform. "Clever."

"I should have come sooner," she said.

He heard the strain in her voice. Shock at seeing him like this? No, he looked normal enough, no scars on his face, no burn marks, just good old Jake lying still. What then? Guilt?

"Can I take your hand?" she said.

"Go ahead."

She reached down below his chin. He felt nothing in his fingers, but he remembered. Her hands were very soft, the hands of a casino "honeybee"—though she was probably making a couple hundred bucks a trick by now.

"We always did meet at night, didn't we?" Jake said.

"Why did you stop coming to see me?" Caitlin asked.

Jake looked at her dark silhouette, wondering what to tell her. That she had become uncomfortable. That her questions about Porter, about his own life, despite their casualness, had become too insistent?

"You were always too classy for me," he said. "A girl from Vassar with a security guard who dropped out of high school."

"Jake, don't con me. Did you get tired of me?"

"You're beautiful, Caitlin. You know that."

"That's not what I asked you."

"My turn to ask you something. Why did you come tonight?"

"I thought you might, for the first time in your life, need me."

"I do."

She bent over and kissed him on the lips, a slow lingering kiss. He tried to return it, the way he used to, but his jaw seemed stiff, his lips made suddenly of stone.

She pulled away. "I'm sorry. Maybe I shouldn't have done that. It's the only thing I have to give you."

"No it's not."

"What can I do? Name it."

Jake hesitated. He was still hooked up to monitors. If she held a pillow over his face, the nurses would get here before he died. If she unplugged the monitor, same thing. Maybe she could make it out of the hospital before the nurses got to the room.

"Did anyone see you come in?"

"Sure," she said. "The guard in the lobby, a nurse on the elevator. But it's all right. They just think I'm another nurse."

Jake's heart sank. Even if she got out, they'd remember her—the beautiful nurse no one had seen here before. He had planned enough hits to know a crash-and-burn when he saw one. The guard and the nurse on the elevator would sit down with a police artist. He was still enough of a celebrity that Caitlin's Indenti-Kit picture would make the papers.

POLICE VICTIM MURDERED IN HOSPITAL BY
MYSTERY WOMAN.

Too many people who didn't give a damn about Caitlin O'Shea knew her face intimately. One of her johns who'd paid her for "nursey" sex would recognize the police drawing and freak. All it would take was an anonymous phone tip to the cops.

No, even if Caitlin could be persuaded to kill him, it couldn't be tonight. He needed time to think, to come up with a way to convince her and a plan that would protect her. The next time she came to visit him, he'd be ready.

The thing to do now was to remind her of what they'd had and hope it was enough—would be enough.

"You said I could do something for you," Caitlin prodded.

"You can tell me something. How did you . . . feel about me?"

He sensed surprise in her hesitation.

"What is this, Jake? I used to try and tell you how I felt, and you'd never let me."

Jake remembered the first few times. During the sex she'd start moaning, "Oh, baby, I love it, you're so good," and so on, and he'd made her stop. He was there to buy sex, not lies. A simple deal, all the cards on the table, no deception. He'd had enough deception from Sarge to last him a lifetime.

"I'm letting you tell me now," he said.

She eyed him. "Okay. At first, you mystified me. So polite. So respectful. Most men can't do that. They have to despise me, especially afterward. You never did. I liked that, very much. I liked your sense of humor. I liked it when you bought me things. Then, after you saved me from that guy Porter . . ."

"Caitlin," Jake said.

She gazed at him. "What?"

He felt the words on his tongue, an inch from coming out. He *could* ask it of her, ask her to do it right now. She had a chance to get away with it. And he needed it so much.

"Jake." She smoothed his forehead. Her hand was as cool and soft as he remembered. "Poor Jake. Are you asking if I *loved* you? Of course I loved you, silly man."

"Don't con me, Caitlin."

She stood there a long time, her hand resting lightly on his forehead.

"All right, Jake," she said softly. "I wish I could be the whore with the heart of gold. But what I do changes a woman. Maybe we're already changed before we go into the life. Whatever, I don't know what love is. I know I need men to adore me. They don't, of course. They only adore my body. But I'm not so good at the distinction. When I look in a mirror, I don't see my brain, I see what men see, what they *desire* . . . " She trailed off. "I liked you, Jake," she said at last. "I liked you best, and that's no lie. If I'd been a different woman, maybe I could've loved you. And if you had been a different man, maybe you could even have loved me."

Jake said nothing. What was there to say?

"Can you still get hard?"

"No."

Jake felt her hand lift from his forehead, saw rather than felt it slide down across his blanketed chest toward his groin.

"Don't," he said. "For both our sakes, don't."

"I'm sorry, Jake. Really sorry." She leaned over and kissed his forehead. "I'll come see you again."

"Good," he said.

But he knew she wouldn't.

11

THE PROMISE

October

Jake walked through the forest. A vague anxiety gripped him. His right hand dangled at his side. He could feel the stock of the Mauser against his palm, the weight of the pistol dragging at the tendons in his arm. Looking up, he glimpsed patches of ultramarine sky through the leafy treetops. The dense color hurt his eyes, buzzing on his retinas like the vibrations of a dentist's drill. He dropped his gaze but could not draw the ground into focus either. Dark leaves blurred around his ankles, dragging at his feet as he tried to slog through. The air stung his lungs with the smell of burning.

"Jake," said a voice ahead of him.

Jake dropped into a crouch. He fought the unnatural weight of the Mauser, dragging it up into firing position.

"Going to get you, boy." The voice was harsh, mocking.

Jake sighted along the short barrel at a bush straight ahead. The voice seemed to be coming from there. He tried to squeeze the trigger, but it had rusted solid.

"Come on, Jake, what are you waiting for, you limp-dick pussy? Couldn't even get it up for that whore last night."

Jake felt a terrible tightness in his throat. "Sarge?"

"Who else would be out here with you? You lost, boy? I see you plain as day. Got you right in my sights. You ain't doin' so well, are you."

"No," Jake said.

"What's the story?"

"Shoot me, Sarge," Jake pleaded. "I'm paralyzed, see?" He dangled his arm for Sarge to see, letting the Mauser swing back and forth like a pendulum. He threw down the pistol. "Shoot me. I don't want to live."

"You're pitiful." Sarge emerged from the bushes and Jake gasped in shock at the blood-soaked apparition. Bullet holes stitched Sarge's camouflage uniform and puckered the blood-drenched skin of his forehead. "You killed me, don't you remember? I was the only friend you had."

Jake swallowed. "You weren't my friend."

"Not your *friend?*" Sarge rolled his eyes at the dark heavens. "I took you in when no one else would have you. I let you share in the most important thing in my life. I taught you. I held back my anger when you screwed up and praised you when you did well. I was the first man in your pathetic no-account life to show an interest in you, to treat you with respect. I gave your life purpose. And you say I wasn't your friend?"

Jake's head ached. He couldn't think. "You betrayed me."

"Bullshit."

"You made me kill you."

"The hell I did. I was only testing you. Shooting blanks. And you failed the test. Was it really so easy to believe I could turn on you? Me, Sarge—your father, your best friend in all the world?"

Jake stared at Sarge, horrified. Shooting blanks? No, that couldn't be right. Hadn't he felt the bullet tear through the leaves next to his head? Or had he only dreamed that in the years since?

"You would've killed me."

Sarge shook his grotesque, bloodied head sadly. Then he wasn't Sarge anymore, he was Mark Porter. One of his eyes was missing where the 9mm slug had entered. Jake's face prickled with anxiety.

Caitlin would be safe now, but he was in immediate danger. He must get Porter into the trunk of his car before someone came down the alley. He could not seem to get a proper hold on the body. It kept slipping from his grasp. It was hideously heavy.

"Jake, Jake," said a woman's voice behind him.

Shocked, he tried to turn, but someone was holding him.

"Jake, wake up."

He opened his eyes. Angel gazed down at him. Her hands gripped his shoulders. He took a slow, deep breath.

"You were having a nightmare," Angel said. "Look at you, you're covered with sweat."

She went into the bathroom and returned with the basin and washcloth. Gently, she sponged off his forehead and face. The water felt cool and good, pulling him clear of the dream's lingering dread.

She looked beautiful. Her soft brown hair shone in a flood of morning sunlight. The scatter of freckles across the tops of her cheeks and the bridge of her nose made him think of a fawn he'd seen once out in the Pine Barrens. She looked so healthy, so alive that it made his breath catch in his chest. He felt suddenly mortified. Had Angel heard him moaning, crying out?

He mustered a quizzical smile. "What makes you think I was dreaming?"

"I watched your eyes."

Jake tried to dredge up what she meant. How could she have seen his eyes? Had they been open? The idea sent a chill through him.

"You know," Angel said with a trace of impatience, "that bump the cornea makes under the eyelid. People look around when they dream. You can see the bumps sliding back and forth, like they're watching a tennis match."

It sank in then that she must have been standing at his bedside, watching him sleep. Why would she do that?

"All right," he said, "but what makes you think it was a nightmare?"

"A guess," she said dryly. "I have good news."

"You're going to transplant my brain into Arnold Schwarzenegger's body."

She held the washrag threateningly over his face as if she were about to squeeze it out.

"Be serious, will you? What I want to tell you is you're ready for physical therapy."

"Great. Roll me over and I'll do push-ups with my lips."

"With your mouth, I do believe you could do it. But maybe we should begin with something a little less strenuous, like your fingers. Start trying to get some feeling back into them."

Jake thought of Fredo's smug face, centered in the crosshairs, his finger curling on the trigger. Great. But who was going to prop him up and hold his arms?

"In most quadriplegics," Angel said, "there's some sense of touch left in the hands. Researchers have been using a biofeedback device to teach some paralyzed men to recover feeling there. We've put together our own version of one of the same machines—"

"Angel, wait. I don't want to start rehab."

"Well, we could put it off a few days, I suppose."

"I don't want it, period."

She gazed at him. "This is the part where you tell me you don't want to go on living, right?"

He said nothing, unnerved by her swift jump ahead. This conversation was an inch from going out of control. The plan was to make her love him, *then* ask her to kill him.

"Jake," she said softly, "a third of all quadriplegics try to commit suicide at some point. If that's what you're feeling, don't be afraid to say it."

He *was* afraid to say it. And not just because it might prevent her from loving him enough for him to use her. He realized with a shock that he cared what she thought of him.

Jake felt a dull alarm. That was no good, no good at all.

"You can't move your body," she said—

Jake's knee jumped in one of the spastic twitches. "Except for that."

"Except for that. But you still have your mind. Your thoughts, your dreams, your imagination . . ."

"I was never much for sitting around thinking," Jake said.

Angel gazed at him. "Then you must have hated your job."

It took him a moment to realize she was talking about his false identity, Jake Nacht the security guard.

"All those nights sitting around in a warehouse guard shack," Angel prompted, "and you're telling me you didn't think? What did you do?"

"I walked around a lot." It sounded lame, even to him.

"Come on, you must have read books, right? Or imagined you were someplace else, doing something exciting?"

"That's different," Jake said. "When the shift was over, I could go out and *do* whatever I'd been thinking about."

"What sort of things did you do?"

Jake did not like the direction the conversation was taking. He did not want to go on inventing a life that never had been to explain the one he no longer wanted.

"From the start," Angel said, "I've had trouble imagining you as a security guard. You're much too bright."

"Yes ma'am, that's me, a real rocket scientist."

A corner of Angel's mouth turned up. "Don't try to hoodwink me, Jake. I've heard every con there is, from the tooth fairy to the bogeyman. My first day in school I got in trouble because one of my sisters had told me to be sure and ask the teacher for my masturbation papers. When I was four, my brother told me if I put a leg out of bed before morning, the crocodiles underneath would bite it."

"You mean that's not true?"

She smiled. "You think you can put me off the point by joking? You're not lazy. You're depressed. You hide it beautifully, and Lord, I do admire that, but if I were you, I'd be crying my eyes out, or cutting down everyone who tried to help me. . . ."

"No, you wouldn't," Jake said. "Not you."

She looked pleased. "I'd like to think you're right. I'd want to be as brave as you've been. But brave or not, I'd be horribly depressed, I know I would. I might even want to die."

"Aren't you making my point for me?" Jake asked gently.

"That you *should* die? Not at all. You should be depressed and angry and scared and you should go on fighting it, with jokes or curses or whatever it takes, until you realize you still have a life."

"I don't want the life I still have." Jake's exasperation gave way to resignation. So much for plan A. She'd been too far ahead of him, anyway.

So what was plan B?

"You're feeling sorry for yourself," Angel said.

Jake considered it. Could she be right? Many times in his life he'd felt sorry for himself—when he was a kid, that is, before Sarge. He'd wanted a family, but no one had wanted him. It had hurt and he'd definitely felt sorry for himself. But as time went on he'd come close to not caring. If no one else gave a damn about him, why care about himself? Then Sarge took him in. Sarge cared. Because of it, he'd begun to believe he mattered again.

Then he'd found out *why* Sarge cared.

Since that day, he could not remember feeling *anything* for himself.

Which was not to say he felt nothing for life. Life was, for the most part, enjoyable. Or had been.

The satisfaction in doing well what you were good at. A cold beer in a dark place. The feel of a smooth gun stock in your hand. You didn't have to feel anything for yourself to love the throb of an open road through your steering wheel at eighty miles an hour or the thrill of burying yourself in the electrifying softness of a woman. His body had come prewired for such pleasures, but now his wiring was cut. A bent cop's bullet had destroyed the only feeling that mattered, putting all the things that kept life interesting forever beyond his reach. The only thing still within his grasp was his self, for which he felt nothing, one way or the other. Hell, if he *could* feel sorry for that self, as Angel was accusing, he might have a reason to live. But feeling nothing at all . . .

Better to die.

How could he make Angel understand that?

"Say something," she said.

"Remember when you told me about what it was like to be the youngest?"

"Yes."

"It made me understand why you wanted to be a cop. I need for you to understand me now, but I can't think what to say that will make you. Nobody patted me on the head until it felt flat. But I have that same need you do to be in control."

Angel lifted his hand from the blanket, studied it as if it were a map to his insides.

"I do understand, Jake—I wanted to be a cop so I could, yeah, give orders to someone for once in my life. That's probably why I'm a nurse. And now you can't even give orders to your hands—but just because I understand doesn't mean I have to agree dying is the best way out. Your body has been changed. Now your mind has to change. It hasn't caught up yet, but it will if you give it a chance. Maybe the way you were before, you didn't have a body, you *were* your body. If this hadn't happened, you could have gone your whole life believing that was all of it—or not thinking about it one way or the other. But this *has* happened. Now you'll be forced to learn the difference between sensations and *feelings*, to realize you were never just your body. Your body was a tool of your mind, like a carpenter's hammer. The hammer is broken, so now you have to go into a new line of work. That means retraining. Easy? No. But if you'll make the effort, that new man will want to live."

"You can't know that."

"And you can't know he won't unless you try."

She looked up from his hand, challenging him with the beautiful, brown-gold gaze. He realized with admiration how intelligent this woman was. What she'd just said was so clear, so logical. The doctor—Graham—could never have put it so simply.

My body, the hammer, Jake thought. Not bad.

If it were possible to persuade me, Angel would be the one to do it. . . .

He realized with a glimmer of excitement that she had just handed him a small opening. Could he make it wider?

"What if I try," he said, "and I still want to die?"

"We'll talk about that then."

"Let's talk about it now."

"You can't project yourself that far now. It's no use talking about it. If you try for a year, and then you still want to discuss it, we will. I promise."

"That's not good enough, Angel. You want me to try. The way I feel right now, make it worth my while. I *will* try—but only if we make an agreement right now."

She said nothing; her gaze stayed on his face.

"I will try my best for the next two weeks. I swear to you that I will give it everything I've got. If, at the end of that time, I still want to die, you will help me."

Angel paled. "Two weeks! That's ridiculous. You—"

"A month, then."

"A year."

I've got her! Jake thought, but kept his face impassive. "Two months."

She stood and stalked to the end of the room and back. "Jake, I'm not going to kill you. No way."

"Angel, if we don't make a deal now, I'm going to give all my attention to dying. And I will make it, I promise you that. I have friends. I'll find someone, some way. You can't stop that." He put absolute confidence in his voice, even though he knew it would not be so easy to find someone, not nearly so easy.

Friends . . . yeah, right. For too many years he had needed no one, and now that's exactly what he had.

"The only thing you can decide," he went on, "is whether I'll try—with genuine effort—to do things your way. I'll do it, give it all I've got, if you'll have the courage to help me if you turn out to be wrong."

"I'm not wrong," she said.

"Then you have no problem."

She paced again, to the wall and back. He saw a thin sheen of sweat on her forehead. "Six months," she said.

"Four. I'll do everything you say. I'll never slack off. If I do, you're off the hook. If I don't, and I still want to die, you'll do what has to be done. We'll make it so no one can guess you helped me."

"Jake—"

"Otherwise, I start working on my friends."

"Four months. You do everything I say? No slacking?"

"I swear it."

"And I'm the one who says whether you've lived up to your end?"

Jake hesitated. "All right."

Angel stared at him. "Deal."

Jake wanted to take her hand. He settled for smiling at her. For the first time since he'd awakened in the hospital, he felt a measure of hope. Four months was a long time. But he'd make it, day by day, week by week. He'd sweat it out.

And then Angel would kill him.

12

ANGEL

Angel yearned for intermission. Time seemed to be slowing, the universe congealing around her. She was conscious of William's arm pressing against hers. Carnegie Hall's graceful white balconies curved away from her on either side, converging again on the glowing stage, where a little orchestra played on and on.

And on.

The best word she could think of for Bach was busy—too many tunes going at once. The harpsichord player was pounding awfully hard for such a tinkle of sound. The violinists sawed in earnest unison, but the beat seemed out of sync with their jerking bows, kind of like a Japanese movie where the actor's lips kept on moving after the English stopped.

Just try Bach, William had said. After you've heard Bach, you'll see why baroque is better than classical.

And here she'd thought baroque *was* classical.

Angel wished William's boss, Senator Harrison, had not insisted on sitting behind them in the box. He'd joked that they wouldn't be able to see over his head—which was true enough. But the thought that the senator could see William snuggling up to her made her a bit uncomfortable tonight. Strange.

Angel imagined what it would have been like to sit this close to Jake. The arm would have felt harder against her. William's was soft, but what could you expect from a Senate staffer? When she'd visited him in Washington, he'd introduced her to a couple of the other guys in his office. Both of them looked soft despite the padded shoulders of their designer sport coats. They were pale as the white rats in Uncle Joe's research study—and not half so cute.

Hill rats . . .

At least William was cute—better than cute, he was drop-dead handsome. And to be fair, it was pretty hard to pick up a tan sitting in front of computer screens under fluorescent lights all day and half the night doing the nation's business. As for muscles, you didn't get those writing speeches. Apparently, a lot more words than weights were lifted under the dome of the U.S. Capitol.

Even after weeks in the hospital, Jake was still tanned.

Thinking about the deal she'd made with him, Angel felt a pulse of dread in her stomach. What would her former nursing instructors say if they knew she'd agreed to snuff a patient? Of course, she was positive Jake wouldn't hold her to it. He'd been working hard for two weeks now, doing everything she asked, really throwing himself into it. He seemed to have an excellent attitude. People with excellent attitudes didn't want to die.

So why did it keep nagging at her?

Because the key word was "seemed." Underneath that excellent-*seeming* attitude, she couldn't tell what Jake Nacht was really thinking.

Angel tried to reassure herself. Even if he didn't yet want to live, he would by the end of the four months. And if he didn't, it would be because he'd stopped trying. So it was a safe bet either way. Perfectly safe.

And besides, what was she supposed to have done? To try, a person had to have hope, or at least motivation. When she'd agreed to the deal, the only motivation Jake had had was his desire to die. So she'd had to go with that, harness it. Anything to get him moving.

And what if he tries real hard, gives it everything he's got, and at the end of four months says, Okay, Angel, now kill me?

I'll tell him the deal is off, Angel thought.

The piece ended and everyone clapped. A few people yelled. Angel took her cue from William, clapping crisply the way he did. His face was alight with pleasure. Say this for him, he wasn't faking. He really did like this Bach stuff. His enthusiasm pleased her. It wasn't often he dropped that grave and superior mask of his. She wished he'd give a little yell, too. It would be good for him. Watching him now, she could almost imagine him as a little boy, grinning as he rode his bike with no hands. She wished she could like Bach too, so that she could share his pleasure.

Soon William would ask her to marry him, she was pretty sure of that. Lately, in her daily phone confabs with one or another of her sisters, subject number one was whether William had popped the question yet. Clearly, they all thought she'd be crazy to turn him down. Even Uncle Joe liked him. Until a few weeks ago, she'd had no doubt she'd marry William if he asked. After all, William Fitzpatrick III was intelligent, handsome, and caring. Senate staffer was an important and powerful job—William was Senator Harrison's point man on world hunger. You had to be impressed with that.

It was just that she and William didn't seem to share many things. He was serious and she liked to joke; he dreaded hospitals, where she spent half her waking life. He liked Bach and she liked Eric Clapton. What about their wedding music? Meet in the middle? Bach, Eric . . . Bacharach!

The orchestra started sawing and tinkling again—apparently their last effort had fallen short of intermission. Angel resisted the urge to squirm. Lord, what these people needed was a couple of saxes—or some *drums.* To keep her sanity, she thought about later, when William would take her home. It still felt a little funny when he walked into her apartment ahead of her with that proprietary air, as if it were really his place and she the guest. Not that Angel had a problem with him living in. It had just naturally evolved that he'd stay with her whenever he was in New York. So far, it had been nice having William around. Of course, he never stayed long enough to wear out his welcome—just the odd weekend and an occasional rare week of leave.

Tonight, they'd go back and he'd carefully take off his tux. He'd kiss her a few times and then hustle her into bed. He'd make love quickly, uttering no sound, keeping his eyes closed, as if he thought she'd be offended for him to look at her.

Jake . . . Jake would look.

She pictured him lying beside her, running a hand over her stomach up to her breasts, his eyes hungry for her. Her skin warmed just thinking about it. So strange that she *could* think of Jake this way. She'd worked with a lot of paralyzed men, some of them as handsome as Jake, but she'd never fantasized making love to them. Knowing they couldn't get it up would make her pity them, and she tried to stay away from pity. But somehow, even lying on his back unable to move, Jake Nacht did not inspire pity. She sensed something about him, an aura of suppressed power. Even in paralysis he seemed just a bit . . . dangerous, and she had to admit it excited her.

Somewhere in his past he had walked through fire. She was sure of it. But whatever it was, he kept it hidden. What was his secret? Had his whole family been killed in a car crash? Or maybe, instead of being a security guard, he was FBI or CIA, doing something so classified he could never talk about it to anyone. Maybe it was a woman. Surely a guy like Jake had been in love. Had it ended tragically, his wife kidnapped by terrorists, then killed before he could save her? Angel wished she knew. Someday, she would. She'd find out, she had to. He fascinated her—

Watch it!

With an effort, she got a grip on herself. She was Jake's nurse, not his confidante or lover. Her job was to make him try, to rehabilitate him to the fullest extent possible. She was good at her job and she would do it and not think about what might have been. When the four months were up, Jake would realize he could live. She would marry William and go on to other patients. With all the money Jake would no doubt get from the city, he'd hire someone to look after him every day. He could get a place overlooking Central Park. He could tilt his bed up and watch the leaves turn in the fall, watch the ice skaters in the winter. He could read, watch television . . .

Angel felt a knot in her throat. Not pity, but dread. Somehow, she just couldn't see Jake doing those things. What she could see was Jake, at the end of four months, asking her to kill him. She kept seeing it over and over.

She had made a very dangerous deal.

She thought about Uncle Joe's studies with the rats. Maybe something would happen in the next four months, even a small break in the long succession of failures. Jake didn't know that the soft-spoken balding guy who came around to examine him every day wasn't just any neurosurgeon, that the slight air of distraction hid a tightly-focused mind, and the subject of that focus was nothing less than curing paralysis.

Uncle Joe had a strict rule of not bringing up his research to his patients. So far, no researcher had been able to effectively regenerate the spinal cord, and until someone did, he did not want to hold out false hope. If anyone could do it, Dr. Joseph Graham would be the one, Angel felt sure.

But it was a very big if.

"May I get you a champagne?" William asked.

Angel realized the orchestra had stopped playing. Everyone was standing, filing from their rows. Intermission—finally.

"Do they have anything stronger?" she asked.

Angel followed William into her apartment, wondering why she felt so cross. After all, the part of the concert following the intermission had been mercifully shorter. William had even let her lead him out during the encore so they could get a cab.

And now he would want to make love.

"Do you want some wine?" she asked, heading for the fridge.

"I want some Angel." He was already standing beside the bedroom door, leaning on the jamb. He *did* look handsome in his tux. He loosened his tie and grinned evilly at her. She felt a faint prickle of desire. But she poured herself a glass of Chardonnay before following him into the bedroom. By the time she got there, he had his coat off.

An impulse seized her. "Put it back on," she said.

William gave her a perplexed look.

"Let's make love with your tux on," she said. "You can just pull your zipper down. I'll slide my dress up and sit on the windowsill."

He gave her a tolerant smile. Taking everything off but his undershirt, he folded the tux carefully, just like always. She thought of asking him to undress her, but she didn't want to see the tolerant smile again, so she did it herself and slid between the sheets. William turned the light out before crawling in beside her, but enough glow from the city came through the window for her to see that his eyes were already closed. Angel closed hers too, and imagined William was Jake. She felt guilty about that . . . but for once, she came before William.

Afterward, when he was asleep, Angel gently eased his now-leaden hand from her thigh. Tuning out his soft snores, she wondered if she should break Uncle Joe's rule and tell Jake about his attending's spinal cord research.

She knew most of what there was to know about it, having put in several hours a day in Uncle Joe's lab. The latest set of rodent trials had been running for over a year; she'd done the anesthesia on each rat, made daily observations, and kept the protocols straight. On the plus side, the approach was highly promising in theory. But so far the rats themselves had not provided the slightest reason to hope. Uncle Joe's three previous studies had ended in failure. However good the theory, she hadn't seen any evidence yet to indicate this time would be different.

No, the rule was a good one. Jake was not the type to trust in theories, and even if she did succeed in raising his hopes, what would happen when those hopes began to fade? He'd be more depressed than before, and in the bargain would lose trust in *her*. That trust was all that was keeping him going, and she must do nothing to undermine it. All the rehab in the world could not restore Jake's spinal cord, and he knew that, but the commitment he was pouring into the effort *could* regenerate his severed will to live.

And she must see that it did, because if Jake kept on giving it his best, and the four months ended, and he still wanted to die, could she betray his trust? Could she really look him in the eye and tell him the deal was off?

13

WORKING

November

As he was about to sign on to the Internet, Jake felt a warning prickle at the nape of his neck. Keeping the "stick" firmly gripped in his teeth, he rolled his head to the side—winning back that simple ability had added a whole new dimension to his existence—half expecting to see Angel standing beside the bed. But no, the room was empty.

Just a touch of paranoia—Angel never sneaked up on him.

Morning light poured through the window, an amber sea teeming with dust-mote fish. A section of the wall blazed in the sunlight, releasing the faint, fruity smell of paint. Out in the hall, where his hearing liked to go without him, the last of the breakfast trays trundled away on creaking carts.

Angel couldn't sneak up on me if she tried, Jake told himself. No one else walks quite like her . . .

He closed his eyes, strangely weighed down by the thought. He knew the light, crisp tread of her feet, yes, and the smell of her skin, her laugh from far down the hall, the whisper of her nylons against each other as she moved around his bed, like another man might know the downy feel of her cheek, the contours of her lips—

Jake's jaws ached suddenly. Easing his grip on the stick, he let the tip settle against the sheet. The important thing, the thing he should be thinking about, was that, even though Angel wouldn't sneak up on him, she was surely aware by now of how much time he was logging on the computer. She'd promised that no one would monitor his screen from another station, but she had other ways to keep track. Nurses and aides darted in and out all day. Asking to have his privacy curtain drawn didn't help—light from the screen gave the curtains a blue flush, especially at night, and they could probably hear the stick tapping out in the hall. And Dr. Graham, popping in at unpredictable moments, had seen him working on the computer several times.

An odd duck, Graham. He'd pick up a hand and bend it back and forth. Can you feel this, Mr. Nacht? No. This? No. Never called him Jake, never much expression on the guy's face. Dr. Graham did not particularly like him, that was clear. Or maybe he was just one of those guys with no personality. Sometimes there'd be a look of speculation, almost greed, in his gaze.

Like I'm the goose that might lay the golden egg, Jake thought. Other times, he treats me like a side of beef.

Not yesterday, though. Graham had seemed to be really paying attention, the "golden egg" look staying on his face for the whole visit.

What's he up to?

Jake hated mysteries, had learned the hard way how much it could cost if you didn't figure out what was really going on inside people. But he couldn't begin to guess what movie was playing inside Graham.

Hell with that. What mattered was that Graham not pop in when he was surfing the wrong part of the Net. Fine for the nurses and Graham to see him using the computer. And by all means let them tell Angel. She'd feel good about that—more evidence he was trying.

As long as Angel didn't know *what* he was trying.

He couldn't blow it now. Nine weeks gone; he was more than

halfway to his goal. Another six and he'd be out of here, away from the ripe paint smell, the floating dust motes, the eternal, fixed-camera view of the world he was coming to loathe with an aching, helpless desperation.

Gripping the stick firmly between his teeth, Jake tapped keys, trying to get to the right section of the Net's bulletin board. Instead, he found himself stumbling through the day's news summaries. Baseball scores, stock prices, politics. . . .

Frustrated, he poked with the stick, trying to remember the command he wanted. As the screen continued stubbornly to scroll through the news, a familiar name leapt out at him. Of its own accord, the stick froze the screen on a story in that day's *New York Times:* Weingarten Blames NRA.

Jake felt a sudden burning itch along the nape of his neck where the bullet had plowed in. Anything Whiny said had to be bullshit and he was not about to waste his time on it . . .

On the other hand, he had nothing but time.

Jake scanned the article—Senator Weingarten theorizing to the *Times* reporter that the hysteria fostered by the NRA over antigun legislation was responsible for the attempt on his life two months ago. "The gun nuts know I'm their fiercest enemy," Senator Weingarten said. "They wanted to silence me. They sense a wavering on the part of some people. I'm just one senator, a public servant, and yet, if they could shut me up, maybe the gun lobby in this country could get a better foothold. But the assassination attempt hasn't intimidated me one bit. I'll go on fighting crime, and I'll do it just as I always have: not by trampling the public's right to privacy and free speech, but by taking the guns off the streets."

Yeah, Jake thought dryly. Whiny has seen the light. Whiny is back in line. Thanks to me, Jake thought.

Fury surged through him, so strong he could almost feel it lifting him from the bed. He embraced the rage, clenching his teeth, feeding it with images of Fredo's smug face.

He imagined leaping from the bed, running down the hospital corridor to get a gun and kill them all, starting with Fredo. Jake could almost feel the tiles slapping his bare feet with cool, stinging blows, doctors and nurses turning, astonished at this miracle. In his mind, he ran past them, clinging to the hem of his rage, knowing if he lost it even for a second he'd slump to the floor in a helpless tangle, his arms and legs useless again. . . .

Drawing a deep breath around the stick, Jake let go of the fantasy. Hate was powerful, maybe the most powerful thing in the world, but it could not raise him off this bed, any more than happy thoughts could make Peter Pan fly.

Jake steadied the stick with his teeth and put it back to work, poking keys with slow deliberation until finally he made it into the section of the Internet called "Writers Corner."

Too bad Dr. Kevorkian didn't have a home page. *Hey, Dr. K, I need a consult. Stat.*

Signing in, he started tapping out the message he had composed in his mind during the night:

Am writing a medical thriller. Need the naem (backspace, backspace) *n-a-m-e of a poison that causes death from heart failure. Must be undetectable at autopsy—*

Jake froze, hearing the familiar energetic tread.

"Ready to work?"

Angel, already through the door—he'd become so engrossed he hadn't processed the sounds! Jake stabbed desperately at the key on the top row, missed, tried again. Sweat stung his eyes, making the screen blur.

"What's that?" Angel asked.

Panic closed his throat. If she saw his message, she'd understand in a flash and two months of daily effort on her useless damned hand "exercises" would be down the drain.

"Hey, I like it."

Relief swept him. He'd managed to switch screens. He gazed at the monitor with her as she read the quote: "It's easier to act yourself into a new way of thinking than to think yourself into a new way of acting." She eyed him speculatively. "Very Zen. Where did you find it?"

"Just something I read in a psychology book once." He kept his voice offhand, not overdoing it. She was smart, and if she thought he was conning her, she'd be doubly on her guard.

"You're sweating," Angel observed.

"It's hot in here," he growled. "All that damned sunlight." He knew he was permitted a little grumpiness—in fact, she seemed almost to encourage it sometimes. Seeing her face relax a fraction, he knew it had been the right touch. The little victory failed to cheer him. Though manipulating her was a game he had to win, he found no pleasure in it.

Maneuvering the stick, Jake exited from the network, turned the power off, and carefully deposited the stick into the slot in the foam cube so that he could reach the bit again when he was ready.

"You're getting good with that."

"I'd prefer opposable thumbs, but I'll take whatever I can get."

"That's the spirit."

"So what's today's shocking episode?"

"Same as yesterday's, I'm afraid."

Turning to the door, she waved the tech in. He pushed the cart with the video monitor and biofeedback machine into the room. Angel kept up a patter while the tech, a big guy named Mustaf, slipped the electrodes on. Today Jake imagined that he could feel the cuffs sliding over his fingers. Or maybe it wasn't imagination. Angel had said he could expect some returning sensation. As usual, Mustaf didn't look at him or speak to him, hooking him up with quick efficiency and heading out with a wave at Angel.

"Is he that talkative with the other patients?" Jake asked.

"Actually, he's usually pretty friendly. I think he may be a little afraid of you."

"Of me or of being paralyzed?"

"Of you. You feel helpless, I know. But that's not the way people see you—"

"Give me a break, Angel—" *Careful.* Jake gave her a strained smile to cover his irritation. "In case you haven't noticed, I can't make a fist. And I couldn't have whipped Mustaf on my best day."

Her face remained serious. "He doesn't think you're going to sit up and punch him, but he sees something in you that scares him."

Jake couldn't quite read her tone. What was this? *That's not the way* people *see you.* "Are you talking about Mustaf or yourself?"

Angel returned his gaze. "I'm a little afraid of you, yes."

Jake felt a sudden stillness inside himself, deeper even than the paralysis. He'd had this same eerie feeling once before, when a target had turned and looked straight at him through the scope. Even though he'd known the man wasn't really seeing him four hundred yards away, it had made his spine crawl. And now Angel seemed to be looking at him, really looking, seeing inside to what he really was. That must never happen. If she knew he had killed seventeen men, she might run from this room and never come back. He needed her right here every day for the next two months. Their deal had to go through, it *had* to.

"Don't get me wrong," Angel said. "I like you. I enjoy being with you, talking to you. You have a good sense of humor, great courage. You've been working hard, doing everything I've asked of you and more. But a part of you is always hidden, and that's the part that scares me. I don't know what that part could do, what it's capable of."

Jake's anxiety eased, but only a little. "I'm just a guy, a security guard who thought a weekend in the big city would be fun."

"Are you snowing me, Jake? Is your trying all an act?"

Jake went cold. "That's not fair, Angel. Trying and acting are the same. Remember those words on the computer screen? Well, I'm trying to act my way into a new way of thinking—that's what our deal was all about. So don't ask me if I'm acting. Yes, I'm acting—I'm *doing.* I promised I'd try hard and I'm trying hard."

"Are you making it, Jake?"

He could hear the fear in her voice now. What should he say? Not yes, or she'd throw it back at him later. But he couldn't say no, either. The deal was four months, and Angel wouldn't kill him a day sooner—if she killed him at all.

"I don't know," Jake lied.

"It's just that I get the feeling your main worry in life is whether I think you're trying, and if that's true, then it's because you still want to die. You've made up your mind and nobody or nothing can change it."

"You're thinking too much, Angel. Stop analyzing and just work with me, all right?"

"At the beginning, when the shock and panic were at their worst, I could understand you thinking you wanted to die. But since we made our . . . deal, I haven't seen the slightest sign of depression or anger in you."

"Do you want me to brood? Fly into rages?"

"It might be just what you need. Our deal is that you try, not that you hide all your feelings. That's not human, Jake. Anger and depression are normal for quadriplegics after the shock and panic wear off. But not you. You look and sound so strong. You give every appearance of a man enjoying life again. If you are, great. But if you're not—and I honestly can't tell which it is—that kind of control, that airtight capacity to *deceive*, is . . . scary."

"Angel, please. I'm *not* trying to deceive you."

She held his gaze a moment; then her eyes faltered away. He felt the guilt again, and it annoyed him. What, after all, did he owe this woman? She had no right to expect him not to deceive her, if that's what it took. It was his life he was fighting for—the right to end it, which any normal person with the use of his arms and legs had. If she couldn't understand that, it was her problem.

All the same, he wished he could take her hand.

"Angel," he said gently, "you're getting way ahead of yourself. This is today. We've got almost two months before *either* of us has to face whether I'll want to die. Neither of us knows the answer to that question today, and it's pointless to jaw about it."

She gazed at him a moment longer, then nodded. "You're right. I'm sorry. Let's get to work."

As she plugged the leads trailing from his fingers into the biofeedback machine, Jake assessed what had just happened. Kind of encouraging, actually. If she didn't mean to keep up her end of the deal, why worry about whether he was still determined to die?

Angel squeezed dollops of electrode paste onto the back of his neck and slipped the disc-type leads into place between his skin and the pillow. She flipped on the monitor and a green line snaked across the screen. At once, small tremors spiked along the line—evidence, according to Angel, of neurological activity in the spinal cord below the point where the bullet had gone in, small firings from the nerves in his neck, mostly. Angel adjusted some knobs below the screen, tuning out the impulses until the line went smooth.

"Ready?"

"Ready," Jake answered, watching the screen.

The green line took a sudden jump, and he knew she'd applied current to one of his fingers. Clearly, the nerve impulse was making it past the rupture in his spinal cord to his brain. The cord had been severed almost through, but the ten percent that remained, holding the cord together, did provide a small passageway for impulses. So why couldn't he feel the shocks? When he'd asked Angel, she'd given him a confusing little lecture about the brain. Apparently, the brain itself had no pain receptors. What it did do was *interpret* the pain registered in other parts of the body. The monitor proved that at least some of the shock impulses from his fingers were making it to the brain, but apparently not in enough force for the brain to notice and interpret them.

No pain, no gain.

"Did you feel that?" Angel asked hopefully.

"Nope."

"Let's try the middle finger."

"Hit me."

The line on the monitor jumped; Jake felt a very slight tingle in the middle finger of his right hand. "Hey!" he said. "I felt that!" Hope rushed through him. Three weeks on the new machine, and this was the first time he'd felt anything. . . .

And then he reminded himself that it didn't matter.

Angel grinned at him. "Wonderful! Okay, again."

"Yes! Just a very faint tingle." He kept enthusiasm in his voice.

"Try and increase it. Watch the screen."

He stared at the screen, for the first time in weeks not having to fake his concentration. He watched the little spikes, timing them. He focused his mind on making the rhythmic spikes bigger. Nothing happened.

"Again."

He gritted his teeth, willing the spike to broaden. Come on, he thought. For Angel.

The spike edged up another millimeter. He could feel the tingle a little more strongly.

"Jake, that's terrific. You're doing it!"

He grinned back at her.

They kept at it for another thirty minutes. He got the spike to broaden by almost three millimeters.

"All right," Angel said. "That's enough for today." She gazed at him, her eyes luminous. She was so happy, it made him feel good, too. She slid the tray table with his computer back into place and stood a moment, looking down at him. "You did fantastic," she said.

"I did, didn't I?"

She picked up his hand and kissed it. He kept the smile on his face until Angel had left the room.

Nice as it had been to see her pleasure, this changed nothing. Jake knew from reading the computer's on-line encyclopedia that the most he could hope for from this new biofeedback training was to be able to feel pressure exerted on his fingers or palms, to be aware when someone moved his hand without having to look at it. Possibly, he might be able to move his fingers just a bit.

Maybe, if Fredo ever came to see him, he could flash him the bird.

Jake carefully clamped the bit of the computer stick between his teeth. Turning the machine on again, he pecked his way back to the Internet, the Writers Corner—

And there it was, beside his sign-on code: Someone had answered his query already. A guy who'd researched plants in the Amazon for a pharmaceutical company. *Claviceps cyanidus:* death by heart attack. The right dosage was all but untraceable at autopsy. It would be a painful death. But Jake was not afraid of pain.

At least he would go out feeling *something.*

14

GREEN MONSTER

"So how's it hangin,' sport?"

Waiting for Angel to come in and start his biofeedback session, Jake felt a second of shocked disorientation at the voice. In the next instant, rage swept him. *Fredo!* The son of a bitch actually had the gall to come here.

Jake rolled his head over. Fredo was holding a huge vase of red roses. His eyes held a mixture of fascination and revulsion; his olive complexion had lightened a shade.

"Come to take my place?"

"Now Jakey, don't be bitter."

Jakey? Fredo had never called him that when he could move. Never would have dared.

He set the flowers on top of the computer monitor. Jake envisioned the water slopping into the computer, cutting off his most important link with the outside world. The thought sent a cool flood of alarm through him.

"Not there," he said as casually as he could. "Over on the windowsill."

Fredo waited long enough to show Jake he would put the flowers where he damn well pleased, then moved them to the bed table.

"What's this?" he asked, poking at the snakelike hump of the catheter line under the covers.

"When you're paralyzed," Jake said, "you don't make piss anymore, so they have to pump it into you from that bag there."

"No shit?" Fredo's eyes narrowed as he realized Jake was pulling his chain. "Real smart-ass, aren't you? So if you're so fuckin' smart, how come I'm standing here and you're lying there like a carp somebody dragged up on the beach?"

"You tell me."

Jake could not take his eyes off Fredo. The tailored Armani suit didn't conceal the fact that he'd got a bit plumper around the middle since their last meeting. His dark hair arched straight back in stiff, shiny grooves left by the broad-toothed comb Fredo favored. Jake could smell his hair spray, a tacky-sweet odor that he now realized had always clung to Fredo. His sense of smell had become much more powerful during the months he'd lain here. But not powerful enough to snort a bullet into Fredo's low forehead.

"You want I should tell you?" Fredo asked. "Okay, I'll tell you. I think you got careless, old buddy."

Jake was suddenly conscious of the bit of his computer stick lying on its pad inches from his cheek. Could he get Fredo to bend over the bed? Then grab the stick, jab it into one of those black button eyes. A scream from Fredo would be the sweetest sound in all the world.

And then Fredo would kill him with the hogleg he always packed under his coat.

Jake imagined Angel coming in to start his rehab session, finding him with a hole blown in his forehead and a greasy guy in an Armani suit with a thick gold chain around his neck staggering around bleeding from one eye. A great picture, except for one thing: Angel was already a minute or two overdue for the session, a rarity. She was probably coming down the hall right now. If so, she would hear the shot and come running, and Fredo would have to kill her too.

Hell with it. He'd never get the stick into Fredo's eye anyway. That was just dreaming. He gave Fredo a cool, inquisitive look.

"How's your boy Danziger? Bet he misses his job on the police force. Who'd you get to replace him?"

A disbelieving smile twisted Fredo's lips. He leaned over the bed. Jake saw rather than felt him prodding his body through the covers. His teeth clenched in outrage. What did the slimy bastard think he was—?

A wire. The idiot thought he was wired!

Jake almost laughed. "I never realized you felt this way about me, Fredo. Are you one of those fancy boys?"

Fredo jerked his hands back and glared at him.

"Usually the DA only wires guys who can walk," Jake said. "When you're paralyzed, they just hide the microphone in your hospital room and wait for the sleazebags to come to you."

Fredo glanced around before he could stop himself. "Asshole," he growled. Fredo had never been good at snappy repartee.

"Red roses," Jake said, glancing at the vase on the bed table. "I'm touched."

"Mr. C wants you to know his regard for you and the way you've taken this," Fredo said. His voice was flat and emotionless. He'd been sent to say it, but he didn't have to sound like he meant it

Interesting, Jake thought. Mr. C is thanking me for not ratting him out. What am I supposed to do now, thank Mr. C for sparing my life?

"Tell Mr. C I'm a stand-up guy," Jake said.

"Is that supposed to be funny? The way I hear it, you won't be standing up no more."

"Anymore."

"Huh?"

"You've got to watch those double negatives, Fredo. Unless you mean to say that I *will* be standing up."

Fredo's lip curled. "You may be flat on your ass, but you still look down on me, don't you. You always did think I was too dumb to pick that up, but I knew how you felt from day one. I'm some dumb Guinea and you're what, Joe Camel? Let you in on a little secret, Jakey: You were never anything but a common whacker, dime a dozen, selling yourself like a gigolo. And you know what I like, Jake? After all your whacking off, you just got five times as much for being the whackee. You ain't a gigolo no more. You're a whore. Maybe you should of tried it sooner."

Five times more? What was Fredo talking about? Ah, the settlement, right. The papers had picked it up two or three days ago. The $5.2 million the city was giving him not to take it to court, where only God knew what a jury might award him. He wouldn't even have to go to court. Whoopee.

"So what you going to do with all that money?" Fredo asked. "You going to hire some girls to come in here? Yeah, have some girls in, give you a nice rubdown. But you wouldn't feel a thing, would you? Hmmmm." Fredo made a show of thinking. "Maybe you could buy one of those yachts, get a crew, have 'em sail you around the world. They could put you in the dinky and row you to shore, have a wheelchair waiting. . . ."

Fredo droned on. Jake wished he'd finish gloating and get out. Angel would be hurrying in any second and he did not want Fredo to see her. He'll leer at her, Jake thought. He'll try and put a hand on her, and I won't be able to do a damn thing about it.

What'll she think of me?

Jake, I don't understand. How did you come to know a slimeball like that? Why did you ever have anything to do with him?

Angel was no fool. Fredo had mob written all over him, wore it like a badge. When Angel was first put on my case, Jake remembered, she asked me, *Did* you shoot at Senator Weingarten? Fredo will bring back all of her suspicions.

Anxiety surged through him. He had to get Fredo out of here.

". . . could hire a guy to move your arms and legs for you," Fredo was saying. "Be the first paralyzed guy to dance the herky-jerky."

"Maybe I'll hire someone to blow you away," Jake said.

Fredo's eyes narrowed again; then he smiled. "Right. Just dial up the yellow pages under whackers. I don't know about piss, but they sure don't have to put the shit back in you, do they?"

This time Jake said nothing. It was as close to a score as Fredo would ever come—the perfect motivation to walk out now, before Jake topped him again.

Sure enough, Fredo sauntered toward the door.

"Don't do anything I wouldn't do, Jakey."

Jake focused all of his mind into the middle finger of his right hand, visualizing it lying there on the covers. Was it palm up? Jake rolled his head to peer down along his arm. His palm was up. Middle finger—just raise it up two inches. Come on, come *on*. He could almost feel the finger moving, rising. But his eyes told him otherwise. His hand lay limp and still on the blanket.

It didn't matter. Fredo was gone.

Jake heard himself chuckling. A dry, terrible sound. He wanted to stop, but he was having trouble. He visualized Fredo's face as seen through a Redfield variable power scope. Centering the cross-hairs in the middle of his forehead, making an extra black eye there.

With an effort, Jake stopped. His throat burned. Pains shot up from his jaws to the side of his head. How had this curse fallen on him? To see Fredo only a few feet away, to have to exist on the same planet with him and not be able to kill him?

I need to die, he thought. I've *got* to die. Got to get out of here, just . . . get . . . *out*.

He lay for a while, eyes closed, trying to empty himself of all feeling. Where the hell was Angel? He needed her. Focusing his mind on her, he felt calmness returning. She was the one bright thing in his life, the one thing he actually looked forward to each day. Angel had thrown herself into bringing him back, knowing it probably couldn't work, but trying anyway. The way she talked to him, not just mindless inanities like the other nurses, but deep and straight from the shoulder, about whatever was on her mind—or his.

The way she looked at him.

Angel felt something for him. It was more than nurse and patient, more even than casual liking. He had never been so sure of anything. He almost wished she didn't care about him. It would be easier for her to keep her end of the deal when the time came. And easier for her to forget what she'd done. He did not want her living with the guilt of killing a man who was totally dependent on her.

I asked her, Jake thought. I begged her.

But he knew it would haunt her anyway.

He ought to wish she did not care.

"Jake!"

He turned his head as she skirted his bed, smiling. Picking up his hand, she pressed her palm against his, watching his eyes to see if he felt it.

"Nothing," he said. "Maybe you should get one of those hand-shake shockers like they sell in novelty shops . . ." He trailed off as she held her hand up and he saw the small round shocker in her palm. "That's right," he groaned, "break it to me gently."

"It's probably not working." She inspected the gadget with a baleful eye.

He caught a sudden, crushed-grass whiff of chlorophyll. "You're wearing different shoes."

"Huh?" She looked down. "Oh, yeah. My running shoes. I was late, so I decided not to change." She turned toward the door and motioned Mustaf in. The cart with the biofeedback machine rolled around the foot of the bed.

"For me?" Angel said.

Jake saw that she was looking at Fredo's roses. His heart sank. Before, on the rare occasion he'd gotten flowers—that arrangement from his lawyer, and the ones Caitlin had sent after her visit—he'd given them to Angel right away. But these . . . he couldn't. Not flowers that had had Fredo's hands on them.

"I'd better not," he said. "They're from my boss, and he said he was coming back tomorrow."

"Your boss?"

"Ex-boss." He grinned, hoping it looked sincere. "Marsh Management in Paterson, New Jersey. Bernie Marsh. He's in the city on business. You know, the guy whose buildings I used to guard."

"They're beautiful."

Jake cringed inwardly as Angel leaned into the roses, inhaling. Mustaf moved his computer aside and started hooking up his fingers. For a second their eyes met and Jake glimpsed his disapproval. Mustaf must have a pretty good bullshit detector.

Angel flipped on the machine. "Today, let's work on some of the other fingers," she said as Mustaf walked out.

"I didn't know you ran," Jake said.

"What? Oh, the shoes. Actually, I don't. I just wear them instead of tennis shoes when I'm doing something outside."

He noticed that the freckles stood out on her face. Her skin had the dark, honeyed tone of someone who has just spent a few hours in the sun.

"Picnic?" he said. "In November?"

"Yup. It's been a warm fall."

Her gaze slid away and a sudden suspicion struck him.

Angel had been with a guy.

Well, of course she had. No ring on her finger, but a woman so beautiful, so wonderful, must date. She'd never mentioned it, but it had to be. Jake tried to let the idea die stillborn, but instead it sank its vicious little milk teeth into him.

The thought of Angel having a guy had crossed his mind before, but had never seemed real, as though this room were the only place in the universe for everyone else as well as for him. But Angel had an existence—a *life*—outside of here. She had other people to talk to. Other men's hearts swelled under that direct, gold-flecked gaze; other men felt the intoxicating fullness of her attention.

Men who could touch her.

The thought became a jab of pain beneath Jake's breastbone, as though he had taken the drug he'd researched on the Internet. A close botanical relative of *Claviceps cyanidus,* only not from the Amazon, but from the dark jungles of his own mind.

"Okay," Angel said. "Ready?"

He realized she'd put the electrode discs under his neck already. He had a dim, echoic awareness of her lifting his head, of the cool slide of electrode paste over his skin. He turned his head toward the monitor screen where the flat green line jumped, then subsided. "Fire away."

The line jumped.

"Which finger?"

"What?"

"Come on, Jake. Which finger did I tickle?"

"Sorry. Hit me again."

The line jumped. "Middle?" he asked.

She sighed. "I told you, we're going to work on some of the others today."

"Oh, right. Sorry." He squinted at the screen. "Go."

The line jumped. He felt nothing. He shook his head.

"That's all right," Angel soothed. "Let's take a minute." She gazed at him. "You all right?"

"Sure." He smelled the grass again . . . crushed grass. It must have gotten on the sides of her shoes. He pictured her sitting down, her feet out to the side, blanket spread on the ground. In the picture, she was not alone, but the man with her refused to come into focus.

"Central Park?" he asked.

She nodded. "Over by the Sheep Meadow."

"Hope you didn't have mutton."

She smiled. "Fried chicken and potato salad. It's required."

He studied her. This time she did not let her gaze slide away, though she looked like she wanted to. The silence grew and took on weight, like a stalactite hovering over them. If it fell, it might skewer them both.

"Okay," he said, "I'm ready."

"No you're not. What's on your mind, Jake?"

"Nothing. What do you mean?"

She blushed slightly, the fresh tan darkening. "You just seem preoccupied."

A queasy feeling spread through him. She wasn't going to risk being wrong, but she wasn't going to let it go, either. And she wasn't wrong. "I guess you didn't go by yourself."

"No-o-o-o."

"What's his name?"

"William Fitzpatrick. He's an aide to Senator Harrison."

Jake looked at her, trying to think of something to say. Her reticence told him everything. This was not just some casual date; this guy was important to her. They'd managed to tiptoe around the subject, but she'd gotten grass on her feet and here they were. He wished he could put his hands under the covers and clench his fists, do something to draw off the pressure that swelled in his throat, making him want to shout at her.

This was crazy. What was happening to him?

"An aide to Senator Harrison," he repeated. His voice felt like it was being pushed out through a sieve.

"Yes," she said brightly. "He gets up to New York every so often. He never gets any sun, so I made him go out to Central Park with me today. He got the sunburn of his life. . . ." She trailed off, shrugging an eyebrow.

"So, are you engaged or what?"

"Not officially."

Not officially. Jake felt the weight of dead air pressing on his chest. The light seemed to drain from the room. "Would I like him?" *That was insipid. And I'll get an insipid answer.*

But he didn't. Angel cocked her head, looking past him for a minute. "I don't know," she said.

"William Fitzpatrick."

"William Fitzpatrick."

I wouldn't like him, Jake thought. I don't like him. I've never met him, and I'm never going to. I never had a chance with Angel—didn't want a chance. I want her to kill me, for Christ's sake.

So how could I be feeling this way? He mustered a smile. "Well, William is lucky to have you." It sounded self-pitying. He suppressed a groan. "Let's try with the machine again."

"Jake. . . . Okay." She drew herself up with a sigh, obviously knowing, as he did, that there was no point letting this get any more absurdly excruciating than it already was.

"Ready?"

"Go."

He felt nothing in his fingers. He wished he could feel nothing anywhere.

After she was gone, Jake booted up the computer and signed on. He stared at the quill-and-inkwell icon for Writers Corner, where he had learned about *Claviceps cyanidus,* the Amazonian poison that stopped the heart.

What had him stumped was how to get some.

He'd been letting that question slide, but it was time to get serious. Because, in four more weeks, Angel *was* going to kill him.

At least he didn't have to worry that it would ruin the rest of her life. William Fitzpatrick, aide to Senator Harrison, would be there to take her mind off it.

15

DOING IT

January

Knowing it was the last night of his life, Jake felt a vast relief. He had expected excitement, but no, only relief. Sweet oblivion was rolling toward him like a soft black cloud.

Lying with the utter stillness he hated, Jake watched shadows slide across the curtains at the end of his room as people passed in the halls. Around nine, he heard the squeak of a wheelchair tooling past his door. He realized he'd been hearing it every night lately about this time—one of the ward's paraplegics making his restless rounds up and down the hall. Jake wondered how the man—if it was a man—felt. Probably devastated that he had lost the use of his legs. No doubt he cursed the fate that had confined him to a chair, forcing him to strain and pull just to make headway. He'd have calluses on his fingers from pulling at the wheel. Right now, his biceps probably burned with exertion.

The squeaks stopped suddenly. Jake caught a whiff of sweat, strong and a little greasy—so it was a man in the chair. Jake pictured the guy pausing to reach up and wipe the sweat from his face. What a simple act. How many times had he done that himself over the years, never thinking about it, certainly finding no pleasure in it? Did the guy out there in that chair think, Well, at least I can still use my arms?

No. He didn't think that. He thought, Damn this chair.

Jake realized he was smiling into the darkness. Smiling though he didn't think it was funny . . . something he'd been doing more and more. He did not like it, but he couldn't seem to stop. Well, tomorrow, when Angel kept her promise, he'd stop.

His sense of smell awakened, Jake picked up other odors—sweet Keri lotion from the next room; a hint of perfume, strong, like old women wear. A trace of cigarette smoke prickled high up in his nose, probably some orderly snatching a few puffs in the stairwell. The tobacco smell made him think of Mrs. Nacht. He pictured her sitting silently on her rocker, smoking, pausing every now and then to lean forward and cough.

Mom.

An arid chuckle escaped him.

And there was Sarge, sitting on the big kitchen chair, cleaning and oiling the Garand M1C with the Lyman Alaskan 2.2 hunting scope. Jake could almost smell the thin scent of the gun oil. *Come over here, son, I want to show you something.*

Why did he call me son? Jake wondered.

He felt a sudden, burning impatience. Come on, morning. Come on, Angel.

He tried to picture what was going to happen, how it would go down when he asked Angel to keep her promise. The picture would not come clear and that made him uneasy. Maybe his old pal paranoia was trying to tell him something—that Angel wasn't going to show. She'd know what day it was as surely as he did.

What if she took off and he never saw her again? Wouldn't be a damned thing he could do about it. Running away from her promise would make her feel like a rat, but she'd probably prefer that to murder.

She'll be here, Jake told himself. She's not the type to run.

He went over in his mind what he would ask her to do. *Claviceps cyanidus,* the heart poison, was out. He'd never had a chance of getting any. Even if the pharmaceutical employee on the computer Net wasn't snowing him, even if the man had his own private stock, he'd never mail a lethal poison, untraceable at autopsy, to some stranger just because the guy claimed to be a writer doing research. Working on the problem had helped pass time, but that was all.

Still, in the end, the computer *had* provided the solution. Jake felt himself grinning again. He sucked his lips in and bit down on them, holding them in place until the urge passed.

The shadows stopped moving on his curtains. The hospital settled into the deep silence of the late shift. Jake thought about Fredo . . . Mr. C . . . Danziger. The familiar anger came, enough to warm him, make him wish he could push back the sheet. The smell of gun oil came to him from memory again, fragrant as incense. Odd, how a word like incense could have two conflicting meanings. Incense the noun—with a tip of the hat to the computer's CD-ROM dictionary—was something the priest burned to give scented smoke during worship. But as a verb, incense meant "to anger." How many people knew that? Or that the term for his former profession—"assassin"—derived from the word hashish, because in the eleventh century the followers of Hasan ibn-al-Sabbah used to smoke the stuff before making murder raids on their enemies? I've learned a lot in the past four months, Jake thought.

But not how to stay alive.

After a long time, he dozed.

Clinking dishes woke him—the nurse's aide with his breakfast. Bright sunlight streamed through now open curtains.

A nice day for dying.

Jake's first impulse was to tell the aide to take the breakfast away. He wasn't hungry. Then he realized eating might give him an edge. When the current coursed through his body, it might make him vomit. Then, even if the shock didn't kill him, he could choke to death.

He let the aide feed him every spoonful of the oatmeal, every bite of toast. He sucked up eight ounces of orange juice and eight of milk through the bent straw. He tasted nothing. As usual, the aide chatted with him. He calibrated his responses carefully. Later, with her perceptions colored by knowing he was dead, she would say, "Come to think of it, Mr. Nacht *did* seem depressed this morning."

But he mustn't make her think it now or they might watch him more closely.

After she was gone, Jake turned on the computer and stared at the screen. He gripped the stick in his mouth and rotated it between his teeth until the notch he'd chewed near the end was facing down. He let the notch settle onto the slight metal lip on the tray stand. By working the stick backward into his mouth, he was able to drag the heavy tray an inch closer. He heard its casters squeak under the bed. Angling the stick slightly, he clamped down with his teeth and scrabbled at the lip of the tray again. He drew it in another half inch toward him. Sweat started up at his hairline.

After fifteen more minutes, the stick was at an extreme angle. The tray had moved three inches, but, with the stick angled so sharply to the side, he could no longer get enough purchase. He'd practiced for two weeks, and this was still the best he could do. Though he'd expected it, he felt a weary disappointment. No way around it—he needed Angel. She'd have to put the computer monitor next to his face and make it look like he'd pulled it down there.

No problem, Jake told himself. The thought that she might have helped me will never enter their minds. To suspect that, someone would have to lie here and try it himself, day after day, for as long as I did. And no one's going to do that. They're going to accept the obvious, that the severely depressed and determined Jake Nacht was able to build up enough strength in his jaws to pull the tray to him and drag the computer monitor over. And fate made it fall so that the power cord was close enough to his face to bite.

He'd wait until Angel was gone to chew through the cord, of course.

One more big shock. *Did you feel that, Jake?*

Not for long.

Jake allowed himself to relax. The sweat had barely dried on his face when Angel came in.

"How are you doing this morning?" Her smile was forced, but he thought he detected something else in her expression, too—a suppressed excitement. Odd.

"I'm ready to go." His voice sounded oddly hoarse.

She gazed at him, the beautiful gold-flecked eyes turning shiny.

Damn, Jake thought. He rolled his head away, so he wouldn't have to see her cry.

The bed sagged a little under his shoulder as Angel settled on the edge beside him, and he could not stop himself from looking at her again. "Would you say I've tried?"

She blinked and brushed a finger across the corner of one eye. "You know you have, Jake."

And he realized it was true. Somewhere along the line, faking it had become really trying.

And still he could not move so much as his index finger.

"Angel, I'm sorry, but I want out."

"No."

He felt a cold rush of dread. "You can't go back on your word."

Tears began to roll down Angel's face. He groaned, overwhelmed with misery, feeling like the world's worst bastard. But he couldn't stay trapped in this useless flesh just to keep a woman from crying.

"Come on, don't do that. It's wrong to be sad. You'll be giving me what I want."

Her tears increased, pouring down her cheeks. Her face was rigid and he knew she was battling for control. A woman like Angel didn't cry easily. Her shoulders twitched with a suppressed sob.

"Oh, Jake. Is it so easy to think of leaving me? Don't you feel anything for me?"

Jake stared at her, astonished. "Of course I do. Don't you know that?"

Angel bit her lip and blotted gently at the tears. "What do I mean to you, Jake?"

He hesitated, unsure what she wanted. Months ago, he'd put the same question to Caitlin, and now Angel was bringing it back to him. Did she want him to say that he loved her? Didn't she know he couldn't love anyone? It was too late for that, had been for a long time.

But he did feel something. If he were a whole man, he would like to be with her every day. He would watch after her, keep her from harm. They would laugh and joke and do things together. He would get her anything she wanted that was within his power. When she got grass on her shoes at a picnic, it would be with him. But he did not love her. Love was not for Jake Nacht.

"Why are you so afraid?" she said softly. "I can say it, even if you can't. I love you, Jake."

Jake felt his heart race suddenly. He felt a powerful urge he'd schooled himself never to permit again—to jump up and cavort around the room. He groaned a second time, unable to help himself. This could not be. Angel in love with him was even more incomprehensible than him in love with Angel. How could she love a man who was bedridden, unable to move? He could never take her for a drive, never climb into bed with her, never hold her in his arms. How could she see him lying here day after day and not grasp that?

"What about your boyfriend?" he asked before he could stop himself. *What did it matter? This could never be.*

"What about him? I've dated lots of guys, Jake. None of them ever looked at me the way you do. None of them listened to me the way you do. You can tell what I'm thinking, read what I'm feeling. Not only can you, you *do* it, all the time. Jake, a man isn't a body. That's just the wrappings. A man is what you find inside. And you are the man I want."

"You're just saying that so you won't have to kill me." Realizing what had just popped out of his mouth, Jake grinned despite himself.

Angel laughed, wiping at a tear.

Stop this, Jake thought. *Now.* You are not what she thinks she sees. You have killed seventeen men. And you want to kill three more. You fall asleep every night lining up their heads in the cross-hairs of an imaginary rifle.

"If you knew the real me," he said, "you wouldn't love me."

Angel gave him a knowing half smile, more enchanting than Mona Lisa's. "I *do* know the real you. Whatever it is you think you've done that's so terrible, those days are behind you."

Right, Jake thought. I'm all done *do*ing anything.

"Angel, it's impossible. Love is a physical thing, too. And I can't give you that."

"Oh? You've still got a tongue, don't you?"

Jake felt himself blushing.

"Jake, you can give me physical love. But I can't give it to you—not at this point, anyway. Is that the problem?"

"Don't be silly—"

"I am *not* being silly. Think about it. Have you had any . . . desire for me? Physical desire?"

Jake felt a horrible, gray dread settling over him. He would rather do anything than talk about this. But he could see she needed the answer.

"Angel, I don't know how it is for a woman. But for a man, physical desire happens in two places at the same time—the head and . . . down there." He motioned with his chin. "Have I wanted you? Yes. You're so beautiful in every way, what man wouldn't want you? But I want you the way a very old man would—with my memory. I remember how it felt to get hard for a woman. I could give you the words for it. But remembering and talking aren't the same as feeling and doing."

Jake stopped, seeing pity in her eyes. It galled him. He fought the urge to turn away again. He ached to die. Why couldn't she understand that?

Just then, something she'd said registered: *Not at this point, anyway.*

He looked at her, frustrated. "Angel, you've got to face it. My condition is permanent . . ." He trailed off. She was smiling. Why was she smiling?

"Maybe not," she said.

"What do you mean, maybe not?" Jake felt an irrational surge of anger. "What the hell do you mean, maybe not?"

Angel got off the bed. "Wait here, Jake."

"Is that supposed to be funny? Angel, come back here. Don't you run out on me, damn it, you promised . . ." He realized she was gone. His heart was pounding again, thumping the mattress so hard that the bed trembled.

Maybe not.

Jake's mind whirled.

Maybe not, maybe not, maybe not . . .

Angel walked back in. He saw that she was carrying a small box. A dusty, grain smell, not unpleasant, wafted ahead of her.

Angel opened the box and took out a white rat. "His name is Jake," she said. "I named him that when he first came on the study."

"What study?"

The rat squirmed out of her hand and ran up over her breast, perching on her shoulder. It nuzzled her ear. Jake found himself envying the rat.

"So what's the plan?" he said. "You going to transplant my brain into Jake junior's body?"

Angel laughed. "Notice anything funny about the way he moves?"

With an effort, Jake controlled his impatience. "No. He pawed your breast and now he's kissing your ear, which is just what I'd like to do. I'd say he has real good moves but needs a little polish in his manners. So what's the point?"

"The point," Angel said, "is that six weeks ago, Jake the rat couldn't move anything but his whiskers. He had a ninety percent severance of his spinal cord. He was a 'permanent, nonreversible' quadriplegic."

Jake felt a rush of vertigo, the bed seeming to spin beneath him as the world changed before his eyes. He locked his gaze on the rat, the most beautiful thing he had ever seen. The bed stopped spinning, but now he seemed to float, an ecstatic sensation so alien it was almost frightening. After a second, he recognized the unfamiliar emotion: *joy!*

"Angel . . . wait a minute now, are you . . . God, I can't believe . . ."

"I'm not putting you on, Jake. I wouldn't do that."

"Jesus, Angel!" Shifting his gaze to her face, he was still hyperaware of the rat crawling along her shoulder. "What is this? You come in here knowing it's day zero and let me go through my whole spiel about wanting to die. Then all that about leaving you and don't I care anything for you? You cry, as if it were really going to be my last day on earth."

"You mean you've changed your mind?" Angel asked innocently.

"Don't change the subject!"

"I cried because you've been through so much. And I brought up . . . that other first, because I knew if I told you about the rat right away, I'd lose the chance to learn how you really feel about me."

Jake tried to sort back through what he'd said to her. Had he told her he loved her or that he couldn't love her? Whatever, it was gone—wiped out by the rat. There it sat on her shoulder, his salvation, grooming its whiskers with rapid but fussy motions of its tiny paws. It stopped and peered back at him. He felt the most incredible, warm lightness flowing through him. His heart was floating on a lake of gold. He wanted to grab Angel and kiss her. Hell, he'd even kiss the rat. "You want to know how I feel about you?" he asked.

"I love you, Angel, of course I love you!"

She gave him a half smile. "Sure, you say that now. If this works, you're going to love everybody for a while."

Not everybody, Jake thought. It took him a second to dredge

Fredo's face into his mind, center it in the crosshairs. *No, think about Fredo later.*

"Angela!"

Jake recognized the voice from the hallway, and then Dr. Graham hurried into his field of vision and snatched the rat from Angel's shoulders, putting it quickly back in the box. He glared at her. "What are you doing?"

"I'm solving two problems at once," Angel said.

Graham gave her a blank look. "Angela? You can't just take a rat from the lab. When I saw one was missing, I was frantic." He sounded incredulous and wounded.

Jake felt a deep inner satisfaction as the missing piece of the Dr. Graham puzzle dropped into place. The guy had been doing research on healing severed spinal cords. And he'd had a big success. That's why he kept looking at me like I might be the goose that laid the golden egg, Jake thought.

He cleared his throat. "Good morning, Doctor. When can you operate?"

Graham's eyes widened; then he frowned furiously at Angel. "You didn't!"

"Don't be mad, Uncle Joe. I had to."

Uncle Joe? Jake thought. Christ, this woman is almost as good at keeping secrets as I am.

"What's the problem, Doc? You're a genius. You made the rat walk again. Now I'm volunteering."

Dr. Graham stared at Jake with a mixture of dismay and greedy speculation so comical Jake had to laugh. Graham rubbed at his thinning hair, making it stand up.

"No. It's out of the question. You have no idea what's involved." He shot Angel another black look. "How much have you told him?"

"Everything."

"Mother of God!" Graham pulled at his hair, turned in a half circle, stared at the ceiling. He muttered under his breath. "If you weren't my only sister's daughter . . ."

Jake felt himself starting to bristle. He did not like the man's tone with Angel. With an effort, he kept his voice calm.

"So, what's the problem, Dr. Graham?"

"What's the problem? What's the *problem?* What *isn't* the problem? This research has to be kept absolutely secret until I have a clear success. If this gets out—"

"I know how to keep quiet."

Graham eyed him, and Jake thought he saw distaste in the man's eyes. "Do you? You've been practicing, have you?"

"Uncle." Angel's voice was low but sharp.

Jake sensed something passing between them. *He still thinks I shot at Whiny. That's why he looks at me sometimes like I'm something he picked up on the heel of his shoe. He and Angel have argued about it.*

Graham looked at him again. "You'd better keep quiet about what you *already* know, or—"

"Doctor, you don't need to threaten me," Jake said quietly. "In fact, it's a bit unwise, don't you think? If I *were* the sort to babble your secret, you'd be better off not insulting me."

"I'm sorry," Graham said, making an imperfect effort to sound it. "It's just that it's far, far too early for human trials. I explained that to Angel yesterday. Just because rat twenty-three has, for the moment, regained full mobility doesn't mean we're home free. Some of the rats receiving the surgery have become psychotic. Others have suffered reversals. God knows how many other problems could crop up."

"So how soon can we operate?"

Graham raised his hands and glared at the ceiling. "You're not listening, man."

Jake was momentarily too fascinated to answer. He would never have imagined that the cool, clinical Dr. Graham who looked spaced-out half the time could become so agitated.

Graham drew a deep breath. "Let me try once more to explain it to you. I'm afraid Angel may have given you false hope, Mr. Nacht. Yes, this rat has regained full use of its limbs. Four others not only regained sensation and motion, they became psychotic.

And we've had other, very bad outcomes. My grant is up for renewal, and NIH, while they are very excited about the few successes, know as I do that we are far from having a workable technique. In fact, they've told me they will only renew my grant if I bring in two of their own researchers."

Graham tramped away from the bed to the window and glowered down at the parking lot.

Jake could see that he was seething. And he could understand why.

"You mean they're blackmailing you into giving them a piece of the action?"

"Not at all," Graham said without turning. But his tone made it clear that it was exactly what he did mean. "They . . . feel that they may be able to help work out the problems."

"They think their boys are smarter than you, even though you're the one who developed this."

This time Graham said nothing.

Grinning, Angel flashed Jake the okay sign.

"Doctor, you say there have been some very bad outcomes. As bad as being paralyzed?"

"Worse," Graham said in a low, tired voice.

"Excuse me, but I believe I'm in a better position to know that than you. You say some of the rats went psychotic. What does that mean?"

Graham turned back to face him. "They wandered around bumping into things. They bit at themselves. Some of them ran in circles until they fell down exhausted. It was clear that they had totally lost touch with reality."

"Doc, would it surprise you to know that I have prayed a hundred times that I could lose touch with reality?"

"It would surprise me to know that you prayed."

"Uncle—"

Jake shot Angel a look, quieting her.

"I'm sorry," Graham said stiffly. "That was uncalled for."

"No problem, Doc. But let me be sure I understand this . . ." Jake stopped as he saw Graham roll his eyes very quickly at the ceiling. Revelation number two: *He not only thinks I might be a killer, he thinks I'm stupid.* Jake was surprised to find that it did not make him angry. If the man could make him walk again, he could be forgiven absolutely anything.

"The rats that turned psychotic were totally paralyzed for how long before you did the surgery on them?"

"It varied," Graham said. "From three or four weeks to three months."

"How do you know they didn't go psychotic while they were paralyzed? What does a rat that can't move do to show it's gone psychotic?"

Graham cocked his head. Suddenly, there was respect in his eyes. But he said, "If that were so, they should have recovered when their motion was restored—"

"Bull. Dr. Graham, you *are* a genius. If this works out, you're going to be one of the great men in history and the first thing I'm going to do after you operate is kiss your feet. But you don't know word one about being paralyzed. I came this close to going insane—imagine I'm holding my hand up, Doc, and you can't see daylight between my thumb and fingers. For two solid months, the only thing I've wanted is to die. I laughed for no reason. I ground my teeth. I had out-of-body experiences, thinking I was floating in space. If I had to go on like this, I can tell you I'd definitely lose touch with reality. And once I did, even if I started walking again, if I realized it at all, I'd probably think it was part of the delusion and be afraid to go sane again."

"I understand what you're saying," Graham said, "but you have to realize that the vast majority of quadriplegics do not go insane."

"Again, how would you know? If you mean we don't stagger down Broadway muttering to ourselves, you can only be right. But I believe I heard someone say that a third of us try to snuff ourselves. Being totally unable to move changes you, Doc—not just your body, your mind. And even if walking would put *me* right again, maybe it's not so easy for a rat. Maybe with their tiny brains, what they went through while they were paralyzed was more irreversible than it would be with humans."

Graham stared at him, almost smiling. "Mr. Nacht, you might have had a decent career in science."

"Operate on me."

"Damn it, man, you don't understand. The FDA would never grant me approval to do surgery on humans at this point."

"So don't ask."

"Ridiculous," Graham sputtered. "I could be severely disciplined. I'd lose my funding for sure. Maybe even my license."

"How does five point two million sound? Would that keep you going?"

Graham stared at him. "Five million?"

"Okay, I'll keep the two hundred thousand. I'm a rich man—or hadn't you heard?"

"You would do that—fund my research?"

"I was thinking of using the money to help retire the federal deficit," Jake said dryly, "but yes. Under the right circumstances, I think I could be talked into funding you instead."

"The right circumstances . . ."

"First, we tell no one. If you get me moving again, I fake that I'm paralyzed until I'm discharged from the hospital and out of everyone's sight." *Which I must do anyway.* "If you don't get me moving, same thing. No one ever knows what you did but you, me, and Angel. Second, if it does somehow get out, and the FDA comes down on you, I take over your funding and you, pardon the expression, tell them to put it where the sun don't shine. Third, I give you five million no matter what happens. But the bottom line is this, Doc. You're going to move up from rats to me."

Graham stared at him for a long time, but it was clear to Jake that he was seeing other things, winnowing through all the possible outcomes, probably imagining the fame, the glory that would be his down the line even though he couldn't publicize Jake right away; the immediate disgrace if he was found out, the loss of funding, and then again, the five million.

"I'm sorry," Graham said at last. "I just can't risk it."

16

UNDER THE KNIFE

Jake felt euphoric as Angel wheeled him toward Dr. Graham's lab. If this worked he was going to dance for an entire night with Angel, dance until they both dropped, then lie on the floor wiggling his feet until he passed out.

I'm out of control, Jake thought.

He tried to focus on the warnings Angel and Dr. Graham had drummed into him for the past week: The surgery might not be a success; and even if it was, despite his smooth reasoning about the rats, it might indeed unbalance his mind.

So what? Nothing could be worse than what he'd gone through the past four months. The surgery *might* make him loco; *not* having the surgery would definitely blow his circuits.

Jake gazed at Angel's beautiful face. It was tense with worry. The halls of the hospital receded endlessly behind her. They seemed to be filled to overflowing with people—especially doctors and other nurses. Angel kept saying hi, how's it going, good morning Dr. this and Dr. that. Her voice sounded calm enough, almost normal, but Jake could tell she was rigid with anxiety. If anyone dreamed that she was wheeling him into Dr. Joseph Graham's lab for surgery rather than just to have a look at his research, it would be the end for Graham.

Jake wondered exactly how Graham was justifying this to himself. It seemed clear he thought Jake was low-life scum, possibly the man who had shot at Senator Weingarten, but maybe that was a plus for him rather than a minus. Maybe in his own mind, Graham thought he would be operating on a convict—or someone who deserved to be a convict. If the operation went wrong, Jake Nacht would get what he deserved—continued punishment.

And if it succeeded?

Had Dr. Graham given any thought to the fact that he might be putting a hit man back out on the street? Maybe he'd decided, even if that was the result, the greater good made it all right. Graham seemed like a driven man, obsessed, completely myopic about what he did.

Obsessed was something Jake understood. Because, if Dr. Graham succeeded today, the first thing Jake was going to do when he could walk again was go after Fredo, Mr. C, and Danziger—the goal he'd fallen asleep to and awakened with every day since his first in the hospital.

He imagined the look on Fredo's face the second before the bullet plowed in.

Hey, Jakey, Jakey, you can walk! What the fuck is—Christ, don't shoot—

Jake felt a jolt in his neck, saw a double door sliding along the side of the gurney. The doors flapped shut behind Angel, and she seemed to relax a bit. She turned and locked them behind her. Jake winked at her. She gave him a quick, nervous smile. Dr. Graham's head floated into view. Apparently he'd already scrubbed for the surgery. He looked strange in the green cap and mask; his eyes seemed magnified. There was an odd light in them, like he'd taken speed.

"Are you clear on the arrangement?" Dr. Graham asked him.

"I'm clear."

"The official story is, I'm checking you out today to a private clinic where you'll undergo evaluation. That should give enough time for any adverse effects of surgery to recede. You must not, in any case, divulge that you came to this lab and underwent surgery."

"I understand, Doctor."

"I hope you do. I could be ruined. If I do restore movement, you might find it hard to fake paralysis, but it's vital that you do. A lot of people have a general idea what my research is about. We must avoid any possibility of suspicion."

"I couldn't agree more, Doc." Jake suppressed a smile. If Graham restored movement to him, he'd have his own very good reasons for pretending that he was still paralyzed.

Until the right moment came.

"You agree to all that?"

"I swear it," Jake said gravely.

"Are you ready, then?"

"I'm beyond ready, Doctor."

Graham's mask billowed and Jake realized he'd blown out a huge breath. Graham nodded at Angel. She moved up beside Jake and he saw her lift his arm. She held a syringe up, giving him a quick look. "Just a barbiturate," she said. "You don't need to be knocked out."

"Good." Jake didn't like the idea of going under anesthesia—counsel from his old pal paranoia.

"This won't sting," Angel said. "Are you sure you want to give up painless shots?"

"Very funny."

She concentrated on his arm. A moment later, her face blurred a little. It seemed to swim in a golden haze. He smelled something wonderful. "Whazzat? Perfume?"

"No, that's Betadine disinfectant," Angel said. "Basically iodine."

"Hah." Jake thought that was quite funny.

"Now we're going to roll you onto the operating table," Graham said. "We'll do our best not to jolt you—usually four people do this part."

"I'm a bit shorthanded myself," Jake said. He could not tell if Graham smiled.

"One, two, three," Graham said, and the world spun around. Green floor tiles jittered in Jake's vision, then steadied up. He felt a cushion against his chin. He gazed at the tiles. They were beautiful. Those barbiturates were all right. Fredo could walk right up and pop him, and he'd die grinning.

"It'll be a few minutes," Graham said. "Angel has to scrub in."

Jake stared at the tiles.

"Now, you understand," Graham said, "this isn't just surgery. In fact, the surgical aspect of it is quite minor. I'm going to expose the point where your cord was cut, check the repair, and then inject the site with fetal nerve tissue in saline solution. Then I'm going to patch over the cut made by the bullet with omentum, which is a tissue that normally drapes between the stomach and colon—"

"Where'd you get it?"

"What?"

"Where'd you get the Oh Mentum. Did'ja have to ice someone?" *Jesus, careful.*

"What do you mean 'ice'?"

"I mean keep it on ice after you cut it out of someone," Jake said, trying to recover.

"Yes. The tissue is from a man who died in a car crash just this morning. He was an organ donor. The omentum contains various biochemicals that encourage blood vessels and nerves to grow. . . ."

Jake let him ramble on. Graham was nervous; he needed to talk. Jake was nervous, too. Talking about icing people. Christ. He made a mental note never to let anyone give him a barbiturate again.

"Ready," said Angel's voice.

Jake gazed at the tiles, woozily determined to keep his mouth shut. Minutes dragged by. Graham mumbled short, cryptic instructions to Angel. Jake heard the tinkle of metal on stainless steel, presumably the surgical instruments. This isn't so bad, he thought—

And then he felt a blow to his spine. Hot pain speared through his back; he gritted his teeth, but instead of subsiding, the pain grew worse, building and building. Distantly, he heard someone scream and realized it was him. Everything went black.

He awoke to pain. He felt like his spine had been shattered and someone was dragging a rake along the splintered ends of bone and nerve. Groaning, he opened his eyes. Angel's head hovered over him. Her face was a pale mask of concern. Graham's face moved up beside Angel's. His skin was the color of ash. He was no longer wearing his mask and cap.

"What happened?" Jake groaned.

"The operation is over," Graham said. "You're still in the lab. How do you feel?"

"Like someone's practicing with Ginsu knives on my back."

"Dear God. I'm sorry. None of the rats reacted this way. But it may be a promising sign." He nodded to Angel. Jake felt a numb pressure on his arm, then a flood of coolness. Almost at once, the pain subsided.

"Better now?" Angel asked.

"Much. There's still some pain, but nothing I can't handle."

Angel and Graham exchanged glances.

"I just shot you up with a big dose of morphine," Angel said. "It should last about four to six hours."

"What did you mean by 'a promising sign'?" Jake asked Graham.

"It means the sensory nerves in your spine are still functional. The motor ones should be too, but I can't be sure."

Jake felt the excitement returning. Of course! If he could feel pain, he could feel other things.

"When will we know?"

"When you can move one of your fingers."

The room blurred around Graham's face. His voice rolled on, but became meaningless babble. Darkness closed over Jake again.

The next time he woke up, he was in a different room. It looked like a hospital room, but Angel informed him he was now at Uncle Joe's clinic in Brooklyn. He coasted in and out of sleep for two days, waking long enough for Angel to feed him. He'd ask Angel the time and day, then submerge again in the warm ocean of morphine.

He lost track of time.

He awoke again. His head was clearer and the pain was back. Rolling his head to the side, he saw Angel sleeping in a chair at the foot of his bed. A second later, agony flared in his spine, making him gasp. Apparently, rolling his head was no longer painless. He dug a hand into the sheet, fighting to keep from groaning—

Dug a hand into the sheet!

Jake gasped with shock and elation. The room spun around him, catching him up in a wave of giddiness. Jesus, his hand, he could feel his right hand groping away from him, clutching the edge of the bed! Pain was still there, but so what, Christ, so what? The pain would pass. He could *move!* Jake felt his face twisting in a savage grin.

I'm coming, Fredo.

PART 3

RESURRECTION

17

REHAB

April

Jake sat on the edge of his bed and squeezed the hollow rubber ball over and over, gritting his teeth at the jolt each rep sent up his forearm.

He told himself he was not in a bad mood. How could he be? Damn it, three months ago he'd been lying in bed unable to move, longing to die, and then a miracle had given him back his body—his life. After a fabulous emotional jackpot like that, he shouldn't be able even to imagine being in a bad mood, now or ever again.

All right, so the body given back to him was a frail, shrunken knockoff of the Jake Nacht from before that bastard Danziger had back-shot him. Frail was better than paralyzed—far better. He'd get back to what he was, he was working on it. He was getting there.

Like hell.

Coming out of the surgery he'd been able to grab the sheets, and now he could grab a rubber ball. Big improvement. Okay, yeah, he could walk—or totter, to be more accurate. The pain had faded, but the weakness seemed to be settling in for a permanent stay.

Those months in bed, not moving unless someone moved him,

had done a job on him. Angel kept assuring him that his soreness, frailty, and lack of coordination were completely natural and to be expected. That the work she and the other nurses had done in the hospital, flexing his arms and legs every day, had slowed the shriveling of his tendons and ligaments, but very little muscle tone could be preserved that way. Translated, his muscles had turned to jelly. Not just the big ones in his arms and legs but the little ones in the pads of his fingers, around his ribs, along his spine. His back ached incessantly from the rehab exercises. Being fifteen pounds thinner than the day he'd been shot, he looked all right, but he hated the flabbiness his probing fingers found in his biceps, his gut. His head had stopped wobbling on top of his shoulders, but his neck was constantly sore.

Even now, after months of work, it took a fierce effort to more than dent a racquetball in his right hand, and his left was weaker still. His coordination was so scrambled he could barely hold a pen; scrawling his name took immense concentration. Here at Graham's clinic he had zero chance to get close to a gun, let alone pick one up, try to aim it, and squeeze the trigger. Even if he could, he had an idea what would happen: He'd be lucky to hit the wall instead of the floor.

If this was going to be it, he had about as much chance of sneaking up on Fredo and putting a bullet in his head as he did of winning the shot put at the next Olympics.

Patience, he told himself. I always had it before. I never capped someone until I'd planned every step, plotted escape routes, gone over all possible outcomes, run through dozens of practice shoots at the same range and light conditions as the hit. Sometimes it took weeks. What's my hurry?

This is personal, that's what.

Squeezing the ball harder, Jake tried to focus on the prize: between the eyes for Fredo, yes, but first the right knee and then the groin, and let him lie there helpless and terrified and in pain until someone came to drag him away. Then a final shot to the head, more merciful than Fredo deserved. All from a distance, all without being seen. In his last seconds of life, Fredo would feel the hatred Jake had kissed into the bullets; as Fredo sucked his last breath, somewhere deep inside, he would realize who had killed him, but it would be far too late.

Then what?

When Fredo went down, what would Mr. C do? Fredo was such a scumbag he must have lots of enemies. None could hate him worse than Jake Nacht, but Jake Nacht was helpless, right?

Mr. C *will* check, Jake thought. Right now he's forgotten me, but if Fredo goes down, he'll look me up, just to be sure there haven't been any miracles. So after I hit Fredo, I get straight back here and lie in bed, be ready any moment, day or night, even if Mr. C sends someone in through my window after midnight. All I have to do is lie still for a few weeks—hell, I've had enough practice at that. Graham and Angel may wonder why I'm suddenly being so careful, but they'll pitch in selling the con, because Graham has his own reasons for wanting to keep me a secret. When Mr. C is satisfied I'm still paralyzed, he'll forget about me again. Then I slip out and do Danziger—from behind, in the back, a single slug at the base of the neck like he did me.

And then, right away, Mr. C himself.

Have to hit him before he finds out about Danziger. Fredo's hit could be anyone, but Danziger will fill the pattern. No time for anything elaborate. Mr. C will be the lucky one—a clean, quick kill, out of the blue—

"You sure look determined!"

Jake felt his frozen grin thawing, warming on his face, as though Angel were a sun that had suddenly dawned in the room. Her gold-flecked eyes, the chestnut hair, the slight skew of her smile, caused a lightness in his chest, a feeling that, if he just took her hands, his pain and awkwardness would drop away and he'd be able to dance her around the room.

"Watch!" he said.

With a savage extra effort, he squeezed the ball almost flat, then tossed it toward the other hand. It bumped off his palm and away before he could close his fingers. Grabbing for it pulled him off balance. He slipped from the edge of the bed and dropped to his knees. His face flamed with mortification.

Wisely, Angel did not try to help him. His legs wallowed, then thrashed, and then he got control, pushing up from the floor and reclaiming his seat on the bed.

"Guess that one needs more practice," he said.

She picked up the ball and put it back in his hand, making sure her fingers touched his, then drawing them away in a soft caress. His heart soared. She worked with him a few minutes—some range-of-motion exercises and then a backrub. When she was gone, he realized that he was, in fact, not in a bad mood.

Two weeks later, he suddenly began to improve very quickly. Angel told him that this, too, was expected, but she hadn't wanted to say anything in case it didn't happen. After all, this was unplowed ground. No one's spinal cord had ever regenerated before.

He continued to improve.

Four months after the surgery, he sat on the examining table in the ridiculous, flappy hospital gown, while Dr. Graham tested his reflexes, whacking at his knees and elbows with that little rubber mallet of his. Outside the window, Jake could hear the traffic in the street, the chortle of pigeons strutting in the casement.

How many times, pacing to his window and back, had he looked out and seen nothing? Then, a few weeks ago, his healing had crossed some magical threshold; the blackout curtain of pain and weakness had lifted and he'd begun to be aware of the world outside this room. The window looked out on a broad Brooklyn street lined with three-story brick and stone buildings. Hanging from half the windows were flower boxes, most of them painted a rich dark blue. Down a few blocks, he could see an old theater whose marquee was permanently christened Sons of Norway Hall. Market stalls gave off the mingled smells of potato pancakes, gefilte fish, and the peculiar brown goat's cheese called *jetost.*

Few native New Yorkers knew about this little Nordic enclave in Brooklyn, but this wasn't the first time he'd been here. He'd found it shortly after he took over Sarge's business, during that month or two when he was mapping the city into his brain. He made sure he reconnoitered a few blocks around each and every subway stop, including the elevated station five blocks down the hill from here.

According to Angel, her uncle's clinic itself had once been a small apartment building owned by Dr. Graham's Norwegian aunt. When Tante Hanna had died, Graham had inherited the place and converted it into a rehab center, but echoes of its past still clung—the transoms over the windows, a slight pitch and roll in parts of the flooring, and an attic out of some gothic novel.

The memory of that dusty top floor burst to life like a mint rolling with sudden flavor against his tongue. Yesterday, he'd finally made it up the last, narrow flight to the attic and found a strange, forgotten world filled with old mirror stands, cobwebbed rocking chairs, and curious wooden equipment that looked like it had been salvaged from the gymnasium of a turn-of-the-century sanatorium. That, and a dog, peering at him with utter, silent stillness from behind an old rowing machine.

Gave him a start, that dog, and then he'd realized it was stuffed, apparently one of Tante Hanna's treasured pets of long ago. Jake could imagine her petting the little dog, cooing endearments, feeding it treats—

What the hell was wrong with him? Looking at a stuffed dog, for Christ's sake, and feeling the love and pain of an old woman he'd never met. Sentimental rubbish. He needed to keep his mind clear, focused on Fredo, Danziger, and Mr. C.

Doc Graham tapped his kneecap and the leg jumped, but not as much as it used to. The doc had told him that was a *good* sign. His skin still had a faraway feel to it, like he was enclosed in soft plastic. He could feel, but every sensation seemed padded. But that was okay too, because the padding was getting thinner and thinner every week.

"Very good," Graham said. "And how are you feeling?"

"Good. No complaints."

"I mean your moods, mental state, so on."

Jake suppressed a groan. Wasn't Graham ever going to stop with this?

"I have a good mental state." He felt the awkwardness of the words, clunking out as though English were suddenly his second language. The only thing stranger than having all these new feelings was having to talk about them.

"No nightmares, no strange impulses?" Graham peered at him with grave concentration.

"Wel-l-l. I do have this occasional urge to void where prohibited."

Graham stared blankly at him.

"You ought to like that joke," Jake said. "It's got one of your doctor words in it."

"Oh, yes, I see." Graham delivered a weak laugh.

The door eased open and Angel slipped inside, closing it again. Her agitated manner triggered a warning; the bottom dropped out of Jake's stomach and then he got himself moving as Angel spoke.

"A man is here to see Jake. I told him to wait downstairs, but I don't know if he will."

Jake slipped into bed, straightened his body, and pulled up the sheets. There was just enough time to lay his arms along his sides before the door opened and Fredo leaned in. "Surprise!"

Graham bristled. "Sir, excuse me, but visiting hours are in the evening."

Fredo ignored him, gazing at Jake, who rolled his head slowly to the side. *That's as much as you can move. Don't forget it for a second.* "Hello, Fredo," he said.

Graham reached to take Fredo's arm, but Angel took his, instead, stopping the motion. The glimmer of fear in her eyes panged Jake. Her intuitions were so finely tuned she could smell what Fredo was—*and I'm in no shape to protect her.*

"I'm sure we can make an exception," Fredo said. "Jakey and I go way back, right, Jake?"

"Right."

"Well, all right then," Graham said. "But in future, please try and come between seven and eight in the evening."

"Sure, Doc," Fredo said, still not looking at Graham or Angel.

When they were gone, he ambled to the bedside. His tan was very deep, Jake saw, except for pale circles sunglasses had left around his eyes.

"No flowers?" Jake asked.

The tan shaded briefly toward red. "Those were from Mr. C. Been me, I'd have brought you fish."

"Wrapped in newspaper."

"You got it. Or maybe a dead canary."

"You always were the subtle one."

"Subtle is for skirts. Speaking of which, that's some nurse you got there, Jakey. Even paralyzed, I think I could get it up for her."

Jake let nothing show in his face. He did not want to talk about Angel.

"If you think I should be sleeping with the fishes," he said, "why don't you do something about it?"

Fredo gave him a cold half smile. "That what you want, Jake? You getting so desperate you'd bite it even from me?"

Jake stared at him, and after a moment, Fredo's gaze faltered, flicking away and back.

"You'd like that, wouldn't you, old buddy? I put one in your brain and then they come and get me. But if you really want it, the time might come Mr. C could arrange it. Have to hang on a few more months until the Dan Rather types forget about you, then make it look like an accident, but it could be done. Mr. C, he still has a soft spot for you."

"I'm touched."

Fredo ran a hand down the sheet, and sweat prickled up on Jake's forehead as he realized what he was looking for.

"That tube you had in the hospital to take the piss out of you. Where is that, Jake?"

"They can't leave it in all the time," he said. "You'd get ulcers."

"So . . . what? They just let you wet the bed?"

"Not the bed." Jake turned his head away.

"Diapers?" Fredo laughed. "That's great. This I gotta see." He pulled the sheet back and then his face took on a calculating, sober cast. "I don't see no diaper, Jake."

"They were changing it when you came. You want the old one? I'm sure they could find it for you." Jake resisted an insane urge to reach up and wipe the sweat away.

"Very funny." Fredo drifted down to the end of the bed, planting his hands on the footrail. "How come they moved you here?"

"Because they couldn't do anything for me at the hospital."

"Yeah? Didn't they even get your fingers moving?"

How did he know about that? He's been keeping closer tabs than I thought.

"No," Jake said. He jerked a leg, trying to mimic the spastic, unconnected movement Fredo had seen before. Fredo's eyes never left his face.

"If the hospital can't help you, what can they do here?"

"Not a damned thing, but it's quieter here, and the staff is good. They keep me turned and dry. What the hell do you care, Fredo? It's not your money."

"Any other live-ins here?"

"I don't know."

"Don't seem to be. I looked around. Seems like this is what they call an 'outpatient facility.' Don't you love doctor talk? No live-ins, but they made an exception for you. How come?"

"Five million buys a lot of exceptions."

Fredo gazed at him. "I'm getting the strangest feeling about you, Jakey. Are you trying to con a con? Jake the snake? Trying to fool your old buddy Fredo? Make him think you can't move or feel anything, when really you can?"

Jake tried to think what Fredo would expect him to say. "I know you're stupid, but do you have to be ignorant, too? I thought you understood: When your spinal cord is cut, it's cut. It doesn't grow back. Why don't you get the hell out of here and leave me alone?"

Fredo smiled. Reaching into his coat, he took out a cigarette and lit it.

Jake's scalp crawled, but he said, "Go ahead. As soon as Doc gets a whiff of that, he'll send in the orderlies. You'd like them, Fredo—I think they both used to be pro wrestlers."

"Oooh, scary," he said, taking a long drag.

"Fine. Puff away. It'll be fun watching them make you put it out."

Fredo lifted the sheet off his feet, and Jake knew what was coming even before Fredo started sucking hard on the cigarette.

Christ!

Panic rose like a fist inside Jake, blocking his throat. His skin sensitivity was down, but could it take this? He tried to picture his foot frozen in a block of ice. The skin was blue and he'd lost all feeling. He desperately needed something warm to touch it or he'd get frostbite—

Fredo lifted his foot—

Cold, so cold, just a touch of warmth would be so nice—

And put the tip of the cigarette against the pad of skin behind his toes—

God, the pain, despite the "padding," turning his brain white, he wanted to scream, had to scream—

Fredo ground the cigarette into his foot until it went out, then dropped his ankle. The disappointed expression on his face wavered and swam in Jake's eyes. For a second, Fredo seemed to be shrinking away down a long, dark tunnel—

No, hang on.

"No one's that tough," Fredo mumbled.

"What did you do, you dumb son of a bitch?" Jake asked. "Did you burn me?"

18

LOVE AND HATE

Sick at heart, Jake waited for Angel to ask her questions. Instead, she seemed totally focused on his foot, making low sympathetic sounds as she smoothed salve on the burn. The seared spot throbbed viciously—Jake could swear the blazing end of the cigarette was still in contact with the flesh. But he was aware, too, of the coolness of her hand around his ankle.

"Lucky I don't have full sensation back," he said, needing to fill the silence.

To his surprise, Angel gave a shaky laugh. "Even so, it must have hurt like a maniac. And you didn't even jerk your foot? Jake, how did you *stand* it?"

"You do what you have to do." Was that vague enough?

She gazed at him and he saw only admiration in her eyes. Damn, this was killing him. When was she going to ask?

"You are a very brave man, Jake Nacht."

"Well, I didn't want to give away your uncle's research."

This time her laugh was more solid. "Right. You took a third-degree burn on your foot to keep your doctor from getting a severe tongue-lashing from some ethics review board."

"And loss of funding. Don't forget that."

Despite the pain, Jake found himself grinning, too. Was it really possible she was not afraid of him? Not scared that Danziger's accusations after shooting him might be true? She was such an acute observer of people and Fredo was obviously mob. Even if she didn't know from mob, she could guess what kind of man would burn another with a cigarette. And she could also figure out that it was done to make sure, very sure, that Jake's move to the rehab center did not mean he was getting his arms and legs back.

What's the matter with me? Forget Angel. I should be feeling on top of the world. I fooled Fredo. He'll never see me coming. A warm, gloating pleasure washed through Jake, and the pain began to dim at last.

"Better?" Angel asked.

"Better."

She wrapped his foot in gauze. "You'll have to stay off this foot. But there's plenty we can do—you need to work on your arms more, anyway—"

Graham stepped into the room and stood watching Angel finish up. His face was grim and Jake knew that, even if Angel didn't have questions, Graham did. Would he ask them in front of her?

"Mr. Nacht, can you explain this, please?"

Jake tried to hide his annoyance. Of course Graham would ask in front of Angel. Why not? He's never really put aside his suspicions that I'm bad news, so why pass up a chance like this to demonstrate it to Angel, undermine any feelings she might have for me. Pompous jerk.

The pompous jerk who gave you back your life.

"Why did this . . . Fredo do this to you?" Graham prompted.

"He wanted to make sure I was really paralyzed."

"Obviously. But why would he, in particular, care about that?"

"Uncle—"

"No, Angela, this is important. It's time we cleared the air. Your safety could be at stake."

Angel picked up the salve and bandages and headed for the door.

"I think you should stay and hear this, too," Graham said.

Bastard. Jake thought. *You've hung out with rats too long.*

Angel turned at the door and gave her uncle a level stare. "You're so full of what you've done for Jake, maybe you should stop and think what he's done for you."

She stepped out while Graham, obviously taken aback, was still groping for an answer. The doctor turned back to Jake, his expression openly angry now.

"I don't want her hurt, Mr. Nacht."

"Neither do I."

"Then I think you'd better level with me. You did shoot the senator, didn't you? And that man, Fredo, is a criminal. You did it for them, but they set you up. They don't dare finish the job because it would strongly imply their part in it, but they're making damned sure you won't be evening the score."

Jake was impressed, but gave no sign of it. He shook his head. "Doc, you just added two and two and got twenty-two."

"Really. Then why did Fredo decide to stub his cigarette out on your foot?"

"Because he hates me."

"And why is that?"

"He tried to bribe me once, and I turned him in to the cops."

"Bribe you? To do what?"

"To let him store certain substances in a warehouse where I was the night watchman."

Graham's suspicious squint was almost comical. Jake felt a sudden, vast weariness. The adrenaline Fredo had torched into him was draining out, and, strangely, it depressed him to lie to Graham. But what choice did he have? The good doctor was the sort of man who did things on principle. His unapproved research was not an exception to this but proof of it. He'd rather face disgrace than waste years going through traditional scientific channels on a discovery that could mean salvation to some of the most wounded, despairing people on earth. And he might well rather turn his prized patient in to the police than give a killer back his legs.

"What substances?" Graham asked.

"Controlled substances."

Graham looked out the window. Darkness was falling on the Norwegian quarter of Brooklyn, deepening the sky to cobalt above the brownstones across the street. As always, Jake found the fading of light soothing. He began to believe he'd succeeded in deflecting Graham. It's a plausible explanation, Jake thought, accounting for all the facts. And I had to master lying when I took on my profession.

Graham looked at him again. "Mr. Nacht, bullshit."

He stalked out. Jake watched him go, surprised and uneasy. Maybe Graham had some of his niece's intuitive skills after all. Or maybe, Jake thought, I'm not so good at deception anymore.

The thought both scared and, in some way he could not fathom, pleased him.

Around midnight, Angel came to him. Jake was already awake—the eight o'clock Demerol had all but evaporated from his system, and his foot was working its way up from sullen throb to raw pain. When he heard the door ease open, Jake lay very still, thinking it might be Fredo. Then he felt her hand settle with the softness of a veil on his forehead. The contact brought with it cool scents of lotion and soap.

"Jake?" she whispered.

He rolled onto his side and gazed at her. Light from the rising half moon flooded through the window, pooling in the soft folds of the oversized T-shirt that reached halfway down her thighs. Something was written on it but he couldn't read it in the dark. Didn't matter. Her hair fanned out from her face and a faint oily musk told him she had just brushed it. He felt himself rising into full hardness—the first time that had happened since the bullet smashed into his neck. An unspeakable joy, mixed with longing, filled him. Sitting up on the bed, he wordlessly held his arms out to her. She came to him, taking his hands, wrapping them back around her waist, leaning into him.

This is wrong, but the thought had no force; it scattered and crumpled to ash on the hot updrafts that rose through him.

He brought his lips to hers, feeling his neck tremble with the effort to be graceful. Their lips matched perfectly, just as he had imagined so many times. She opened to him and he let his tongue dally just inside her mouth, tasting its heat, its flavor of toothpaste and her sweet moistness. She brought her knees up on the bed, straddling him. He realized with a pleasurable start as his hardness rested near her other lips that she wore nothing under the T-shirt. He throbbed against her softness, his flesh magnetized to her. Her swollen nipples settled with exquisite gentleness against his chest.

He groaned. *Don't come—not yet.*

He tried to think about baseball—How about them Mets?—but the second she began to rotate her hips over him, he shot up into her.

To his surprise, she moaned with pleasure, sitting down hard on him, slipping him into her. He pumped out of control, dizzied, clamping his teeth to keep from shouting. Afterward, still hard, he started to pull from her but she clamped him with her legs.

"No."

He sat very still.

"Good," she murmured.

She kissed him, thrusting her tongue deep inside him. He cupped her firm buttocks in his hands and began moving them gently. He kissed her breasts, sucking at them through the T-shirt fabric, tasting her sweat. She moved up and down on him, slowly, gently, and he felt her orgasm start around him, a long, luxuriant squirm of supercharged flesh. She let out a long, low moan, then slumped against him.

"Jake—ahhhhhh."

He rolled over slowly, pulling her with him, holding her against him. An expansive ecstasy filled him, as though all the cells of his body, suddenly discovering they were half-empty, were drinking in the night, the moonlight, everything good they could find. With astonishment, he recognized what he was feeling: love.

What he did not recognize was what to do about it. Did what just happened mean that Angel did, in fact, love him too, as she'd said the day he'd meant to die? That she hadn't just been trying to con him into holding on to life? For many women making love did not mean being in love.

But Angel was not many women.

What about her almost-fiancé? Or was that off? They had only talked about him that one time, and he was afraid to ask even now. But surely she had called it off. Angel was not the sort to bed another man while she was still engaged. She loves me too, Jake thought. Loves me and is free to act on that love. We could be together.

His heart began to pound so hard he was afraid she would feel it. Relax, he told himself. Calm down.

After a while, still locked together, they slept.

When Jake drifted back to wakefulness, the ascending moon had dragged its cape of milky light back to the foot of the window. Glancing over Angel's shoulder at the red numerals of the clock on his bed table, he realized it was almost three o'clock. His foot hurt again, but the pain was miles away.

He lay there, cataloging her smells. The soap and lotion now mingled with the heady musk of their coupling, enough to make him hard all over again. Her flank was perfectly smooth beneath his hand, and then he felt the slight bubbling of goose bumps.

"Oh," she said, lifting her head, then letting it drop back to the pillow. He felt her shudder.

"Bad dream?" he asked softly.

"Mmmm. I was on a bus for some reason, and then as I was getting off, I realized I was part of a choir, a touring choir. People were waiting for us, so we started to sing as we got off the bus. It was such a sad song, in my dream I was crying. The people waiting in the depot just looked at us and I couldn't tell if they liked the song or not."

"Weird. Are all your dreams like that?"

"Hey, I can't help it. You were expecting me to dream about you, maybe?"

"I wouldn't have minded."

She poked him in the ribs. He hoped she would not become aware of his hardness. He wanted to make love to her again, but it would be wrong, because he had to get out of here, now, before the light came. He could see that with sudden clarity, as if it had sprung to him from her muddled dream. Not the bus, though. The subway, get lost in Manhattan, rent a car—no, a Jeep. And no sad songs.

"What are you thinking?" she asked softly.

"That your dream wasn't so weird. You know I have to go."

"Do I?" She rose to one elbow and looked at him, her face capturing a faint scatter of light. "Go where?"

"Someplace safe."

"You think Fredo will come back?"

"No. But if he does, tell him if he shows up again you'll have him arrested. It won't scare him, but it's what he'd expect you to say. You'd also tell him I've set up home care back at my house in New Jersey, and that I've hired guards around the clock who will be glad to shoot him if he puts a foot on my property. He'll understand that, too, after what he did to me."

"Jake, slow down. We can have guards brought here. Your money is as good in Brooklyn as New Jersey. And you need more rehab. You can't walk on that foot—"

"Can't?"

"All right, shouldn't." She put a hand on his shoulder. "What is it? Is it . . . what happened tonight between us?"

"No." He hoped she would see the truth in his eyes, sense it through his skin.

"All right," she said. "Home care. I'll come with you. I'll be your home care."

He suppressed a groan. "Angel, there's nothing I'd like more, but you can't."

"Why not? Uncle won't need me here—especially if you're gone. And you can't find a better rehab nurse. Besides, you made a promise to keep your recovery secret from everyone until Uncle Joe can publish, so I'm just about the only nurse you dare have around."

Jake tried to frame an answer that would not be a lie. "I'll be doing the rehab on my own—I know the drill now and I'll keep at it until I'm fit again. Fredo is bad news, Angel. I don't need to tell you that. It's possible he'll come back, and if he does, I want us to be in two different places. Your uncle and you will be safer if Fredo thinks you're no longer connected with me."

She continued to gaze at him. "Jake, I don't care about Fredo. I didn't even ask about Fredo and I don't want to know now. I know he's from your past, and I don't care about your past, because it is over. The day I first saw you, you frightened me. And then, over the months, I watched you change. Even before you got your body back, you became a different man. But now, suddenly, I'm afraid again."

"Of me?"

"That you are about to do something that will take you back to what you were."

He looked at her, amazed. She did know at least a part of what he was, had known for a long time—knew and didn't care. How was that possible?

A sense of wonder filled him. He found himself looking at his hands, and then Angel sat up and took them in hers, gently toying with the fingers that had held the stocks of a dozen exotic rifles—grim reapers who had harvested the lives of seventeen men at a hundred yards, two hundred, four hundred.

"I don't care, Jake. I don't *care.* As long as it's over. It has to be over. Forget Fredo. You did a fantastic thing today, a monumentally brave thing, and you succeeded. You're safe—we're both safe. We can be together, you and me, if you'll just let the rest of it go."

Jake thought about it. About Fredo coming to the bar and negotiating the biggest price he'd ever gotten, sucking him into a deal that had smelled wrong from the start, blinding him with a million dollars because they weren't planning to pay. He thought about Danziger shooting him in the back—the crushing pain, the way his body had vanished, as if turned to smoke. He thought about the months lying paralyzed, fighting madness, longing to die.

He thought about the look on Fredo's face today, the savage pleasure in his fat, stupid mug as he'd pushed the red tip of the cigarette into his foot.

"I'm sorry," Jake said softly.

Her tears dropped on their hands, burning him worse than the cigarette.

19

BARON OF THE PINES

May

Out in the lost reaches of the Pine Barrens for five days now, Jake thought not about Fredo or Danziger or the bullet that had made them his life's work, but of Angel. It was exasperating, agonizing.

And it was just plain *weird.*

When he was with her, all he could think about was Fredo and the others. Now, when he most needed to focus on them, Angel dominated his thoughts.

He did love her, oh yes. Leaving her was the hardest thing he'd ever done. He could feel it every minute, sitting inside his chest like a cold, scaly fish that had swallowed his heart. Five days, and the pain was only getting worse. He'd loved Angel before he could move, loved her while he'd wanted to die, but he hadn't known it. Fighting to master the body that had been restored to him, he'd loved her, loved her when she was in the room with him and loved her even more when she wasn't, and still hadn't understood that he loved her. And then, that last night together, that incredible, sweet, beautiful midnight, had driven it home to him. He'd finally realized it.

And then he'd walked away anyway.

Sighting through the modified Redfield scope, Jake squeezed

off a shot and watched the pinecone continue to swing, undisturbed, on its string. He cursed and rubbed his shoulder, trying to ease the hammering aftershocks of the AR-10. Had he even come close? No way to tell—the bullet had zipped soundlessly into the stunted pines beyond the swaying cone, disturbing nothing.

Was he ever going to hit the damned thing? Or was the skill that had defined him gone forever?

Jake sat down in the weeds, disheartened, resting the gun across his thighs. A jay called raucously from a box elder bush, mocking him. He was aware of a dull flame of nerve on the sole of his foot where Fredo had burned him. Tromping around over the uneven ground had inflamed it. But he couldn't worry about that now.

Sweat trickled from Jake's headband and rolled down to the tip of his nose, making him aware that the spring sun had found its way through the low, sparse canopy onto the back of his neck. Not a breath of wind, just warm and still, like so many days he remembered out here.

He hadn't realized how much he hated this place until he came back, but he could think of no better arena to practice undisturbed. He still knew this godforsaken patch of woods as well as any man could, which was not all that well. Out here, where each scraggly pine or bush looked pretty much like every other, even experienced woodsmen got lost.

The thought roused a tremor of dread in Jake. Not to be able to find the Jeep and get back to his motel, to have to sit out here while darkness fell, knowing he'd see Sarge's ghost in every shadow, hear him in every rustle of raccoon or snake. Sarge, the dead king of the Pine Barrens.

Jake shook off the pang of superstition. This was where he'd learned to shoot, and maybe he could still find some lingering magic here. Maybe the familiar tangles of brambles and pine boughs could help him visualize the inner branches of nerve he'd learned to navigate in this place. His shooting skills, the knack—whatever it was—must still be there in his brain. All he had to do was find the right pathways to and from his eyes and hands, the exquisite control of his trigger finger, the peculiar, still voice that told him just when to squeeze.

Jake clambered up, stiff from just a few moments of sitting, and walked to the dangling pinecone, setting it in motion again.

Hurrying back into position, he sighted through the Redfield, finding the swaying cone, letting its motion soak into his brain. *Now.*

Jake squeezed the trigger and the cone shattered. He felt no triumph, only a dull satisfaction. He'd been working toward this for five days, but by itself it was nothing. What mattered was that it had felt right, and maybe now that he'd gotten that feeling, he'd get it again, and again, until it was his to command again.

Jake hit two out of the next ten.

Then four.

Three. Six. Seven out of ten. Seven. Seven. Six. Seven.

Darkness began to fall. Hurrying back to his Jeep, Jake felt a mixture of hope and frustration. Seven out of ten wasn't good enough. The first bullet had to go straight into Fredo's kneecap. And then Fredo would be writhing on the ground, a jerky series of spasmodic movements, not a predictable pendulum swing of pinecone. One in the kneecap, then the gut, and finally, as Fredo lay shocked and dying, the easy one straight into the brain.

Jake tried to visualize it, but all he could see was Angel's face, the enchanting off-center smile that he would never, except in his mind, see again.

By evening of the next day, Jake could hit the swinging pinecone 9.5 times out of 10. The day after, he backed up to a slight knoll a hundred yards away and used the first shot to snap the branch the pinecone was sitting on, kicking the cone into a crazed pirouette on its string. The pirouette smoothed into wide swings that gave him several shots at a small moving target before entropy ran the motion down. Within three days, he could hit the swinging cone 9 times out of 10 at a hundred yards.

The old reflexes, the automatic responses and adjustments, were awakening. His nervous system had been beat up, but it still remembered. The satisfaction felt arid, though; nothing like what he'd expected all the times he'd dreamed of it. He was still good—or good again, whatever the right neurologic characterization might be. Very probably he was once again the best shooter there was. He was ready to go after Fredo. That was when the joy, the dark ecstasy would hit him, when he squeezed the trigger and watched the bastard who had smashed his life fall. He would kill Fredo, then Danziger, then Mr. C.

And after that, what would he do with the rest of his life?

That Sunday, Jake sat high in an oak tree near Bedminster, New Jersey, watching Fredo's black Cadillac limousine cruise up the long drive to his country house. Horse country out here, zoned for a five-acre minimum. Peopled by the likes of Whitney Houston . . . and Fredo Papillardi.

Nice car. Mr. C must have given his nephew some new responsibilities. Remembering Fredo's mahogany tan, Jake decided it was probably Atlantic City—Fredo had wanted for years to handle his uncle's interests there. Looked like he'd got his wish.

Jake eased the AR-10 up and sighted through the scope, feeling no nervousness, knowing this wasn't the moment yet. First a bodyguard got out, followed by Fredo's number one man, Vito Cangemi, a little younger than Fredo, but equally vicious. Then the man himself emerged, his dark suit giving off a faint sheen in the sunlight. Jake felt an abortive movement in his trigger finger. No—under that suit, Fredo would be wearing body armor. Ever since he'd seen *The Godfather,* he'd always worn a bulletproof vest to services, even though mob hits in church were practically nonexistent.

He was back home today only because Mr. C believed his capos should be at church on Sundays, then spend the day with their families. What a joke, like a shark saying a blessing before it bit off your leg.

Fredo's wife, a thin, brittle-looking woman with high hair, followed him, and they all disappeared into the shadow of the portico, except for the guard, who took up a station lounging against a white pillar.

One big happy family. Jake wondered if the wife knew—or cared—how many women Fredo kept on the side.

Jake let out a breath he had not known he was holding. Automatically, he checked the sun's angle, though he already knew there was no chance of a reflection off his scope. He turned his attention to the pool, a sparkling aquamarine gemstone set in the lush grass behind and to the left of the house. On a warm day like this, after Fredo had filled himself with rare roast beef and Chianti, he'd trade the church suit for a swimsuit and go out to the pool. The sun would be behind this oak about then, and Fredo would pull his chair around to face it, put on his sunglasses, and sleep off the wine in the warm summer rays.

Until a slug in the kneecap woke him up.

Then he'd be on the cement beside the pool, thrashing like a gaffed fish, and it would get tricky.

The gut, Jake thought with icy determination. Then the head.

In the first shock, it would take at least ten seconds for someone to think to get to him and drag him off. These bodyguards weren't selfless Secret Service agents and Fredo was hardly the sort you jump in front of when the shooting starts.

I'll take as long as they give me. He doesn't get the slug in the brain until he's known pain. Will I hear him screaming this far away? Depends on the wind.

Jake was surprised to feel a qualm in his stomach. He'd eaten nothing but the usual prehit breakfast of bread and tea. What was this? A touch of nerves? Or was the foot getting infected from all this unaccustomed activity? He'd put salve on it last night, but the area around the burn had turned an angry red.

Before he could stop himself, Jake wished Angel was around to take care of it.

But Angel would not be around again. His choice, and he'd made it.

So just put it out of your mind.

Knee, gut, watch Fredo writhe, listen to the sweet music of his screams, then one in the head. Take that, you fucking bastard, you Judas, you filthy back-shooter. You screwed up my life. You put me in hell for four fucking months. Because of you, I couldn't lift a hand. They drained the piss out of me in tubes. Because of you, I wasn't a man at all.

Because of you I met Angel.

Angrily, Jake shook off the thought. Right, and because of Lee Harvey Oswald, Jackie Kennedy got to date around again.

I'm not meant for Angel, Jake thought. Angel is beautiful. Angel is good in bed. But how could she love me? How could she ignore what I was? She'd—

Jake realized with a start that Fredo had entered the pool area. His heart began to pound as he lifted the rifle and sighted through the scope. Oh, God, the stupid bastard was wearing Speedo trunks—for that alone, he deserved to die. Did he have any idea how he looked, his belly hanging in a slab over the black nut-huggers? Look at all that hair—not just his chest, but his shoulders, even his back. Jake's gorge rose. What a loathsome creature. Sit down there, yes. Pull your chair around, that's it. Adjust the sunglasses. Okay, nice and comfy?

Jake eased the AR-10 against his shoulder and centered the crosshairs on Fredo's chest, then tracked down one meaty thigh to his knee. In the crosshairs, the kneecap sat, round and pale as a biscuit.

If ever a man deserved to die, this one did.

Jake found the trigger, curled his finger around it.

He remembered Angel's tears falling onto his hands. He heard her voice in his mind: *Let it go, Jake.*

The rim of the scope dug into the flesh above his eyebrow. Jake swallowed, sick to his stomach.

He hated Fredo, *hated* him.

So go ahead, this is the moment you've dreamed of. You can't walk away now.

She loves you. It can be over. All you have to do is let it go.

And then he saw his life stretching before him, a shining new life, scoured clean by the fire of the last nine months.

Nine months . . . like a pregnancy. And now the moment of truth: What was he going to deliver from that womb of fear and pain and utter desperation? A new life was out there, waiting. Did he want to sully it with Fredo's blood?

Let it go.

I can't.

Jake raised the scope to Fredo's head. He centered the crosshairs above the sunglasses, then brought it down, right between the eyes. . . .

And hesitated.

"Bang," he said.

He lowered the rifle.

Let it go.

He didn't know if he could.

But he could try. Like a drunk . . . one day at a time.

Jake waited in the tree for nightfall, smiling as Fredo moved his chair around to keep the sun on him. Fredo didn't matter, Fredo was on another planet now.

When the grove of oaks was steeped in darkness, Jake eased himself down the rope, feeling light and strong, and more sure of himself than he ever had in his life. He put the gun in its case and carried it back to the rented 4 × 4 he'd hidden in some bushes. He would return to Brooklyn and go back to Angel. He would tell her it was over—that he had turned his back on Fredo and all the old bad deals. Tonight they would start over.

In the privacy of the Jeep, Jake broke down the AR-10 and scope. He'd find a bay or river to throw them into on his way out of here. First, he needed a phone. He couldn't wait until he saw Angel, he had to tell her now, as soon as possible. *Angel, I'm clean, and I'm going to stay that way. Angel, I love you.*

Jake drove until he spotted one of the quaint roadside watering holes along Route 24—Dew Drop Inn, comfortingly unoriginal. A blue neon sign ticked and buzzed above the door, casting its soft glow on the pay phone. Jake dialed Graham's clinic, inhaling the smells of frying fish, the malty tang of beer. The chatter from inside the restaurant filled him with delicious, floating ease.

"Hello!"

Graham's voice, and at once Jake's sense of serenity fled. Something was wrong.

"This is Jake. Is Angel there?"

"Jake? Oh, yes. Jake Nacht."

The man sounded half-stupefied. Jake's stomach went hollow with dread. "What is it?"

"She's gone. They took her, and it's your fault."

PART 4

REBIRTH

20

TEAMWORK

Jake's mind raced, slipping and sliding over the appalling words Graham had just uttered. Angel, abducted?

Fredo's boys must have decided to check the clinic again, and I was gone, so they went to my house, and I wasn't there either.

But *why*? After he burned me, Fredo should have been satisfied. Why check again?

Jake thrust the question from his mind, struck by a more immediate worry: *They grabbed her to flush me out. If they're that suspicious, they've tapped Graham's phone.*

"You seem to forget," Jake said, "that I'm paralyzed. How could it be my fault Angel is gone?"

An interval of silence told Jake that Graham was digesting the hidden message—was starting to think, thank God. But would someone listening in guess that, too?

"Your friends from your old life must have done this." Graham gave "friends" a bitter twist. "Before you came along, Angela didn't know anyone like Fredo. You brought him down on us—you and whatever it was you did with him before you were paralyzed. If he hates you enough to burn a helpless man, then he hates you enough to kidnap someone he thinks might matter to you."

Jake, listening with the ears of Fredo's eavesdropper, decided it was an adequate response. Never mind if Graham didn't have all the logic straight—Fredo wouldn't expect him to. The important thing was for them to keep Fredo thinking he was paralyzed.

And to give no sign of just how deeply Angel did matter to him. Luckily, Graham himself probably didn't grasp that, and so could not give it away.

Jake tried to pull his scrambled thoughts together. "When did this happen?"

"I don't *know*. Sometime earlier today. I just discovered she was gone. Her room was . . . a shambles." Graham's voice hitched on the last word.

"Have you called the police?"

"Not yet. They left a note warning me not to. They said if I did they'd *kill* her."

"Do exactly as they say," Jake said firmly. "It's me they want. I think I can get this straightened out."

"So you admit it's your fault."

Yes, Jake thought, but he said, "It's the fault of whoever grabbed her—and I agree it's probably Fredo. In spite of everything, he must still doubt I'm really paralyzed. If so, he could have checked my house after he knew I wasn't with you. Trouble is, I didn't go back there because I didn't want him coming back and burning something besides my foot."

"Where are you?"

Jake winced. It was not a question Graham should have asked. He still wasn't thinking very well. I've got to get off the line, Jake thought. I've got to get to Graham, as quick as I can, and make *sure* he doesn't call the police or do something stupid.

"Don't worry about where I am," Jake said. "I'm going to call Fredo and tell *him*. That's all he wants. If he grabbed your niece, he'll give her back when he verifies I'm still paralyzed. If I can get enough people here to protect me, I'll call Fredo and let him come here, check me over again. I'll work something out. The main thing is, whatever you do, don't call the police. Just wait there, stay by the phone, and I'll call you as soon as I know anything."

Silence.

"Doctor Graham?"

"I hear you. I'm not prepared to wait very long. I have to do something, do you hear me? They could be hurting her, or . . ."

"Stay by the phone." Jake emphasized each word, then hung up.

Christ! A sick dread filled Jake. He felt his hands shaking in reaction and pressed them against his face to stop the tremors. At least he hadn't yet thrown away the AR-10, or the .45 he'd brought along in case he got into close quarters.

And thank God he hadn't dropped the hammer on Fredo. If he had, Angel would be dead by now.

Taking slow, even breaths, Jake battled a smothering attack of claustrophobia. So dark here; hard to breathe. The oily stench of spoiled sardines seemed to ooze from the walls that brushed either shoulder as he crept along, hands out front. A vertical slice of lighter gray ahead drew him deeper. He tried not to think what would happen if someone stepped into that gray crease and fired a shot down the alley. Wouldn't even have to aim—a sure bank shot—and he wouldn't have room to fall down.

But if he could get through this crease between buildings undetected, he'd be in the alley proper, an ancient, cobblestoned service lane that bisected the center of the block, giving access to the backs of shops and brownstones that faced out toward either street. Graham's rehab center was one of those buildings. A right turn out of the crease, then a twenty foot diagonal across the alley to the rear entrance.

If Fredo had it staked out as he did the front, it might as well be twenty miles.

Jake put the negative thought from his mind. He listened,

searching for any sound at the end of the crease. At two A.M., the Norwegian quarter was eerily quiet for any part of Brooklyn. The good Gunnars and Dagnes were apparently all in bed; with luck, someone watching the rear of the clinic might have dozed off as well.

But Jake did not believe in luck.

Which was why his right hand pointed the .45 ahead of him. If one of Fredo's men caught him slipping into the clinic, Angel's rescue could be all over before it started. Maybe he should have carried out the charade he'd described to Graham—find a place, hire in some muscle, then try again to reassure Fredo.

But what if he flunked the new test?

Or what if Fredo already knows?

Then he puts a round into my head, Jake thought. A Jake Nacht with working arms and legs is too dangerous to let live, and to hell with the newspapers and the D.A.

The nagging suspicion that Fredo might already *know* galled Jake. He'd made a big mistake. He let his hate—and Fredo's dumb-guinea act—blind him. The guy was such a caricature, his greaseball looks, his wise-ass swagger, the ignorant way he talked. Hell, it wasn't an act, it was him. But it wasn't all of him. If he was so dumb, why was Jake the one who got backshot and couldn't move for months, who had to lie still and let a sadistic bastard grind a cigarette out on his foot, who went out shooting pine cones while that same bastard snatched the woman he loved?

Jake felt his teeth grinding together in rage and chagrin. Closing his eyes, he stood still in the darkness, willing himself to calmness. Rage was what had put him in this hole. Now it was time for cold calculation—time to see who was really smarter, him or Fredo. If it was Fredo, Angel would die, and so would Jake Nacht, because even if he didn't go down with her, losing her was not something he could endure.

At the end of the crease, Jake stopped and listened again. Lowering himself to his belly, he eased his head out and peered through the murk. Why was it so dark back here? No streetlights, but at least a shop or two should have a back light on. The only illumination came from far down the alley, diluting the darkness just enough to detect movement. The conditions were perfect for a stakeout. If someone *was* out there, he could remain invisible so long as he didn't move.

He doesn't have to move, Jake thought. But I do.

Just take your time. Wait. Listen.

After almost fifteen minutes, he heard it—a faint scrape, brief and very even—a sound that was somehow familiar, but Jake couldn't pin it down. A few seconds later, he smelled coffee.

A thermos.

Jake remembered lying paralyzed, smelling his way around his hospital room. Being unable to move had sharpened his hearing and sense of smell, and he had gone to them, relying on the scent of Angel's perfume or the distinctive squeak of her sneakers to tell him when she was in the hall, the chalky smell of meds to tell him when the nurse was tiptoeing in so that he could pretend to be asleep—grabbing desperately for smidgeons of control to keep himself from going crazy. Who knew then that he was practicing a new art, honing senses that might save his life?

But he had to do more than save his life. He had to get into Graham's. The front and rear entrances were covered. What now? There had to be a way.

And then he saw what it might be—if he was patient enough, strong enough, quiet enough.

Still on his belly, Jake inched into the alley. Keeping his face down on the gritty pavement, he pushed off gently with his toes, wormed his shoulders. His fingers, splayed to the sides, added an extra centimeter or two to each small push. It took him ten minutes to ooze fully into the open. His spine crawled with dread, pleading with him to hurry, itching in anticipation of a bullet. One more into the back and then he would die. Would they let Angel go then?

Not Fredo.

Ten more minutes, and now he was lying squarely in the middle of the alley, one more body length to go before he could squeeze into the crease on the other side. His ears strained for any sound, dreading it like a blow. When it came, a rustle of clothes, he froze, then almost scrambled up—

Don't!

Staying facedown, completely motionless, he listened. Nothing for a few seconds, and then he heard the spatter of piss against a brick wall.

Jake rose to a crouch and ducked into the crease, pulling his .45, and facing back into the alley. His heart hammered so fiercely he could feel the pulse between his finger and the trigger. Fredo's man would come now and be killed, or not. Five seconds, a minute, and Jake knew he had made it.

Halfway.

Now came the hard part. Time to see where all his rehab had brought him. And how much pain he could really stand.

Clicking the safety on, he shoved the pistol back into his pocket. He felt his way along until he judged he was halfway down the crease. Backing against the wall opposite the rehab center, he raised a foot and planted it about waist level against the center's wall. He stood that way a moment, gathering himself, wishing the place had windows at ground level. In New York, nearsighted vistas of brick walls were not unheard of, but Jake knew from the months he'd spent here that there were no windows on this side.

Just that small, louvered opening for ventilation in the attic, three stories above.

Keeping his foot planted, Jake pushed off it, sliding his back a few feet up the opposite wall, then planting the other foot. He felt a dull pain in the area of the cigarette burn as he ground his sole into the brick, but the Nike Airs he wore cushioned the seared spot.

The motions, the technique, were familiar. He'd got in and out of perches this way on more than one hit. But how strong were his legs now? He was far from peak condition. What if he got two stories up and they gave out?

Then he'd fall.

Jake worked his way up the wall a foot at a time. The pressure of brick against his spine wrung spasms of pain from his back; he had the sudden, panicky fear that he might somehow damage his spinal cord again.

Just keep going.

As he reached the top, the nerves of his legs began firing in ragged bursts, like bolts of electricity arcing from hip to heel. He found it harder and harder to keep the tension on. He was glad for the darkness, but he could feel the three stories of air beneath him, imagine the impact if he fell.

Hang in there, he told his legs. Just a little ways to go.

And then his leg muscles went into spasm, contracting and relaxing to some chaotic up-tempo rhythm only they could hear. His legs began to jitter like a bad Elvis impersonation. It might have been funny if he weren't three goddamn stories up.

But even worse, Jake could feel the strength oozing out of his legs.

Sweat popped out on his forehead. Clenching his teeth to keep up the pressure, he looked around for that damned attic air vent.

There—about four feet to his left.

Suppressing a groan, Jake edged sideways as quickly as he dared until his trembling feet straddled the base of the small, square portal. His legs were damn near gone now and he had to use his hands to keep him aloft, digging his fingers and palms into the bricks behind him.

He lifted his right foot from the opposite wall and pushed it against the wooden louvers, hoping they were as rotten as they'd looked from the inside. They gave way with only a slight push, dropping inside with a dull thump. Jake didn't think there was any way the sound would make it down three stories and around the corner in the alley, but even if it did, so what? He was in big trouble here.

He also realized he had done this wrong.

He should have planted his back against the clinic wall so that his arms would be in reach of the opening.

No time to worry about it. He couldn't feel his legs anymore. As his feet slipped from the rehab center's wall, Jake pushed off the bricks behind him and lunged for the opening.

For a horrible, dizzying second, he thought he was going to fall short, but then his right hand caught the edge of the opening. He swung there, hanging from the vent by four fingers—and they were slipping—for a few eternal seconds before he got his left hand up to help out.

Banzai!

Now what? His legs were useless. Worse than useless. They dangled below him like counterweights. His arms . . . his arms were all he had now. And if they started to go like his legs . . .

He began hauling himself up, inch by inch, working his hands farther and farther into the opening. His fingers screamed in agony but he kept pushing them forward until he got an elbow hooked into the opening.

After that he made better progress, squeezing his head and shoulders through, then sliding the rest of the way inside like a snake entering its burrow.

Finally he lay on the floor, massaging his legs, trying not to gasp. Christ, he still couldn't feel them. They were dead meat. What was happening?

He fought a rising tide of panic. Had the surgery been only temporary? Was he reverting to a vegetable again? Not now. Please, not *now*, when he needed them to get to Angel.

Jake fought to calm himself. He took a deep breath, and the attic's familiar dusty smells of old wood and insulation filled his lungs. He choked back a fit of coughing.

And while he was coughing, his leg moved.

He tried to move it himself, voluntarily. The right knee bent—just a little—and then the left knee followed. And then the tingling began.

They're coming back.

He heard a strange sound in the attic and realized he'd just sobbed out loud.

All right, get yourself together. Get going.

A grimy front window let enough street light into the attic to navigate by. Walking was out, but he could belly crawl. Jake dragged himself to the door by his arms. On his way he stopped for a moment and ran his hand through the fur of the stuffed dog. Wish me luck, he thought.

He slid down the attic stairs as quietly as he could, then took a breather on the rehab center's upper floor. He heard footsteps down on the first floor. Had to be Graham.

Jake waited a little longer, testing his legs. The strength was returning quickly now, but they were still wobbly. He didn't trust them to support him, so he crawled to the top of the stairway and peered through the railings.

Graham was sitting by the phone in the foyer. The problem now was to get his attention without startling him into a sound. At most, they'd bug one or two strategic places in the building—but the phone where Graham was sitting would definitely be one of them. Ideally, he should sneak up on Graham and clap a hand over his mouth. . . .

But no way he could sneak up on anyone now with these legs.

Jake put a finger to his lips, then cleared his throat softly.

Graham whirled and blanched white. Then his shoulders sagged.

Jake motioned him upstairs. When Graham was close enough, Jake cupped his hands and whispered into his ear.

"My legs gave out. Help me up to the attic."

Graham jerked back and looked at him with alarm. He started to say something but Jake put his hand over his open mouth.

He whispered again. "Bugs."

Graham's eyes widened, then narrowed. He helped Jake to his feet and supported him as they climbed back to the attic.

As soon as they reached the top step, Jake turned and sat. His legs were definitely stronger, but that wasn't uppermost in his mind right now.

"Have they called you?"

"No." Graham's head swiveled nervously in the half-light, as if afraid the dark silhouettes of rockers and ancient mechanical gym equipment might hide one of Fredo's men. He said, "If my phone is bugged—and I take it that's what you believe—then they heard us earlier and must be expecting you to call them. Did you?"

"No."

"Why not? What are you doing here?"

"I have to have your promise that you won't call the police, no matter what."

"Forget it. I'm not going to sit here doing nothing and hope you can straighten this mess out—"

"Yes, you are."

"Or what? You'll kill me?"

Jake closed his eyes. Why did the man have to be so damn difficult?

"Dr. Graham, you gave me back my life, but now I'm going to go get Angel, and if you do anything to screw that up, I *will* kill you, yes."

Graham stared at him, his eyes suddenly showing as pale crescents in the murk. "Like you tried to kill the senator?"

"We're not going to talk about my past," Jake said, "one way or the other. I was a night watchman, that's all."

"Right. A night watchman who is now going to rescue my niece from mobsters. My God, Mr. Nacht, for once I actually hope you've been lying to us. If I'm going to let you go after her, I have to believe you are as . . . as dangerous as they are. Are you?"

"I would be if I could count on my legs."

Jake explained what had happened.

"Some sort of neuronal fatigue, I imagine," Graham said. "You overloaded your lower limbs with all that exertion. Your neurons shut down. That's all I can tell you without running some tests. How are they now?"

Jake grabbed the newel post and pushed himself to his feet. His legs felt shaky, but they supported him.

"I can walk, but not that far. Will they be okay by the time I reach Fredo?"

"How can I say? You're my first human case." Graham sighed in the near darkness. "I should never have given you back your legs. And when I did, I should have called the DA."

"But you were afraid to wreck your own research."

"That's not true, I—"

"You knew what you were doing every step of the way, Doc. You were willing to experiment on me because you considered my life worthless, no better than a convict's. Based on your rat studies, you believed the operation might cause deep psychosis in me, and yet you went ahead because, to you, I was a rat. What does that make you, I wonder?"

Jake knew he was being too hard on Graham, but there was no choice.

For a moment, Graham said nothing. "Why are you so determined not to go to the police? Are you afraid they'll take you in along with Fredo?"

Yes, Jake thought. But that was the least of it, and certainly not the part Graham needed to know.

"You call the police and the bent cops on Fredo's payroll will be on the phone to him before you hang up. And then he'll do what he said he'd do: kill Angel. Whether you believe it or not, I'm not Fredo's kind." *Not anymore.* "But I know them. I know how their minds work. You call the police, Angel dies."

A choked suggestion of a sob came from deep in Graham's throat. "All right. But I'm going with you."

Jake stared at him. "The hell you are."

"You need me."

"Have you ever shot a gun, Doc?"

"I served in Nam."

Okay, Jake thought. There goes that objection.

"But more important than shooting is the fact that I made a

paralyzed man get up and walk. How do you think I did that, Mr. Nacht? By pouring brightly colored chemicals back and forth between two test tubes?"

Jake waited.

"I did it by *thinking*. And I believe that's an area where you could use some help."

Jake felt himself bristling, then forced himself to run Graham's words by again. The man was a genius, no question. And only ignoramuses believed that genius was a narrow thing, useful only in the laboratory or at the drafting table. He did not know where Fredo was keeping Angel. And he didn't know how to find out. Was it possible Graham could think of a way?

But I have to keep my head down, Jake thought, and this man has no practice at concealment or stealth, no physical skills useful in a crunch. He'd do more harm than good.

"No," Jake said. "It's out of the question."

"Tell me, Mr. Nacht, how are you going to get out of here?"

"What do you mean?"

"There's a man watching the front entrance and one in back, too. I'm amazed you got inside."

"I'll go out the way I came in," Jake said, "through the attic air vent."

His legs pulsed in protest, and he knew with a sinking feeling that they'd never get him down the wall.

"Neither of us believes that," Graham said. "So wouldn't you rather lie down in the backseat of my car and let me drive you out?"

Jake tried to make sense of the words. "I explored this place, and I never found any door to a garage."

Graham gave him a wan smile. "Of course you didn't, because it's not there anymore. But that garage between this brownstone and the next actually belongs to this building. And sitting in it is a 1975 Chrysler with only eight thousand miles on it. It was the last car of my aunt Hanna, who owned this place. She became such a terrible driver near the end that I took the keys from her. I walled over the door to make sure she didn't go back on her word, but you could probably put your fist right through the drywall and peel it away. I take the Chrysler out every so often. Last time I looked, the gas gauge was on empty, but we don't have to get far. There's a gas station six blocks away."

Jake thought about it. He could not simply take the car himself, even if Graham would give him the key. Too much risk that the stakeout would spot him at the wheel. He'd have to lie down in the backseat, just as Graham had suggested.

Might work, he thought. Fredo doesn't care about Graham, he only cares whether I'm able to show up here. They'd only follow Graham if they thought he could lead them to me, and in our one phone call Graham asked where I was and I wouldn't tell him. They'll think he's driving back to the hospital or heading off on some crazy attempt to find Angel. . . .

Angel . . . visions of her, locked up, maybe even tied to a chair in one of Fredo's safe houses, filled his brain. Chances are she was in Atlantic City—Fredo would want her near where he spent most of his time. Terrific, Jake—how many houses in Atlantic City? He could not suppress an image of her, bound and gagged, lying on a bed, perhaps. He could feel her terror mingling with his own. She was not the kind to accept her situation passively. She'd try to escape, and if she got very far with it, Fredo would punish her. Fredo the sadist. Every moment counted, and his legs, his burned foot, were in no shape to take him back down that wall.

"Get your keys, Doc," Jake said. "I don't like it, but it looks like you're the only game in town."

21

SADIST

Angel was determined not to give in to her terror. She stood ramrod straight, her back pressed against the cold, damp stone of the basement. It was not enough to prevent the iron collar around her throat from digging into her jaw, but at least it kept her from choking. The collar was chained to an iron loop bolted to the wall above her head. By rising on tiptoe, she could free the angles of her jaw from the chill grasp of the collar, but then her calves would begin to ache and she'd have to stand flat-footed again and the chain would stretch her neck. Still groggy from the drugs, she had actually dozed off once or twice, to be jerked awake as her weight sagged against the collar and she began to strangle.

They'd left lighted the bare bulb that hung from the center rafter, but it wasn't much of a mercy. The basement was a stark, windowless room walled and floored in cement. In the center of the floor, a drain cover mottled with rust—or was it dried blood?—made a mute but chilling statement. Pegged to the opposite wall, within the arc she could manage to see without choking, were a coiled whip, a policeman's sap, needle-nosed pliers, and a pair of jumper cables. A car battery sat on the floor beside a brazier. A black fireplace poker leaned against the brazier. She could not see the charcoal, but she could smell it—an ethery whiff of lighter fluid. A vent in the ceiling, darkened with the smoke of past fires, told her the brazier had been used—she was not the first to stand chained to this wall.

It told her that the real terror had not yet begun.

Angel groaned softly, hoping it would release some of the fear. Why were they doing this to her?

Jake. He killed one of them—probably Fredo. I'm their revenge.

She sorted back through the past few hours—it felt like about eight but she couldn't be sure. The two men had worn ski masks. She hadn't even had time to scream. The shock—probably from a taser—had scrambled her brain and turned her body stiff as a corpse. She remembered darkness and the musty smell of carpet against her nose—had they carried her out of the clinic wrapped in a rug? She had swum in and out of consciousness, which, together with her groggy spells now, indicated some kind of sedative. The first thing she really remembered was the two men carrying her down the steps to this place, walking her around and around until they were sure she could stand, then snapping the collar on her neck. Neither of them had spoken, but the memory of the hand groping her breast was worse than anything they could have said.

At least they had left her clothes on.

What a break for me!

A strangled laugh pushed up Angel's throat, then turned into a sob. *Oh, Jake.*

She fantasized him coming for her. But no. He had left without giving her any hope of that. She still could not understand it. He loved her, she had been so sure of that. She'd seen it in his eyes every time he looked at her. And yet he had turned away, gone back to what he was. A killer? It hadn't mattered while they were together, because she'd sensed the change in him and had resolved not to care, so long as it was truly behind him. But if he'd shot Fredo . . .

Footsteps clumped down the basement steps, and she felt a mixture of fear and relief. Now at least someone would talk to her, explain things.

The face that moved into view in front of her was Fredo's. *Jake! You didn't kill him.* Angel felt a sudden access of hope.

Then why am I here?

"How ya doin?" Fredo asked.

"I've been better." She tried to make sense of this. Why would Fredo let her see his face when the two underlings he'd sent after her had covered theirs?

Because, on the way here, there was some chance I might escape. Now there's none. I won't leave here alive.

A cold tremor of panic shook her. Fredo smiled and Angel felt a bracing rush of anger. He wants me to be afraid, she thought. The only way I can fight him is to not be afraid. How can I do that? I'm terrified—I can't help it.

But maybe I can fake it.

"So, tell me something, Angel," Fredo said. "Is Jake really paralyzed?"

And then it made sense. This wasn't about revenge, this was about Fredo's paranoia, his fear of Jake. Jake hadn't killed anyone. Angel felt an irrational moment of joy. There was still hope for them.

If I can survive.

"Of course he's paralyzed," she said. "No one recovers from a severed spinal cord."

"There's always a first time," Fredo said mildly.

"No, there isn't. Not with this."

"You wouldn't lie to me, would you, Angel?"

"Sure I would, but not about something so obvious. The only way to lie about this would be to say that a quadriplegic with a severed cord *could* walk again. That would be a lie—and silly, because no one who understands medicine would believe it. It's as impossible as pigs flying."

Fredo gazed at her, and she forced herself not to look away, though his face revolted her. Her mind raced, trying to parse out the hours that lay ahead. No matter what, she would not betray

Jake by telling Fredo he could move again, could more than move.

She'd protect Jake, and maybe she could lull Fredo. If she could convince him Jake was no threat, maybe he'd keep her alive for a while—the messenger that brought the *good* news. It was too much to hope that he'd let her go—he'd never believe she wouldn't bring the cops down on him—but survival was everything. By now, Uncle Joe would know she was gone, and would suspect Fredo. He'd have called the police. They'd be looking for her now. All she had to do was stay alive long enough for them to find her.

"Why did Jake leave your clinic?"

Angel remembered what Jake had told her to say. "He was afraid you might come back and hurt him again."

"Hurt him? He feels pain?"

Angel went cold. "I mean hurt as in injure. Just because he can't feel pain doesn't mean it isn't very unhealthy for him to have the skin burned off his foot."

Fredo's eyes were watchful now. He said, "I sent one of my guys instead, just to double-check he's still lying there nice and still. But he's not lying there at all. So now I'm wondering if he was just plain lying—if old Jake could really be tough enough to pass the Marlboro test."

Angel said, "If you mean could he fake being paralyzed while you held a lighted cigarette against his foot, no one is that tough." *Almost no one.* "He hired an ambulance to take him back to his place in New Jersey. He was going to arrange for home care, there."

"Yeah, except we thought of that and checked it out and he's not there either. So why don't you just tell me where he *did* go?"

"All I know is what he told me. He said he was going to hire some bodyguards along with the home care nurses—he's got all that money from the lawsuit, you know. If he didn't go home, I have no idea where he went. He was really afraid of you."

She saw a look of gratification pass over Fredo's face, and knew she was on the right track.

She said, "Maybe Mr. Nacht just decided the best way to be clear of you was go someplace you wouldn't think to look, and set up his home care there."

Quit while you're ahead. Don't overdo it.

"Okay, but are you telling me old Jake wouldn't give his new address to his nurse, a gorgeous babe who waited on him hand and foot for months? He must have had a serious case of the hots for you, right?"

Angel remembered the last time she had seen Jake, the wonderful feel of his hands on her face, his body against her. She said, "I don't know what Jake thought of me. I don't think he thought anything. What would be the use?"

Fredo leaned back a few inches, giving her a look of incredulity. "You saying because he couldn't get it up, he wouldn't even *think* about it?"

"Would you?"

Fredo pursed his lips. "You bet I would. You were my nurse, I'd think about you all the time. I might wish I didn't, but I would."

"That's . . . very flattering. But you're not really putting yourself in Jake's position. His body feels nothing. He is chronically depressed. What he thinks most about is dying."

Fredo took a deep breath, let it out. She could almost see the tense muscles in his neck and shoulders winding down a notch.

"I'd like to believe you, Angel."

I'll bet you would.

"But I'd like it even better if I could just drop in on Jake in his new digs. Maybe if you think about it a little longer, you'll come up with an address."

"I'm telling you, I don't know."

"How's that collar? Getting a little tight?"

Angel swallowed. "Couldn't you take it off? There's no way out of here. Where am I going to go?"

"I think we'll leave it on a little longer."

"My knees keep giving out. If I choke to death, I'm no good to you."

Fredo cocked his head. "Good for what? You think maybe you *will* remember where Jake went? Or are you making me some other kind of offer?"

"I'm telling you, I don't know where Jake is." Angel hesitated, sensing the slippery ground they were now treading. Despite his crude manner, Fredo was not a stupid man. He would not believe that she could willingly make love to him. "There's nothing I can give you," she said, "but if I die, there won't be much you can take either, will there?"

Fredo's eyes went moist with lust; she suppressed a shudder. "You make a good point," he said.

Reaching above her, Fredo did something to the chain and she felt it slacken. At once, she sank down, hearing the links rattle through the hoop above her. The relief in her legs was wonderful, but when her rear met the floor, the chain stopped rattling, pulling her up short. Now, instead of having to stand very straight, she had to sit straight. "Couldn't you let the chain out a little more so I could lie down on the floor?"

Fredo shook his head. "A little tension will be good for you, help you think. I believe we may still have business, sweet thing, and I never mix business with pleasure. You be a good girl and tell me what I want to know, and the lying down will come later."

Angel felt the tears welling up and stopped them, but not before he saw. A new, sick greed in his eyes made her throat close with nausea. He knelt in front of her. "Maybe just a little sample won't hurt." His voice was hoarse now. Twining a hand into her hair, he pressed his face against hers, mashing her lips, kissing her throat just above the chain. Instinctively, she held very still, terrified of bringing the predator in him fully awake. Her passivity seemed to work. He released her hair with a rough shove that banged her head against the wall.

"You think I'm bad?" he asked. "I'll tell you who's bad. Your Jake. It wasn't just Senator Weingarten, you know. In fact, Weingarten is the only one he ever missed. Your patient made his living as a contract killer. Cash for a corpse. Seventeen corpses that I know of. Who knows how many more? Now *that's* bad."

All the horror she had managed until now to hold at bay welled up in her. *It was true, then. Jake was an assassin. Seventeen men. Dear God, NO—*

She realized Fredo was gazing keenly at her, wanting to know if she cared about Jake, if she might actually have *loved* Jake, and she knew that if he decided that, he would throw away everything she had said. With a fierce effort, she kept her face impassive.

But when Fredo was gone, Angel cried until there were no more tears.

22

ON THE MOVE

"You can get up now," Graham said from the front seat.

Jake raised his head and stared out the car's rear window. The street behind them stretched away dark and empty.

"I'll be damned," he said. "It worked. I guess they're not interested where you go."

"I can live with that," Graham said. "Where do *we* go now?"

Jake had been thinking about the next step as he'd lain on the floor. "Get me back to the hospital and find me a phone so I can call Fredo."

"Why the hospital?"

"You can bet he's got caller ID. If he traces me, I want him to find out I called from some sort of medical place."

"You're worried about being traced?" Graham said, reaching into his coat pocket. "Let him trace this." He handed something over his shoulder.

Jake recognized the object as soon as he touched it. A cell phone. "Great. Why didn't you tell me you had one?"

"Why didn't you ask? I doubt there's a surgeon in the country who isn't attached to one."

This was perfect. Cellular calls were only sightly more secure than two people shouting back and forth across an alley, but as long as Jake turned it off between calls, Fredo would never be able to trace him through it.

Jake knew how to reach Fredo. He placed a call to Mr. C's restaurant supply company in Atlantic City. The New Jersey Gaming Commission made a big deal of keeping anyone with mob connections from owning the smallest piece of an AC casino. But that didn't stop AC from being the Lucanza family's top profit center. Mr. C and his boys saw to it that every tablecloth, every bedsheet, every morsel of food going through those casinos came—at premium prices—from First Class Restaurant Supplies, Inc. If not, all sorts of unfortunate foul-ups happened . . . plumbing backups, air-conditioning breakdowns, fires, power failures . . . worse than breaking a hundred mirrors.

The First Class office also doubled as a control center for the family's drug and prostitution networks in Fun City.

That was where Fredo would be.

"Hello, First Class," a gruff male voice said after Jake had dialed.

"Lemme speak to Fredo."

"Yeah?" The voice became cautious. "Fredo who?"

"Fredo Papillardi." Jake knew Fredo wouldn't be there at this hour, but they'd damn well know where to find him.

"Who's calling?"

"Just tell him it's a guy with a burn on his foot. And he can reach me here." Jake gave him the cellular phone number, then hung up.

"Won't be long," he told Graham. "Meanwhile, let's find my car."

They spent the next fifteen minutes switching to the Jeep and starting for New Jersey. Jake let Graham do the driving while he rehearsed how he'd play Fredo. His next conversation was going to be *very* tricky. His delivery had to be perfect, his timing flawless.

The cell phone began chirping as they hit the westbound upslope of the Verrazano Narrows Bridge. Jake composed himself, sealing off his emotions so he wouldn't start shouting at the sound of the weasel's voice. Had to act cool, dispassionate. He let it ring three times, then hit the send button.

"Hello, Fredo."

"Jakey!" said Fredo's voice with patently false joviality. "I miss ya, buddy! Where the hell are you?"

"Where the hell do you think? In bed . . . with someone holding the phone to my ear."

"That must be uncomfortable. Give me your address and we'll have a nice face-to-face, just like the old days."

"And let you burn another hole in my foot? Not a chance. You shouldn't have done that, Fredo."

"Hey, I was just testing you."

"Did I pass?"

"I thought so. But then I sent someone around to keep tabs on you and you were gone. You flew the coop, Jakey, and didn't leave no forwarding address." An edge crept into his voice. "*You* shouldn't have done *that*."

"Hey, Fredo. You had me at a disadvantage. I don't like being at a disadvantage. So I moved. Now I'm set up in new digs."

"Yeah? Where?"

Jake forced a laugh. "Uh-uh. That's my secret. I just called to let you know that burning me was a big mistake."

"What? You still whining about that little cigarette thing. You oughta—"

"No, Fredo. Not the little burn . . . the *big* burn. The one last year."

"Now you wait just a fuckin' minute. I didn't have nothin'—"

"Yes, you did, Fredo," Jake said softly. "And now it's payback time."

"Like I'm shakin'!" The laugh sounded forced. "Like you can do shit!"

"Not personally. But I've got plenty of money. And I'm going to spend it all. I'm hiring some talent—a few Dominicans, a few Colombians, all of who'd like a piece of your action anyway—and I'm sending them after you."

"Yeah, right. Like you'd be warning me."

Now came the hairy part. He was going to hang up on Fredo.

"Oh, I *want* you to know, Fredo. I want you looking over your shoulder. And before you go, I'm gonna see you crawl. You're gonna *look* bad before you *feel* bad. It's coming, Fredo. See ya."

He hit the End button and leaned back, praying. . . .

Graham was staring at him. "What are you *doing*? You didn't find out anything about—"

"Just wait . . . and hope he calls back. And no matter what you hear me say—no matter *what*—don't make a sound."

The phone chirped again. Jake closed his eyes and bit his upper lip. It had worked.

He let it go only two rings this time, then hit Send and said, "You're not going to change my mind, Fredo. Good-bye."

"Hey, wait!" Fredo said. "Don't you want to hear about the girl?"

"What girl?"

"Your girlfriend! Don't you want to know how she's doing?"

"You're really asking for it, aren't you, Fredo. Good-bye."

"Your nurse, asshole! Angel Whatever-her-name-is!"

"Angel?" Jake said, controlling his voice. "What about her?"

"She's, um, visiting me." Good old Fredo—always worried about a tap.

"Didn't her uncle tell you?"

"Who gives a damn if he did or didn't. What I can't figure is why you think you need leverage on Graham—"

"Not Graham, you jerk—*you*."

"Me? I don't get it, Fredo."

"Don't bullshit me, man. I know you've got the hots for her."

"Hots? My hots days are gone forever. She was good to me, and I hate to think of anything bad happening to her, but I know you, Fredo. She's probably fish food already. So what's the point?"

"No, listen. She's fine. You can talk to her if you want."

"Put her on, then."

"Hey, she's not with me at the moment. She's out at one of the casinos, but I could have her call you. Better yet, have her come visit you. She wants to see you. And I know you want that, too."

"Let me tell you what I want," Jake said, letting his true emotions leak through. "I want your head. That's all I want from life. You made me dead from the neck down, so I'm gonna see you *gone* from the neck down. And after they bring me your head, my life will be complete. So I'm gonna have them sit me in a chair with your head in my lap, and then put a bullet through my brain. That's how they'll find you, Fredo—that's how you'll be remembered: facedown in Jake Nacht's lap."

He cut the connection then, turned off the phone, and leaned back, sweating.

"Are you *crazy?*" Graham shouted. He was glaring at Jake, and the Jeep was drifting toward the median on 278 at a good sixty miles an hour.

"Watch where you're going," Jake said.

Graham straightened the wheel but kept on shouting. "That was the most idiotic thing I've ever heard! You deliberately provoked him! God knows what he'll do to Angel now!"

"Take it easy, Doctor. Now we know she's still alive, and—"

"She won't be for long, no thanks to you! Why did you *do* that?"

"To keep him off balance." With an effort, Jake kept his patience. "Look, now Fredo doesn't know what to think. Am I bluffing or have I really hired some shooters? He'll be circling the wagons, but being low-key about it. He won't want to look like he's been spooked by a cripple, but the fact is, now he'll be too busy watching his back to pay much attention to Angel. I've put her out of focus for him. He'll find it hard to believe I feel nothing for her, but since he can't be sure, it'll take steam out of his plans to hurt her to get to me. But he'll keep her around, don't worry about that. He's too smart to throw out any options at this point."

"You *hope.*" Graham's voice had lost some volume now.

"I know Fredo—a hell of a lot better than I want to, and a far sight better than you do. I'm telling you, he won't kill her—not yet." Jake wished he could be as sure as he sounded.

"Not yet," Graham repeated. "Why doesn't that reassure me? How long do you think you can draw out this bluff?"

"Who says it's a bluff? And worse comes to worst, I'll trade myself for her." His own words startled him. Where the hell had *that* come from?

And yet he meant it. He'd do it. Christ, it was crazy—precisely as crazy as the way he'd let himself fall in love with her. Put himself in the hands of the man he hated more than anyone, let that man gloat over him, torture him, then kill him?

Right; he'd do it, no question.

Amazing—and scary.

Graham was staring at him again. "You'd give your life for her?"

Jake shrugged. "Why not?"

He was uncomfortable with the scrutiny. How had he fallen into the role of self-sacrificing hero? He wasn't a hero. He simply couldn't let anything happen to Angel.

He noticed the Jeep veering across the lanes again.

"I won't be able to do a damn thing if you break my neck again. I mean, I'd like to get off Staten Island alive, okay?"

Graham faced front and made the turn for the West Shore Parkway. "Why do I believe you . . . a man like you?"

"That *is* a real stumper," Jake said dryly. "Maybe it's because you're desperate, and I'm all she's got right now."

"There's the police—"

"Forget the police, will you. I told you, soon as you call in, Fredo will know."

"Even in Atlantic City?"

"*Especially* in AC."

"But what's going to happen to Angel when this attack on Fredo doesn't materialize?"

"Oh, it's going to materialize. I'm going to materialize it. And when I do, sooner or later he'll lead us to Angel."

Graham went quiet for a while, leaving Jake free to puzzle out how he was going to bring this off. Trading himself for Angel was pretty far down his list of preferences—Plan X. Plan A was to get himself and her out of AC in one piece.

He wondered if he had a chance. His legs seemed okay now, but the way they'd given out on him earlier still scared him. Was it "neuronal fatigue" like the doc had said, or something else? Something worse? Some sort of breakdown that would put him back in bed . . . ?

"You're going to need help," Graham said as they came off the Outerbridge Crossing into Jersey. "I mean, if you want to convince this Fredo you've really hired people to get him."

"That's what I've been trying to figure out: how to split myself into a couple of pieces."

"I'll help."

Jake glanced at Graham's pinched face peering intently through the windshield, the overhead lights strobing off his wire-rimmed glasses. "You kidding me?"

"I'm quite serious. I *want* to do this. Angel isn't just my niece. She's the closest thing I'll ever have to a daughter. How can I go back to my sister—hell, how can I live with *myself* if I don't do everything possible to get her back?"

"Can you shoot?"

"I told you I was in Nam. And what's there to shooting? You point, pull a trigger—"

"And maybe try to hit something. You have any *recent* shooting experience? Like a pistol range or something?"

"No, but—"

"But nothing. Forget it. You'll only get in the way."

"I can pull a trigger, damnit! That doesn't take any skill. Look at the morons running around the streets shooting at each other. What training have they had? I can do what they do. If I hit something, fine. But even if I don't, I can make a lot of noise. I can be another gunman after Fredo, which will make him think you really *have* hired people to get him."

Jake thought about that. Not a bad idea, really. With Graham he could attack Fredo from two angles. Really scare him.

"You might have an idea there, Doc. Maybe you do a drive-by or two—you shoot 'em up one side while I take the other—then we're out of there. Hit and run. High noise, low precision. Just the opposite of what they'd expect if it was me."

"As I told you before, I *do* have a brain."

"And a brain is a terrible thing to waste." Jake paused. He didn't want Graham to take this too lightly. "They *will* be shooting back. I hope you realize that."

Graham glanced at him, then back to the road. He took a deep breath.

Jake said, "You still want in?"

Graham nodded.

Jake wondered about the doc. Could he rely on him to pull that trigger, to fire *at* someone if the need arose? Or would he freeze and get himself killed? Shame to let one of the Boys snuff all that medical talent. But if it served to get Angel out . . .

Would he trade the doc for Angel?

In a New York minute.

23

LOCK AND LOAD

Jake yawned and glanced at his glowing watch face in the darkness.

Twenty-eight long hours since he'd got word Angel had been snatched. He glanced over at Graham in the driver's seat and saw him staring down at the pistol in his hands.

"I thought you said you had a 'little' stash of weapons," Graham said. "That was more like a small arms depot."

"What can I say, Doc? I'm naturally modest."

Graham shook his head. "I still can't believe a private citizen can get hold of that kind of firepower. I mean, there are laws—"

Jack had to laugh. These citizens were a riot. "The laws only prevent *you* from buying guns. Not me. I've never bought so much as a single bullet from a licensed dealer. Last thing I want to do is leave a trail from a gun shop."

"Great," Graham said wearily.

"You call it gun control if you want, but I call it victim disarmament—because if it goes much further it will be only you law-abiding citizens who can't get guns."

"Does that include disgruntled postal workers?"

Jake glanced at him, surprised. The man had actually made a joke. "Give yourself an eight point five on that one, Doc."

He yawned again—long day. In the wee hours of this morning they'd rented a room in a nameless motel on Route 9 south of Absecon and he'd slept, but not well. After that, he'd taken Graham into the woods to his stash—actually a one-man, single-piece fiberglass bomb shelter he'd buried deep in the pines after cleaning out Sarge's gun room. So deep in the pines that he needed a GPS unit to find it.

He'd given Graham a Glock, shown him how to use it, and let him get some target practice. The man was a great neurosurgeon, but quite possibly the worst shot Jake had ever seen. Drop him in the woods with Jake's entire arsenal and unlimited ammo and still he'd starve to death.

But he was game, you had to give him that. And after a few fifteen-round clips of 9mms, he'd lost his fear of the Glock's noise and kick.

The next step had been wheels. One thing AC had no shortage of was cars. The casinos had built multistory palaces to house the cars of all the gamblers driving in from New York, Philly, Wilmington, Baltimore, and D.C. Borrowing one had been easy. Between hits, Jake had educated himself in the fine art of car theft. Never knew when you might need wheels in a hurry.

Only a matter of sixty seconds to slim-jim the door lock, rip out the key cylinder, insert his own, and *bingo*—new wheels.

Well, not exactly new. Jake had chosen an older car, a 1985 Riviera, figuring it would be less likely to have an alarm system.

So now they sat two blocks down from the First Class Restaurant Supplies office, waiting. First Class sat on Mediterranean in the mostly black neighborhood in northwest AC between the rail terminal and White Horse Pike. A mix of warehouses, plumbing supply places, burned-out row houses, bars—a Bronx look, but shaved down to two stories.

"How do we know he's coming?" Graham said.

"Fredo? Oh, he'll show up. First Class is his gig and he's got to stay on top of the operation. He starts screwing up there, Mr. C'll have him out on his ass, nephew or no nephew."

Just then Fredo's black limo pulled up to the front entrance.

"And speak of the devil," Jake said.

The limo stopped by the front door of the First Class building. Jake watched Vito Cangemi get out, followed by Fredo. They crossed the sidewalk and Cangemi held the front door as Fredo strolled through.

The limo pulled away.

"Pardon the expression," Jake said, "but follow that car."

"Why? Fredo's in the office."

"We don't want Fredo. Not yet. But it's time we announced our presence."

Graham started the Riv and eased out onto Mediterranean.

"Get behind him and stay close," Jake said as he climbed into the backseat. "Be ready to pull alongside when I tell you."

He figured the limo driver would either cruise around or head for a coffee shop until he got beeped to come back. Fredo was playing it smart: A limo sitting out front of First Class was like a neon sign flashing, *I'm here! . . . I'm here! . . .*

The limo made a right onto South Carolina Avenue. Looked like he was heading for White Horse Pike. That was bad. Too many cars there. But he swung around and started driving up North Carolina, back toward Mediterranean. Making a big loop? Maybe Fredo wasn't planning to stay long. If that was true, Jake knew he'd have to make his move soon. Pulling the blanket off the Ingram Mac-10 on the seat beside him, he seated the thirty-shot clip and worked the slide to chamber a round. Crude little weapon. No skill involved. Like spraying with a fire hose—and about as accurate. But the Colombians loved these things and Fredo would know that.

"Time to suit up, Doc," Jake said.

He pulled on his own ski mask, adjusted the eyeholes, and checked to see that Graham was wearing his. Everything looked set. He scanned the area. This section of North Carolina was mostly warehouses and they were the only two cars moving.

"Okay. This is it. Make your move, just like I told you."

As Graham accelerated and pulled alongside the limo, Jake rolled down the window, leaned out, and opened fire. The Mac-10 jumped and roared in his hands as the limo's rear side windows dissolved into countless fragments that fanned out behind it in a glittering contrail. He peppered the passenger compartment, sending slug after slug into the upholstery, the minibar, the TV. Two one-second bursts and the clip was empty. The limo swerved and slammed against the cars parked along the curb.

"Get out of here!" Jake shouted.

As Graham floored the Riv, Jake leaned out the rear window and gave the limo driver the finger, leaving no doubt more than one guy was involved in this hit.

"I—I—I can't believe I'm doing this!" Graham babbled as Jake slipped back inside and rolled up the window.

"Believe it, Doc."

"I must be insane! I could get arrested! I'll lose my medical license!"

"You could lose your life, Doc."

"Yes," Graham said, softly. "I could get killed. And for what? What's all this supposed to prove?"

"It proves Jake Nacht wasn't blowing smoke when he said he'd hired guys to hit Fredo."

"All right, but we just shot up an empty car. Isn't that pretty dumb?"

Jake leaned over the front seat. "Doc, it doesn't matter—these particular hit men might not be the brightest bulbs in the box, but Fredo will now be ready to jump out of his skin. He might swagger around and laugh at how stupid we are, but he'll also get a look at what thirty steel-jacketed .45 caliber slugs did to the place where he'd been sitting minutes before. He'll be very scared. He'll be even more scared after we botch a few more hits. So scared he'll head for a safer place to stay."

"The place where he's keeping Angel?"

"You got it."

"And then what?"

"Then we stop botching."

Jake turned on the cell phone when they got back to the Jeep. Within minutes it began to ring.

"Hello?" Jake said after the third chirp.

A bilingual stream of obscenities gushed from the receiver. Jake waited for Fredo to run out of gas, then said nothing. This apparently was more than Fredo could stand.

"Hey, asshole!" he screamed. "Did you hear me?"

"Fredo?" Jake said softly. "Is that you? So sorry to hear your voice."

Fredo laughed but it sounded forced. He probably had an audience for the call. "Yeah? I'll bet you are. Your boys missed, Jakey. Missed big-time. What'd you hire? A bunch of amateurs?" Another laugh.

"I guess you got them, then," Jake said.

Fredo didn't answer.

"You *did* get them, didn't you, Fredo? Because if you didn't, you can expect another visit real soon. Maybe even tonight."

"Nobody takes potshots at me, Nacht. When I get my hands on you I'm gonna—"

"You're gonna what? Break my legs? Cut off my fingers? I won't even feel it. Try to think of something you can do to me that's worse than what's been done, Fredo."

No response from Fredo, so Jake went on, rubbing it in, enjoying it.

"How's it feel, Fredo? I know where you are but you can't find me. I can hurt you, but you can't hurt me. You've got businesses, a reputation, a life . . . a lot to lose, Fredo. I don't have a thing."

"You can die, Nacht!"

"I fully intend to. In fact, I'm looking forward to it. I believe I told you that. And I told you *how* I was going to die, didn't I."

"Your girlfriend might like a few more years," Fredo said. "Ever think of that?"

Jake closed his eyes and strained to keep his voice calm. *Thank you for bringing her up.*

"I assume you're referring to Angel." He saw Graham straighten in the passenger seat at the mention of her name. "You're not still trying to convince me she's alive."

"Alive and well."

She'd better be, Jake thought.

How did he play this? Show he cared a little—or show nothing at all?

A little . . . he'd show just a little. . . .

"She was good to me, Fredo, and I'm not totally heartless, so if she really is alive, I guess letting her go might buy you something."

Another laugh—harsher, more genuine than the others. "So! You do have a thing for her! I knew it!"

"Don't get your hopes up, Fredo. If I hear she's back in Brooklyn, I maybe just have you killed and forget about your face in my lap. But don't think she buys your life. Nothing buys your life, Fredo. That's mine. I want it, and I'm gonna get it. See ya."

Jake cut the connection and turned off the power. No more talking to Fredo tonight. Let him stew.

"You really think she's alive?" Graham said.

Jake nodded.

"That part about letting her go—that was well done."

Jake raised an eyebrow. "Was that a compliment?"

"Yes . . ." Graham seemed as shocked as Jake. "Yes, I believe it was."

"I'll be damned."

"On that we agree. But on the phone just now, I think you struck the perfect balance. You gave him just enough to make him hope that Angel might be an asset . . . not enough to be sure he can trade her, but enough to make it worth his while to keep her alive."

"Right—and we've got to keep the upper hand. Can't let Fredo guess at even one-tenth of what she really means to me. He does that, all of a sudden, *he's* calling the shots."

He noticed Graham watching him. "You really do care, don't you?"

"That's right," Jake said, once again uncomfortable with the scrutiny. "You think it worked?"

Graham rubbed his eyes and sighed. "I pray it did. Otherwise, this is all for nothing."

"Not quite, Doc. I meant what I said. Either way, Fredo winds up dead."

"I thought you said you were a changed man."

"I am. But I can't live the life that changed man wants to live as long as Fredo is walking around. So it's very simple: He's got to go."

24

TRICKS

Instead of heading back to the motel after shooting up Fredo's limo, Jake hot-wired another car—a beat-up Honda Accord. He and Graham drove north separately, Jake in the Honda, the doc in the Jeep. They left the Jeep in Jersey City and took the Honda into lower Manhattan. They spent the wee hours cruising the Fulton Fish Market until Jake spotted a First Class truck.

That was the problem with posing as a legit businessman—you had to make a show of doing some legit business.

They waited till the truck was loaded, then followed it out the all but empty Holland Tunnel. As the truck hit the uphill ramp toward the turnpike, Jake used the Mac-10 to riddle its body and tires. It fishtailed back and forth and finally shuddered to a halt, but Jake kept firing. He saw the driver and his helper clamber out the far side of the cab and jump over the ramp railing.

"Stop by the door," he told Graham.

As the Honda pulled even with he truck's shattered driver window, Jake scratched the top of a flare and tossed it into the cab.

"Go!" he said, and Graham zoomed up the ramp.

As they reached the top he looked back and saw flames starting to flicker from the truck's windows.

"Scratch one from Fredo's rolling stock."

The sun had been up for an hour by the time Jake pulled the Jeep into the parking lot of their motel. He managed to doze through the morning, but every time he woke up a little, he saw that Graham wasn't sleeping. The man seemed in constant movement—even lying on the room's other bed, he squirmed and shifted constantly. Once, awakened by a soft tread, Jake cracked an eyelid and found him pacing up and down the narrow pass at the foot of the beds. Not a good sign, but Jake knew it wouldn't do any good to nag or coddle him. No way could the man, in just a few short days, pick up the seasoning to sleep even when his guts were in a knot.

After sunset, Jake acquired new wheels—a 1988 Olds Ciera this time—and in the heart of night, at 2 A.M., began cruising the AC Expressway. Nothing there, so he took the ramp onto the northbound parkway. Another few minutes and he'd found his quarry. Up ahead, doing a cautious sixty in the right lane, was another of Fredo's First Class Restaurant Supplies delivery trucks, heading north for a pickup—either to Hunt's Point or the Fulton Fish Market. Didn't matter. It wasn't going to get there.

Jake fell in behind the truck.

"We're going to get caught," Graham said from the backseat. "We can't keep this up and not get caught."

"Who's going to catch us?" Jake said. "State cops? I don't think Fredo wants them sniffing around his business. He hauls more than fish and vegetables in those trucks."

"Well, they do patrol the parkway. I've seen them."

"Sure. Looking for speeders. Relax. You're just strung out from lack of sleep."

"I'm more than strung out. I'm dead on my feet."

"Been a long twenty-four hours, hasn't it." Jake glanced over his shoulder at Graham, trying not to let his concern show. The man was like an overwound clock. Before long he'd be jittery as all hell. Speak to him and he'd jump. Tap him on the shoulder and he'd yelp and bounce off the nearest wall. The doc definitely wasn't cut out for this sort of thing. But he wasn't backing down, and you had to admire that. Hopefully, the guy wouldn't go blooey before they found Angel.

"Listen," Jake said. "We'll do this truck, then call it quits on this phase of the operation. We'll hustle back to the motel and get a good night's sleep."

"And then what?"

"And then tomorrow we start phase three."

"What's that going to be?"

"I haven't entirely worked that out yet." Actually, Jake knew exactly what phase three would be, but he didn't want Graham stewing over it.

He checked the rearview mirror: nobody in sight behind him. He pulled out to the left: two empty lanes of blacktop stretching ahead of the truck. About what you'd expect at this hour of the morning.

"Okay. This is it. You go for the tires, I'll put a few through the cargo area, and then we're outta here. All right?"

"Right." Graham's voice quavered a little. "Fine."

"Just don't miss the tires. Get at least one of them."

"I said, *fine!* Let's just get this over with!"

Oh, yes, Jake thought. The doc's spring is wound about as far as it goes.

He wished Graham were behind the wheel instead of him, but he didn't trust the doc's high-speed driving skills. The idea here was to put a few holes in the truck, knock out a couple of tires, and then scoot ahead to the next exit, where they'd left the Jeep in a movie multiplex parking lot. Timing was everything. If Graham missed the exit stop, they'd be stuck on the parkway for miles, sitting ducks for any state troopers who'd heard reports of a northbound Ciera shooting at a truck.

Graham's shooting skills were still nonexistent, but Jake was going to get close enough to those tires so that even the doc couldn't miss . . . with a Glock. Jake was not going to give Graham the Mac-10.

"All right," Jake said. "Here we go. Work the slide like I showed you and get ready."

He heard Graham chamber a round. Jake did the same with his Tokarev and gripped it in his left hand. Another check ahead and in the rearview—all clear—and then he gunned the Ciera.

He pulled alongside the truck, got close, and yelled, "Now!"

As he heard Graham's Glock begin to fire from the rear, Jake stuck his arm out his own window and began firing over the Ciera's roof. He wasn't a lefty but he wasn't looking for accuracy, just to put holes in the truck.

"I got it!" Graham shouted. "I got a tire!"

"Go for another one."

But too late. The truck was rolling across the shoulder, dropping quickly behind as the driver braked and slewed to a stop on the grass.

"Good work!" Jake said. "End of phase two."

"I did it! I shot that tire flat. I don't believe—" His voice faded, then: "Where'd *he* come from?"

Jake tensed and looked in his rearview. A car was racing up behind them, lights out. Damn good question. Where *had* it come from? And who was inside? He relaxed a little as it passed under a light and he saw it was a Firebird. Good. Not a car favored by the Boys. They tended toward—

And then he saw a tiny strobing flash from the Firebird's passenger side.

"Duck!"

As he slid down as far as he could without losing sight of the road, he heard the faint chatter of a machine pistol, but nothing hit the car. He put the pedal to the metal.

"They're shooting at us!" Graham cried. "It must be Fredo!"

No, not Fredo. He'd be back in AC. Must have sent a couple of guys out to follow the truck, just in case someone tried to shoot this one up. They'd been hanging back all this time with their lights out, waiting for something to happen.

And now they were closing in for the kill.

Jake's eyes were level with the dashboard. He reached up and adjusted his mirror. The Firebird was closer—*much* closer. No more than fifty yards now. Then he glanced ahead at the road just in time to see his exit ramp flash by.

"Damn!"

What the hell was he going to do now? This cowboy stuff was going to attract a lot of attention, and that was bad for everybody. He had to get off the parkway.

More flashes from the Firebird, but nothing touched the Ciera. The guy back there was probably using an M-11—light enough to hold in one hand but about as accurate as Graham on a bad day. He'd have been better off with—

The rear window imploded.

"Oh, God!" Graham screamed. "Oh God oh God oh God!"

"Are you hit?"

"Oh God oh God oh God!"

Jake started weaving the Ciera back and forth. "For Christ's sake, Doc! *Are . . . you . . . hit?*"

"No!"

"Then fire back!"

"I can't! I'm out of shots!"

"You've got extra clips back there. You know how to change them. Get a new one in and start pulling the trigger!"

"I'll get shot!"

Another glance in the rearview showed the Firebird closing in on thirty yards.

"He was just lucky. And look at it this way: You let him get much closer, we're both dead men."

"Oh, God!" Graham said again, and kept repeating it over and over as Jake listened to him fumble with the empty clip and slip a new one in.

Jake kept glancing at the rearview mirror, watching the Firebird draw closer and closer, wanting to yell at Graham to hurry but knowing it would only worsen his already near-terminal case of fumblefingers.

If only they could change places.

The Firebird was just twenty yards back now but the guy hadn't fired any more bursts. Probably waiting till his driver got him good and close . . . where he could make every round count. And Jake couldn't get any more speed out of the Ciera. A hundred seemed the best it could do.

Just then he saw a sign: Toll Plaza—1 Mile.

Toll plaza! What else could go wrong? He couldn't thread a toll lane at this speed. He'd have to slow down. And then the M-11 would make Swiss cheese out of the Ciera.

"Got it!" Graham cried.

"Well don't just sit there! Empty it out the back window as fast as you can, then reload!"

Graham peeked over the top of the backseat, extended his arm, and began firing. Jake saw a spark flare on the Firebird's hood, watched it wobble, then drop back to fifty yards.

"A hit! Reload quick!"

The M-11 started chattering again.

"Really? I hit it?"

"Yes, goddamn it. Ricocheted one off the hood. Now reload! You've got to time the next shots just right."

The brightly lit toll plaza hove into view as Graham worked with a new clip. Jake kept the Ciera floored.

"Come on, Doc. You've gotta be ready."

"It's in."

"Great. Now . . . as soon as I pass the booths up ahead, start shooting. Do exactly what you did before. Exactly."

One hit, he was thinking. One nothing ricochet like the last time . . . make them wobble like the last time . . . just enough to throw them a little bit off course . . . and then it's bye-bye toll booth and bye-bye Firebird.

The Firebird was shooting again, and Jake saw a row of holes stitch across the toll-booth glass as he flashed through an Exact Change or Token lane. He had a glimpse of a toll taker's pale, terrified face two lanes away crouching behind his change maker.

"Now, Doc!" he yelled as soon as they were in the clear. "Start shooting!"

Graham did just that. And managed to miss with all fifteen rounds. The Firebird roared through the toll lane and accelerated toward them.

"Christ, Doc. You hit everything in the toll plaza but their car!"

"Sorry."

Yeah. Sorry. Now what? Wasn't there a service island somewhere up ahead? Right—he'd passed it countless times. And a state trooper detail attached, if he remembered.

Maybe we're not dead yet.

"Load up another clip, Doc. Just keep firing. Keep 'em honest for another couple of minutes and we may have a chance."

He spotted the sign for Burger King and TCBY and Mobil gas. Seconds later he came over a rise and saw the rest stop huddled on the median island. The police office sat on its south end.

Jake kept up his speed for as long as he dared, then hit the brakes and slid toward the rest-stop entrance. He hoped the Firebird would miss it, or better yet, lose control and smash into the fuel pumps.

As he screeched into the turn he glanced in the rearview, hoping to see the Firebird flash on by. But no, the bastard was following him, fishtailing into the lot right behind him.

At least his buddy had stopped shooting. For now.

Jake gunned the Ciera across the lot and back onto the southbound lanes of the parkway. If nothing else, this would trigger a call to the state troopers, and they'd be on the Firebird's tail before they'd be on his. All Jake had to do was stay alive until then.

The toll booths were coming up again. He started to tell Graham to load up and fire again but let it go. Why bother? There wasn't enough time, and he wouldn't hit the car anyway. Waste of good ammo.

A couple of 9mms from the M-11 hit the trunk. Jake saw the Firebird pulling closer and a sinking feeling crept into his gut. No troopers in sight yet. This wasn't going to work out.

The next sign announced the exit where they'd left the Jeep. If he was getting off anywhere, it had to be here.

Just as before, he waited till the last second, then jammed the brakes and turned the wheel. The tires howled in agony as the car slid into the off-ramp's steep 270-degree turn. The rearview showed the Firebird right behind them. Good wheelman, whoever he was. At least the gunner had given up trying to shoot until they got back on level ground.

But not Graham. Jake started as he heard the doc's Glock start blasting away through the rear window.

Jake was about to tell him not to bother when he saw cracks spiderwebbing across the Firebird's windshield. The car lurched left, hit the curb and became airborne.

"You got him!" Jake shouted. "I don't believe it, Doc! You *got* him!"

The Firebird did a graceful swan dive over the embankment, tilting to its left as it flew. Then the front bumper caught the grass. The car upended, flipped, and landed on its roof.

"I—I don't believe it either," Graham said. "Oh, thank God! I thought we were goners."

And then the Firebird earned its name: The gas tank exploded, filling the night with flames and flying steel.

As Jake floored the Ciera onto the highway, heading for the Jeep, he heard Graham's voice plunge from elation to despair.

"Dear God! What have I done?"

"You saved our butts, Doc."

"I just killed two men! I *killed* two men!"

"Who were trying to kill you, Doc. Don't give them a second thought. If places were reversed they'd be high-fiving each other right about now."

Silence from the back.

"You were in Nam, weren't you? This shouldn't be anything new."

"I was a general medical officer. I worked in a base hospital trying to put our guys back together. I *saved* lives. I never . . ."

Jake heard another sound from the backseat. It sounded like a sob. He didn't look around.

25

FAKING IT

"I don't think I can do this."

They sat in a beat-up old yellow Ford Country Squire wagon—Jake didn't know the model year because the damn things all looked alike. They'd parked on Virginia Avenue down near White Horse Pike, around the corner and a few blocks from the First Class office. Jake had the passenger seat. He chewed his lip as he watched Graham sit behind the wheel and shake like a guy on a Magic Fingers bed in an earthquake.

"You've got to hold on, Doc. This one is the last. We pull this off and you won't ever have to touch a gun again."

"You're sure of that?"

"Absolutely."

Jake wasn't promising that this little stunt would resolve the situation, but he knew this would be the last time he'd be able to get a gun into Graham's hands. Resisting the urge to shake his head, Jake stared out his window into the night. Graham had been a basket case since last night. If Jake hadn't fed him four stiff drinks at the motel to calm him down, the man would have gone another night without sleep.

"What if I kill somebody else?" Graham mumbled.

"You won't. But even if you do, it's no loss to the world. In fact, it'll make the world a cleaner place. An environmental cleanup of sorts. Really, you shouldn't feel that bad about those bastards in the Firebird."

"Don't tell me how I *should* feel," Graham flared. "I know I should feel glad that I killed a couple of the animals that kidnapped Angel. But I don't. I've spent my whole life trying to improve lives, not end them. And I know it was self-defense, but somehow that doesn't justify the obscene celebrating I was doing right after seeing my bullet go through their windshield. I feel dirty. Does that make any sense to you? Can you understand that?"

Jake was surprised to realize he did understand. A year ago, Graham might as well have been babbling in Chinese for all the sense it would have made. But now, after getting close to Angel, after daily contact with all the people who'd dedicated themselves to restoring his nervous system—who'd worked not just on him but with him—he could somehow grasp what Graham was saying.

But understanding wasn't the same as agreeing. Come on—someone threatens you or someone you love, they go down. How else could it be?

"I don't want to kill again," Graham said in a low voice.

"You won't. I guarantee it. All you have to do is make noise. Shoot at the street, shoot straight up in the air, I don't care. You're not out there to hurt anybody, Doc. All you've got to do is get their attention."

I'll take care of the hurting part, he thought.

Graham nodded, but none too confidently. "I guess I can handle that."

"Got to do better than guess, Doc. You've got to do it. For Angel."

Graham's nod was more resolute now. "For Angel."

Jake clapped him on the shoulder. "There you go." But his worry about Graham eased only a little. The man was close to breaking. Bringing him along was risking his life in a big way. The last thing he wanted was to get the man killed, but he needed a diversion to make this work, so there were no other options.

Shell-shocked as he was, Graham was all he had.

"All right," he said to the doctor. "You've got your walkie-talkie. You've got your trusty Glock—"

"Oh, yes," Graham choked. "Real trusty."

Jake suppressed a groan, remembering how Graham hadn't wanted even to touch the pistol again. Before they'd hit the road tonight, Jake had spent twenty minutes coaxing and pleading before he'd finally managed to force the gun into Graham's hand and make him hold it until he got over the worst of his revulsion.

"It's just metal, Doc. And tonight it's nothing more than a noisemaker. That's all."

Graham swallowed hard and gave a slight nod.

"Good. Let's go over it one more time: You hang back here while I get into position. Keep the motor running. Listen for my go-ahead. You do your drive-by shooting, ditch the car, then wait for me at the pickup spot. Got that?"

Another nod. "Got it."

"I hope so, Doc. A lot's riding on this."

Jake got out and trotted around the corner. Halfway down the block he stopped by another borrowed car—a royal blue Torino he'd parked before a strip of boarded-up, partially burned-out row houses. Looking around, he saw no one, so he opened the trunk and pulled out a Colt AR-15 A2 H-BAR, chambered for .223 ammo. He needed a semiautomatic for this shoot and the AR-15 was as good as they came. Usually he'd have fitted it with a cheek mount and a Tasco scope, but since he'd be leaving it behind, he didn't want it gussied up with sniper paraphernalia.

No scope tonight—a naked-eye shot.

He hurried up the steps of the nearest row house and pulled back the sheet of plywood over the front door. He'd loosened it earlier and it moved easily. He made his way to the second-floor perch he'd scouted earlier and peered through the shattered panes of one of the front windows. He would have preferred higher, like the rooftop, but he didn't trust these roofs—barely trusted the flooring in this rat trap. This would have to do.

He settled the AR-15 across his lap and pulled out his binoculars. The front door of First Class Restaurant Services swam into view. Two black Lincoln Town Cars sat out front. Fredo was inside, he knew. Jake had watched his grand entrance about an hour ago.

The Town Cars had pulled up, the second riding low. The doors of the trailing car opened first and five hulks emerged, all cut from the NFL lineman mold.

Jake had watched the soldiers' little show. They glowered up and down the street, hands inside their jackets, game faces on. Tough guys.

Idiots.

Like they were going to scare off a bullet zooming in the length of a football field. What a nice, tight little group they made. If he'd wanted to start shooting, three of them could be dead before the other two heard the first shot.

Two more hotshots had got out of the first car and the seven of them formed a semicircle around the rear door. From his vantage point, at street level, Jake hadn't been able to see Fredo as his guards clustered around him and escorted him through the door. All those arms and legs . . . like some big ungainly bug. Three went in with him, the other four stayed outside.

Jake had let him go. He wanted to catch Fredo on the way out.

Lowering the binoculars, he leaned on the windowsill, smiling. Fredo had to be ready to jump out of his skin by now. And with good reason. His limo had been hit here in AC; one of his trucks had got ventilated in north Jersey and another on the parkway; he'd sent out two of his gunners to take care of the problem and they'd come back fricasseed. The guy had to believe a small army was gunning for him. By now he'd be wetting his pants every time a car backfired.

How fitting that Fredo, who'd taunted him about the catheter when he'd lain helpless in his bed, should now be experiencing the catheterizing effects of fear.

Jake dwelled pleasantly on the notion until, shortly after midnight, he spotted some activity around the door. Four of the soldiers stepped out on the sidewalk and lit up some smokes. They were trying real hard to look casual but they were lousy actors: If they weren't looking back at the door, they were scoping the street. Something was going to happen, and Jake knew what.

He hit the talk button on his walkie-talkie.

"Yo, Doc. I think he's coming. Start moving, but slow. Just edge in his direction and be ready to floor it."

Graham's reply squawked in his earplug. "Roger wilco."

Jake stared at the walkie-talkie. " 'Roger wilco'?" He shook his head. "Just hold together a little while longer, Doc. Help me pull this off, then you can go to pieces."

Up ahead two more beef jerkies had stepped out onto the sidewalk in front of First Class, milling around with the others, trying to look like they were on a break. A break from what? Practicing with their ice picks?

He hit the talk button again.

"Start picking up a little speed, Doc. Won't be long now. Do as I showed you: Get low in the seat, steer with your left hand, shove your right hand out the window, and pop away." He released the button and added, "And don't get hurt."

Someone stuck his head out the First Class door and said something. Suddenly the Boys had a purpose. They formed a reverse gauntlet just like they'd done before, facing out, hands in pockets. One of them opened the rear door on the first car. Jake hit the talk button again.

"It's now, Doc. Do it!"

Jake heard the roar of the Country Squire's big eight-cylinder engine as Graham hit the gas. He saw it rounding the corner, lights out, gathering speed.

"Don't fail me now, Doc," he whispered.

Up ahead, the front door to First Class was opening. Vito

Cangemi stuck his head out again and checked that the troops were all in position.

Jake shouldered the AR-15 and nestled his cheek against the stock.

Still accelerating, the Country Squire trundled past Jake, leaving a thin trail of smoke in its wake.

Cangemi turned and nodded to someone behind him.

And then Fredo appeared, head down, making a beeline for the open car door.

Jake fixed his sights on the knot of suits by the car.

And Graham was almost there. He was going to be a hair late, but that was okay. As long as he fired his Glock.

Graham was practically on top of them and still no shots. The beef sticks had spotted him and were alerting each other—old car with no lights. What gives? Fredo's lieutenant pushed him into the car and pulled his pistols. A couple of his men followed suit. . . .

"Come on, Doc!" Jake said. "Now, goddamn it! *Now!*"

But no shots. No nothing. The wagon rumbled by without incident.

Jake saw relieved grins and shrugs as weapons were tucked away and jackets were straightened.

The bastards thought they'd got off easy.

Jake forgot about Graham and began pulling the trigger.

He fired a three-round burst into the cluster of bodies. Pissed as he was, he wasn't in a killing mood. But he had to reduce the manpower against him. So he avoided head shots, going for arms and legs instead. The AR-15 gave its slugs a one-in-twelve twist that did enormous damage when they hit. No simple flesh wounds with that kind of rotation. These babies left behind broken bones and messy exits.

Two guards went down with the first salvo and, an instant later, two more with the second before it dawned on them that they were under attack. And then they were diving in all directions. A pair ducked behind the Town Car and probably thought they were safe until it burned rubber away from the curb and left them exposed and frozen like wide-eyed deer caught in the oncoming headlights of a Mack truck. Jake took them down with two shots, then put a couple into the Lincoln's trunk, just so Fredo wouldn't think he got off too easy.

The Lincoln screeched around a corner and headed east. Fredo was running. Good. That had been the whole idea behind this staged event: Make him duck for cover and find out where he went. Had to be someplace he thought was safe and secure—maybe even secure enough for extended boarding of a hostage?

Jake pounded down to the first floor, leaped off the porch, tossed the AR-15 onto the front seat of the Torino, and jumped in after it. He'd left the motor running, so all he had to do was jump behind the wheel and throw her into gear.

As he roared past First Class he emptied the AR-15's clip into the guard car, making sure he got the two street-side tires. The remaining pair of guards returned fire but too little too late. They popped Jake's rear window, hit the body a few times, and then he was gone.

He followed Fredo's taillights up Tennessee and watched him make a right on Atlantic Avenue, AC's main drag. Falling in behind the Lincoln, he pulled to within a block and a half before easing back. He scanned the sidewalks. The plan had been to pick up Graham somewhere around here after he dumped the wagon, but it was up for grabs right now whether he'd even stop for the wimp. Christ, all the doc had needed to do was fire a couple of blind shots, just to maintain the illusion that there was a whole crew of gunnies after Fredo. But no. He'd crapped out. It'd serve him right now if—

The Torino coughed and slowed, then picked up speed, then coughed again . . . and died. Heart sinking, Jake checked the gas gauge. It said half full but he knew the sound of a thirsty engine. He was out of gas.

And up ahead, Fredo's taillights were shrinking in the distance.

Damnit!

Jake jumped out of the car and looked around. He needed

wheels—and fast, even if he had to hijack at gunpoint the next car that came by—

Yes—do it!

He opened the trunk, and was pulling out the duffel bag with all his weaponry when he heard a car horn toot nearby. Looking up, he saw a beat-up old station wagon.

"Need a lift?" Graham said.

Seconds ago, he'd have been happy never to see Graham again; now he was overjoyed. Jumping into the front seat, Jake pointed down Atlantic. "Straight ahead. And step on it. We might have lost him."

"Not unless he wants to get picked up for running a red. These lights are murder."

The wagon took off with a screech.

"Breakdown?" Graham said after a couple of blocks.

"Gas gauge lied to me. What happened to you?"

Graham stared at the street ahead as he picked up speed. "I got cold feet." He shrugged. "Then they warmed up again. But only for driving. I can't do any more shooting. Sorry."

"Forget about it. I'll take care of that from here on. Just find that car."

"I'll do my best—hey!" Graham's eyes widened and he pointed ahead as they rounded the monument at Albany Avenue. "Isn't that him? Three blocks up. Looks like a Lincoln."

Jake pulled out a nightscope, clicked it on, and focused. A black Lincoln Town Car with holes through its trunk.

"That's him." As Graham closed to within a block of the Lincoln, a vast relief shot through Jake. Fredo could have been heading inland, in which case he'd have turned at Albany, caught 40, and been gone.

Watching Fredo's car, Jake said, "Okay. He's going toward Ventnor—"

"What's that? A street? I used to own that in Monopoly."

"It's the next town south. A lot classier than AC."

The casinos and hotels and high-rises abruptly gave way to Ventnor's tree-lined residential streets with their large, stately homes settled within an easy walk to the ocean. But the further they left AC behind, the more the traffic thinned, until Jake was sure Fredo would spot them.

"Turn your headlights out," he told Graham.

"What if a cop spots us? We'll get stopped."

"Have to risk it."

They hung back as far as they dared without risking losing the Lincoln as it wound along the dark streets, turning this way and that, until Jake saw its brake lights flare in midblock as the car made a turn.

"Stop here," he said, grabbing Graham's arm. "Let's see what happens."

Graham pulled the wagon into the curb; they sat in the dark with the engine running.

"What are we waiting for?"

"To see if he pulls out again."

"Why would he do that?"

"An old trick, Doc—part of a procedure Fredo's boys call 'dry cleaning.' You pull into a strange driveway and wait to see if anybody suspicious drives by. When you get on your way again, you've got a pretty good idea whether or not you're being followed, and what kind of car to be on the lookout for."

"You think he's coming out?"

Jake shook his head. "Nope. I think Fredo's home for the night. Hang a U here and circle around so we can pass the place going the other way."

A few minutes later, with their headlights on and the speedometer fixed at twenty-five miles an hour, they cruised past the house—a mansion, rather. Jake squinted through the dark at the glowering conglomeration of white porticoes and stuccoed walls set on a fifteen-foot rise in the center of a thickly wooded yard. Light leaked through heavily curtained windows and French doors. He was sure he spotted at least two figures patrolling the yard. He felt a quick exhilaration. He knew where Fredo lived—officially, that is—and this was nowhere near it. Fredo would never stash Angel in any house known to be his, so that made this one a good candidate.

And there was something else, too.

"Built pretty high," Graham said.

Jake wondered if he was clairvoyant. "Exactly," he said. "That's a man-made mound. Water table's high here. You build your house on a mound like that for one reason: You want a basement."

Graham took a deep breath. "Angel. We've found her."

"There's a good chance. Keep moving. Two blocks, then make a left and find a dark spot to park."

By the time Graham had pulled to a stop in the shadows under a dense maple, Jake was up to his elbows in his duffel.

"What do you think you're doing?" Graham said.

"Going in."

"No-no!" Graham said, grabbing his arm. "You'll get her killed. I won't allow it."

"You won't—?" Jake stared at him. "You've got to be kidding."

"I know a better way. Listen to me: We know where he's hiding her now. We can call the police, tell them Fredo Papillardi has kidnapped a woman and is holding her hostage there. They'll—"

"Doc—Joseph, listen to me. We've been through this. How long do you think before Fredo knows about the call? I'd bet ten minutes, fifteen outside."

"I hope it's *five* minutes. The point is, as soon as he finds out, he'll have to move Angel. And we'll be waiting outside. Don't you see? We won't have go to him, he'll bring Angel to us."

For a few seconds, Jake wondered if the doc might be onto something here, but then he saw the fatal flaw in the plan.

"Uh-uh," he said, shaking his head. "Too risky. Reporting Angel as Fredo's hostage turns her from a possible asset into a dangerous liability. And I know how Fredo handles liabilities. He'd bring Angel out, all right, but it would be her body."

Graham shuddered, saying nothing more as Jake took his Glock and added it to the two others he had, plus his Tokarev. The four automatics would give him about sixty rounds to work with. He began emptying the Glock clips.

Graham watched without comprehension. "You're going in without bullets?"

Jake barked a laugh. "In Fredo's dreams, maybe. I'm just changing ammo in a couple." He pulled a box of shells out of the duffel and tossed them to Graham. "To these."

Graham studied the label. " 'Prefragmented'? What does that mean?"

"It means I don't have to hit anyone twice."

26

THE POOL

"All right, bitch—no more Mr. Nice Guy!"

Angel cringed back against the wall as Fredo strode across the cellar with two of his men—one in a suit like his, and one in a sweatshirt. She saw the fury in his eyes and knew with a rush of fear that she was going to be its target.

"What?" she said, trying to keep her voice from scaling up. *"What?"*

Fredo pointed to the collar around her neck. "Unhook her from the wall, but keep the chain on her." He flashed an icy smile as the suit handed some keys to the sweatshirt. "Like a leash."

Angel struggled to her feet. So weak. They fed her only once a day—leftovers from dinner upstairs—and let her go to the bathroom when they felt like it. She looked down at her hands, her arms, her clothes—all filthy. She wondered if she'd ever feel warm again—feel *clean* again, inside and out. This has been the most terrifying, utterly humiliating experience in her—

"Move!"

Fredo grabbed the end of the chain and yanked it, forcing her into a stumbling walk toward the doorway as his men closed in behind.

Were they taking her upstairs? Was she actually getting out of this basement? "Where are we going?"

"Not 'we,' " Fredo said. "*You*. You're going for a little swim."

"What do you mean?"

He didn't answer, but the way his two men chuckled behind her made her stomach turn.

Angel knew there was a pool somewhere on this level—she'd smelled the chlorine at times, and often heard faint splashes, as if someone were using a diving board.

They led her down a hallway, past a staircase leading up, and then the chlorine smell got stronger as they approached a doorway filled with wavering light.

Fredo led her into a warm, steamy room all tiled in white with a large aqua-bottomed pool. At first she thought the ceiling was black, then realized it was all glass—skylights, dark with the night sky. But during the day . . . she imagined how beautiful and warm it must be with the sunlight streaming through and—

She started as she felt something clasp around her wrists and dig into the skin. Wild panic raced through her as she looked down and saw handcuffs—two sets, with one bracelet of each around her wrists, and the other closed around the handle of a dumbbell. Sweatshirt let the weights down until they hung against her legs, dragging at her sockets, making her arms feel as if they weighed a ton each.

"What are you doing?"

"Doing?" Fredo gave her his sickening smile again. "I guess you could say I'm going on a fishing expedition." She heard appreciative chuckles from Fredo's two sidekicks. Her spine crawled.

"We've used this method before," Fredo said, "and found it to be real persuasive. You see, I'm gonna find out once and for all how much you really know about your boyfriend's whereabouts."

"But I told you—"

"I *know* what you told me." Now the smile was gone. "But I don't *believe* what you told me. So here's where you can make a believer out of me. This is how it's gonna go down: We dunk you a few times, then you tell us all you know about Nacht."

"But I don't know any—"

He slapped her face and Angel staggered back, her cheek stinging.

"Don't interrupt me when I'm talking!" he snapped. He turned to the suit. "Vito. Get her out of those clothes."

Horrified, Angel tried to run but couldn't—the collar, the weights—*trapped!* She struggled anyway as one of them grabbed and held her while the other began cutting the back of her T-shirt.

"Easy with that razor," the one in the suit said. "Don't want to damage this fine merchandise."

"Please!" she cried. "Don't do this!"

"Like I was saying," Fredo said, "if I don't think you're telling me everything after you been dunked, what I do is, I give you to the boys to play with. We got some very horny guys here, and since you arrived they've been buggin' the hell outta me to let them at you. But I've been a good guy up to now. I been protecting you. But like I said before, no more Mr. Nice Guy. You don't convince me, I let them have you. And after an all night session with them in which you've been had six ways from Sunday, we bring you back here and dunk you again. And if I'm still not convinced, then it's back to the boys. And so it will go, around and around, until you tell me what I want to know."

Angel cringed as the slashed remnants of her T-shirt tore away, leaving her with only a thin bra above the waist. Then they went to work on her shorts.

"But I've already told you everything I know! How can I tell you something I don't know?"

"Good question," Fredo said. "I guess we'll find out, won't we."

Angel felt her shorts tear away then and saw Fredo's gaze wander down her body. As fingers gripped her bra strap she twisted away. The sudden move caused her feet to slip on the wet tiles and the next thing she knew she was falling.

She hit the water on her side and went under . . . and down. And kept going down. The dumbbells attached to her wrists made her arms useless, and no matter how hard she kicked, her legs couldn't overcome the extra weight.

She sank toward the bottom.

During the first few seconds she felt oddly at peace in the warm water.

I'm dead, she thought.

No matter what she told him, no way Fredo was going to let her leave this house alive. So better to die down here than be subjected to the rest of what he had planned for her.

But as her air ran out, as the bubbles leaked from her lips and raced to the surface, her peace turned to distress, then panic. Against her will, her legs began to thrash and her arms to struggle in pursuit of those bubbles as her lungs cried out for air.

The weights kept her securely trapped on the bottom. Black splotches sparkled before her eyes, swelling, exploding as she struggled more frantically.

Air! Dear God, give me air!

And just as her limbs were giving out and her chest felt as if it were about to explode, she felt the collar dig into her chin and throat, tugging her toward the surface. But so slowly! She needed air *now!* The black spots invaded her brain, taking over her body. She didn't fight the collar, couldn't if she'd wanted to. Instead she allowed herself to be reeled toward the surface like some log that had fouled a fisherman's line . . . like a dead thing . . .

And then she felt something bump against her knees—

Steps! The pool steps in the shallow end! She reached out with her weighted arms and clutched them. She climbed them with her hands, and then it happened—her head broke the surface and she coughed and gagged and retched. This was a nightmare—even though she felt air all around her, she couldn't draw it past her spasming throat.

A final cough and suddenly she *was* gulping air, her sharp gasps bouncing off the walls and glass above as she pulled it into her starving lungs. One, two, three breaths—was there anything in this world as sweet as air?

And then the collar tugged again, dragging her back from the steps. She had no time to scream, barely enough time for a final breath before she sank beneath the surface again.

How long would they keep this up? How long could she take it?

Please, Jake! Where are you? Don't let them do this to me!

27

GOING IN

Jake watched the two outside guards until he had their routine down. The one wearing the warm-up and the Jets cap patrolled the north side with a shotgun while the bareheaded other wandered the south, both taking the same route each time. They'd meet at the front porch to smoke and gab awhile, then go strolling again.

He decided to take the guy with the cap.

Jake crept up behind one of the oaks that the north-side guard passed regularly. While he waited, he noticed an illuminated expanse of glass panes toward the rear of the house. He wondered what it was. The glass was only three or four feet off the ground—too low for a greenhouse. But maybe it offered a way in. He'd have to check it out.

But first, the guards.

As they finished their cigarettes and started on their rounds, Jake pulled a twelve-ounce sap from his pocket and raised it high above his head. He tightened his grip on the leather handle as he heard the scuffing footsteps approach.

Had to do this right, put this guy down without a sound, no backswing to give warning—

Footsteps getting louder now . . . wait . . . wait . . .

The instant the peak of the cap entered his line of sight, Jake brought the sap down, putting his body behind the swing, and snapping his wrist to give it a little extra oomph.

Mr. Jets-cap dropped to his knees, where he remained upright for a few heartbeats, as if praying—long enough for Jake to grab the shotgun as it dropped from his fingers—then toppled forward face first.

Jake yanked off the Jets cap before it got too bloody, then stripped off the warm-up jacket. Slipping into it, he put on the cap and stepped into the guard's expected route, in case anyone was watching the front of the house. When he reached the porch, he crouched down with his back to it.

A few minutes crawled by and then he heard a voice behind him.

"Hey, Joey. What's doin'?"

Without turning, Jake motioned the other guard forward with his left arm and pointed ahead into the trees.

"You spot someone?" the guy said in a lower voice as he hurried up behind Jake.

Jake waited until the guard was crouched almost even with his left shoulder before he whirled and rammed the butt of the shotgun into the man's face, followed by a Babe Ruth swing of the barrel against the side of his head.

Guard number two dropped without a sound.

Jake dragged him into the shadows and left him next to his buddy. Keeping the shotgun, he headed for the lighted area toward the rear. The closer he got, the more it looked like some sort of low greenhouse, but when he tried to see through the panes, he found them fogged with condensation on their undersides. He noticed panes with heavier frames spaced at regular intervals. Moving to one, he found that it was hinged so it could be opened as a vent. He pried it up and peered inside.

Not a greenhouse, an indoor pool, fifteen feet below.

And someone was taking a swim—

Jake blinked as he realized it was a woman in her underwear . . . with a long chain dragging behind her neck . . . three people standing at poolside . . . the one in a sweatshirt pulling her toward the steps . . . reeling her in, under water . . .

Jake's intestines knotted fiercely. *No!*

He didn't want to believe . . . not even Fredo could—

The woman's head broke the surface, coughing, gagging, gasping, and he saw her face, and what he had already known in his gut became fact.

"Angel!"

As he screamed the word he shoved the barrel of the shotgun through the opening and fired at the bastard holding the chain. He saw the man's face disappear in a spray of red, then swiveled the barrel to go for the other two, but they were already at the exit and stumbling through the door. He fired anyway, on the outside chance a few pellets would strike home.

Finding Angel again, he saw that she'd pulled herself up the steps and was clutching the pool coping, sobbing, retching, but alive. He wanted to break through the glass and jump into the pool to reach her, but that would leave him a sitting duck—and do neither of them any good.

Then he saw the weights cuffed to her wrists.

And something snapped inside.

He tried to shout to her to hold on, that he was coming for her, but his jaw was locked. With his blood turning to ice, he straightened and ran toward the front of the house. The glass bubble of an electric meter budded from the siding. He pumped two blasts into it, jerking his head away as the meter exploded in a brilliant shower of sparks. The house went dark.

On autopilot now, his mind racing a hundred feet ahead of him, he rounded the corner of the front porch and knew what he was going to do. Hitting the steps at a run, he pumped a shotgun round through the glass of the front door's upper half. As return fire blew out whatever glass was left, Jake twisted in midair, hitting one of the gaping window frames rump first. He lost the Jets cap and shredded the borrowed warm-up top on the shattering glass as he hurtled into a living room dark as midnight. He pumped off shotgun rounds in a wild barrage as he hit the floor and rolled. Pumping and firing, he sprayed the room until he ran out of shells, then pulled two of his pistols.

The darkness echoed with screams and groans, punctuated by the muzzle flashes of panicked shooting. Lying flat, he watched them empty their pistols in all directions—*Christ, they're shooting each other.*

Suddenly he realized that he could see and they couldn't. He'd been out in the dark and they'd been inside in the light.

Rough estimate: Four soldiers up and three down.

When two of them stopped firing and reached for fresh clips, Jake squeezed off a pair of rounds at the two who were still shooting, then picked off the reloaders before they could insert their clips.

Four shots, four down—gotta love those prefrags.

A hysterical laugh boiled in Jake's throat. Choking it down, he rolled to his left just as someone opened fire from above, pouring bullets down the stairway from the second floor, riddling the spot he'd just vacated. Jake let out a scream and crouched behind a sofa.

Another fusillade from the stairwell, but Jake didn't return fire. He waited.

"Hey, Eddie," someone cried. "I think I got the fucker."

"Yeah?" shouted a second voice. "Hey, guys! What's happening down there?"

The groans of the wounded were the only replies.

"Oh, fuck, man," said the first voice. "You don't think everybody's down, do you?"

A few heartbeats of silence, then a creak on the steps. Watching from the corner of his eye to maximize his night vision, Jake spotted the pale blur of a face peeking around the edge of the stairwell, soon joined by another.

"I can't see a fuckin' thing, man. You got a light?"

"Got a penlight on my keys."

From the stairs, a tiny beam of light wavered from a shaking hand, cutting through the darkness below.

Thank you very much, Jake thought. He opened fire and Eddie and his friend joined their buddies on the floor.

He listened for the sound of footsteps retreating up the steps but heard none. He chewed his lip. Decision time: Forget the second floor? Risky, but he'd be in worse shape if he got cornered up there.

And time was short. The lights had been out about two minutes. In another two, he wouldn't be the only one with night-adapted eyes. He had to push his advantage.

Jumping to his feet, Jake lifted one of the bodies and held it before him as he pushed into the next room.

As he turned the corner he said, "Hey, it's me—Eddie. Don't shoot!"

Someone opened fire, hitting the corpse twice. Either they didn't buy his mimicry or didn't care too much for Eddie. Jake pumped two rounds at the muzzle flashes and the shooting stopped.

Ahead and to his right he heard footsteps pounding down steps to the basement.

Creeping forward, he found himself in a hall, standing at the door to the basement. He stood to the side and slammed it shut; at once, a barrage from below shredded the door.

At the same time, the sound drew fire from a doorway at the far end of the hall—a bathroom?

Jake lunged back out of the hall and pulled out his Tokarev, still loaded with the steel-jacketed rounds he'd used to riddle the First Class truck last night. He edged his head around the corner into the hall just enough to get his right eye clear for a look down to the door at the far end. It was now closed again, after the burst of gunfire from down there.

Snaking his arm around the corner, Jake started firing the Tokarev. His first shot hit the center of the paneled door at its thickest point, blowing it open. Then he placed one round to either side, each about three feet off the floor.

A dark figure fell foward through the doorway with a satisfying thump.

Jake put the Tokarev away and retrieved his Glocks. Making a quick check of the rest of the rooms along the hall, he closed each door as he passed, throwing the hallway into even deeper darkness. Then he returned to the shredded basement door, his mind racing. The pool was one level down, and this must be the way to it. At last sight, Angel had been alone beside the pool, gasping for air, in no shape to run. He had to get to her. But how? He had to assume that whoever had turned the door into Swiss cheese was still down there—no doubt, more than one man.

Jake groped around him until he found a body. The Hey-it's-me-Eddie routine wouldn't work twice, but maybe he could improvise a variation on it. He dragged the body into the hallway next to what was left of the cellar door. Keeping well to the side, he grabbed the knob and yanked the door open, drawing another fierce barrage that temporarily deafened him.

When it stopped, he fired off three shots down the well, then rolled away, but not before his muzzle flashes had given him a look at the stairwell.

This time the answering volley from below continued until he heard a familiar voice. "Stop it, you assholes! Shit! Can't you see what he's doing? He's trying to run us out of ammo. Hold your goddamn fire till you got something to shoot at!"

Fredo!

Jake felt a savage grin twist his face. Brave Fredo—declining to join the upstairs greeting party.

Slipping off his shoes, Jake reviewed the images strobed into his brain by his muzzle flashes a moment ago: a handrail on the right of the stairwell and four-inch ledges on both sides that continued out straight at floor level as the steps descended between them. The stairwell ceiling descended until it met the ledges on either side, ending them about ten feet away.

All at once, Jake saw how to do it.

"Yo, Fredo?" he called.

The silence stretched to the breaking point before Fredo replied.

"Nacht! I knew it had to be you."

"A Kewpie doll for fat Freddie. It's me, all right. And it's payback time."

"Vito," Fredo said in a low voice. "Get into the pool room and bring me that bitch."

Jake's jaw clenched so hard he felt a tooth crack. *No way do you come out of this alive, Fredo.* Jamming his pistols back into his belt, Jake grabbed the corpse under the armpits, hoisted it to its knees, and waited for Fredo to open his fat mouth again, knowing the silence would break him down.

For a moment, nothing, and then: "There's a dozen of us, and only one of you, Nacht."

Despite the loud bravado, Fredo didn't sound very confident. As he kept talking, blustering, Jake used the sound to cover his own movements, edging through the doorway and straddling the stairwell with a foot on each ledge. He kept one hand planted against the wall for support as he used the other to drag the corpse forward by the hair. He felt naked, exposed. If just one of the men below heard a squeak or a creak and send a random shot up the steps, he'd be finished.

Luckily Fredo loved the sound of his own voice.

"You can't take us all, Jakey. All we gotta do is charge up those steps and sure as shit one of us'll get you."

Jake inched forward with the corpse, still straddling the stairwell, crouching now as the lowering ceiling forced him down. How many soldiers did Fredo have at the foot of the steps? Maybe half a dozen?

"Where's that fuckin' *broad?*" Fredo said, whispering again.

Jake couldn't hear the reply, but whatever it was, it didn't make Fredo happy.

"Fuck!" Fredo yelled in obvious exasperation. "You three—up the steps. We'll be right behind you. Go! *Go!*"

Silence, and then another voice at the bottom of the stairs said, "Tell you what, boss: *You* go first and *we'll* bring up the rear."

Jake almost laughed, and then a cold dash of terror cleansed him as his legs began to tremble. He was bent over now, near the point of the triangle formed by the descent of the ceiling into the ends of the ledges. The body dangled beneath him, damned heavy, the hair starting to slip from his aching fingers now—and then he felt another tremor in his straining legs. Even charged with adrenaline, his muscles weren't up to this. Any second, his legs might go out on him again.

Had to do it *now*.

Bracing the crown of his head against the downward-sloping ceiling of the stairwell, he twined his other hand into the corpse's hair and dragged the body forward. The feet bumped on the steps, and then the body swung free into a forward arc.

"Die, Fredo!" he screamed as he let go.

An explosion of gunfire rocked the basement, throwing more strobe flashes, making the corpse seem to jerk and flop as it sailed down into the midst of Fredo and his soldiers. Head still braced, Jake drew his pistols, then pulled his feet from the ledges, dropping onto the steps. Stumbling down into the basement, he fired left and right, cross-armed to brace both hands.

Hitting the bottom, he dived to the floor and lay flat.

Panic reigned in long, wild bursts of gunfire, and then, at last, the shooting stopped. Jake lay still, ears ringing, gaping his mouth open so no one would hear him sucking air.

"Did we get him?" someone cried.

"Anybody got a light?" Fredo's voice.

Homing on the voice, aiming at it, Jake caught himself just in time. A muzzle flash now would be his death warrant.

"I got a cigarette lighter," a voice replied.

"Use it," Fredo said. "Hold it up so we can see what's going on here."

"Fuck that, man. Like I'm gonna sit here holding up a flame like I'm at some fuckin' Springsteen concert?"

Jake grinned. Morale gone, chain of command breaking down . . . before long they'd be ready to start capping each other. But he couldn't wait around hoping for that—not while Angel was somewhere ahead, half-drowned, probably still hanging on to the edge of the pool—

"Jake?" called a voice from upstairs. "Jake, are you down there?"

"Who the fuck is *that?*" Fredo whispered.

Doc Graham. Jake suppressed a groan. Christ, what was Graham doing here?

"Get ready, Jake," Graham said. "I'm doing the Jersey City truck thing."

Jersey City truck thing? What—?

And then Jake remembered. He covered his eyes just in time, as a flare came flying down the steps and bounced across the basement floor.

Squinting, Jake saw four of them freeze in the piercing red glare—two wincing and shielding their eyes, one turned away and covering his head as if the flare were a stick of dynamite. He shot them all, the bullets spinning them away and down.

But where was Fredo—?

There—running away down a hall toward the rear of the house . . . toward the pool!

Legs, don't fail me now! Staggering up, Jake ran after Fredo. "Stay there, Doc!" he shouted over his shoulder, hoping Graham would hear him at the head of the stairwell and know he was still in business.

A muzzle flashed at the far end of the hall, and a bullet grazed his flank. Realizing he was backlit by the flare, Jake ducked back to the base of the steps. Another shot sent a bullet ricocheting off the floor and past him.

"Shit!" Fredo gasped.

Then Jake heard him working the slide of his automatic: empty or jammed? No time to wait and find out. Grabbing the flare, he flung it down the hall, then rolled into firing position. He got one glimpse of Fredo's back dodging into the pool area—not enough time for a shot—then heard Cangemi's voice call out from the darkness beyond the end of the flare-lit corridor. The voice had a peculiar water-slapped sound, and Jake realized Cangemi was already in the pool chamber—he was the one who'd gone after Angel.

Jake ran down the hall toward the pool.

"Hey!" Cangemi shouted again. "Who's there? Tell the boss I got her. Finally found her in this fuckin' dark."

Angel!

The flare lay on the floor ahead of Jake. Scooping it up as he ran, he flipped it through the doorway. The red glare arced through the air and landed with a splash on the water . . .

Where it kept on burning . . .

Crouching, Jake slipped through into the pool area, pistols out, ready to fire. Where was Fredo?

The floating flare had turned the big glass chamber into an eerie place, a chaotic web of wavering red lines that swirled across the walls, ceiling, and pool bottom. *Where are you, you bastard? I saw you come in here, I know I did.*

To his right, at the far end of the pool, Jake spotted Cangemi standing over Angel's limp body, blinking into the glare.

"Christ, Fredo, is that you? I got her. Now what do I do with her?"

"You leave her right where she is," Jake whispered.

He fired once. The lieutenant's face exploded as the impact slammed him against the wall. The back of his head left a wide dark streak on the tiles as he slowly sank to a sitting position.

And still Angel didn't move.

A cold dread settled in Jake's gut. Dear God, she looked dead. He had to get to her. CPR had never been his line—more the reverse—but he'd seen it done, and there was no one else.

But first he had to get past Fredo.

Where the hell was he?

Scanning the pool area again, Jake still saw only Angel and two bodies—Cangemi and the guy he'd shot earlier, from the skylight.

All the rest was white tile and wavering red light. Fredo had been wearing a dark suit when he'd left First Class tonight. No way he could blend in with the background here.

Jake's heart sank as he realized Fredo might have gotten away clean. Angel would never be safe as long as Fredo was alive.

Worry about that later. Get Angel out of here.

As he started toward her, a weight slammed against his back and something hard smashed against his skull. Cracks spidered across his vision and he felt consciousness slipping, shattering into a million pieces. With a fierce effort of will, he held it together. *He got behind you. Run!*

But before he could gather his legs, Fredo plowed into him again; dropping his pistols, Jake grabbed behind him, catching an arm, and carrying Fredo with him as he fell. Cool water shocked him as they hit the pool together, reviving him, hosing away the fuzz of confusion on his brain. Kicking free, he broke the surface and looked for Fredo. The pool surface was still unbroken. Above it he glimpsed the dark doorway opening on the pool, and above the door, a wide ledge of molding. Fredo must have clambered up there, then jumped down on him.

Hearing a splash beside him, Jake twisted in time to see Fredo's enraged face surging from the water, and above it, his pistol held high and arcing toward him for a knockout blow.

Jake blocked the blow with his wrist, then grabbed the arm, and they both went under again as they struggled for possession of the weapon. Jake managed to twist it from Fredo's fingers but lost his grip on it. He watched the automatic sink to the pool floor. He wanted to go after it but his lungs were clamoring for air.

He and Fredo broke the surface together. Now it would be a test of endurance. Jake dragged his arms, laden with sodden clothing, from the water and grappled with Fredo, as the other man flailed back. Jake felt him kicking and kicked back, trying to get a grip on him so he could drag him under the water, a bizarre, clumsy ballet, but one look in Fredo's eyes told him this was to the death, the last fight for one of them.

Almost at once, Jake began to tire. Struggling against Fredo while fighting the extra weight of the saturated clothes that tried to drag him under, he felt the water slap his chin, then spike up into his nose. He had to maneuver Fredo to the side where, with his feet on the bottom, he might have a better chance to gain the upper hand. The closest edge of the pool was maybe a dozen feet behind him. Right near Angel . . .

His heart leaped as he caught a glimpse of Angel raising her head. She stared at them dully for a second, then sank down against the tiles again.

She's alive! She's going to make it!

And so am I, damn it!

Suddenly Fredo was all over him. Jake grappled with him and, as they went under together, began kicking to steer them toward Angel.

Then he felt the tingling in his legs again.

A scream rang in his mind: *Not now! Jesus God, not now!*

Using Fredo as a human ladder, Jake climbed back to the surface, giving Fredo's head a final downward thrust before he broke the surface.

Panic clutched him in an icy fist—his legs weren't just going numb, they were *dying* on him. Now more than ever he had to get to the side, away from Fredo. Without the full strength of his legs, Jake could barely keep his head above water. If Fredo got hold of him now . . .

Powered almost entirely by his arms, Jake began thrashing his way to the side.

Eight feet to go . . . six feet . . . he felt his legs dying on him with every foot . . . four feet . . . had to rest them, just for a minute or two . . .

He heard Fredo splashing up behind him.

You're not going to make it!

Twisting around, Jake flung an arm out, catching Fredo's nose with the heel of his palm. Fredo's head shot back and he turned away, cupping his bleeding nose with one hand.

No time to press the advantage—another few seconds and he was going down.

Three feet . . . two feet . . .

He reached out with a sobbing gasp and grabbed the coping tile.

Saved. Now, all he had to do was get himself out of the water.

Grasping the coping with both hands, Jake began to pull himself up. But his arms were tired and the wet clothes were heavy, and without a boosting kick from the sandbags that had once been his legs, he was getting nowhere.

He heard splashing behind him, but not close. It seemed to be heading away.

Fredo on the run? Christ, he hoped so. Let him go—if Fredo got to him now, it would be the end for him, not Fredo.

Now, if he could just get *out!*

He tried to lever himself up again and managed to get one elbow, then the other atop the coping. All he had to do was find a handhold of some sort and haul himself out of the water. But the only thing in sight was tile . . . and more tile . . .

"What's the matter, Jakey?" said a voice above as two bare feet and a dripping pair of pant legs stepped in front of him. "A little trouble with the legs?"

Before Jake could push away, a set of fingers dug into his scalp, grabbed his hair, and twisted.

He looked up into the face of a madman—wide grin, wild bright eyes, hair plastered against Fredo's forehead, blood running down from his smashed nose over his lip and into his mouth, reddening his teeth.

"Looks like the cure didn't take," Fredo said. "Too bad."

Jake reached up and tried to knock Fredo's grip loose—if he'd had his legs he could have kicked away from the wall and pulled Fredo back into the water—but even his arms seemed to be weakening.

Fredo hung on. "Let's see if shit floats."

He pushed Jake's head under water. Jake flailed his arms above him, hoping to land a lucky shot, but Fredo had entwined his other hand in Jake's hair and was holding him firm. He'd had time only for half a breath and now that had gone stale. His lungs screamed for air, but his arms were not strong enough to overcome Fredo's leverage and the weight of his wet clothes.

I'm dying! he thought.

Worse, he was all that had stood between Angel and death. Once he was gone, Angel would be next.

Filled with a galling bitterness, he lashed up with his arms one last time, but the strength wasn't there. He felt his hands slipping impotently down Fredo's meaty wrists. The world was dimming . . . dimming . . .

And suddenly he was free. Fredo's death grip on his hair relaxed. With a desperate lurch, Jake found the coping with his fingers. He pulled, and slowly, too slowly, began to rise. *Hang on—one more second.*

His face broke the water, and air—wonderful, miraculous air—surged into his lungs. As he gulped it, he twisted around, looking for Fredo, waiting for the sadistic bastard to dunk him again.

"You!"

Angel's voice. Fear struck Jake through. Fredo would get her—

"You!"

Jake realized he was staring at Fredo's face—not above him, but directly at eye level on the coping. The rest of Fredo was sprawled like a beached whale on the tiles.

Above him, Angel knelt. Clutching the dumbbells shackled to her wrists, she raised them and smashed them down on Fredo, one and then the other, like clubs.

"You!"

Her eyes had a vacant look, her teeth were clenched, bared. She pounded at him, her rage leaving her only one word, screeching through her gritted teeth with each blow.

"You!"

And suddenly Graham was there, grabbing her arms, gently restraining her.

"Angel, stop! He's down, he's out, he can't hurt you anymore!"

Angel stared at her uncle as if she didn't recognize him. Then her eyes cleared and she began to wail. She dropped the dumbbells and sagged against him, sobbing.

Jake hung on the coping and watched her cry, wishing he could be at her side to help comfort her. His legs seemed to be coming back now, starting to twitch and move, but they still weren't strong enough to get him out of the water.

"Give me a hand, will you, Doc?"

"Not now." Graham frowned over the shoulder of his sobbing niece. "Give her a minute."

"We may not have a minute. If the cops aren't already on their way, they will be soon. No way we can explain what's happened here without doing some hard time."

Graham's eyes widened—remembering the two dead guys on the parkway off-ramp, maybe? Pulling free of Angel, he extended a hand. Jake grabbed it and, with Graham's help and a few feeble kicks from his awakening legs, hauled himself out of the water.

"Angel," Jake said. "Angel, listen to me. Who has the keys to those cuffs? And that collar?" *Christ,* a collar—*may you rot in hell, Fredo.*

Angel straightened and looked around, eyes red, her gaze darting about, as if expecting someone to leap out at her. Finally she pointed.

"Him."

She was pointing to the first guy Jake had shot, lying a dozen feet away.

As Graham ran over to search the dead man, Jake noticed an extra flare sticking out of his back pocket. Turning to Fredo, Jake looked for any sign he might be coming to. Nothing. He realized with a sinking feeling that Fredo wasn't breathing.

Angel had killed him.

Jake prayed that she would not notice it too.

Graham hurried up with a key ring. "These could be it—they don't look like car keys."

A few tries, a few more seconds, and Angel was free of the weights and the collar.

"Get her out of here, Doc," Jake urged. "Use that other flare to help her find a blanket or something."

"What about you?"

"My legs'll be strong enough to walk in a little bit. Just get her out of here."

As soon as Graham and Angel were gone, Jake checked Fredo's throat for a pulse. None. He looked into his eyes and saw that fixed, forever stare.

And then he saw the back of Fredo's head and winced. His skull was caved in. Angel had kept hitting him and hitting . . . must have been in the same spot . . .

Jake felt sick for Angel. This would destroy her. She'd never get over this, never be able to look at herself in the mirror.

Christ, what was he going to do?

And then he knew . . .

Maneuvering his legs under him, Jake forced himself to a kneeling position. He grabbed two fistfuls of Fredo's wet shirt and slid him into the water. For a moment, he watched Fredo float facedown toward the center of the pool, then struggled to his feet and, holding on to the wall for support, began a slow, unsteady walk toward the entry passage.

He made himself move even more slowly than necessary; still, he was almost to the door before Angel came back, stepping from the darkness into the light.

The worried expression fell from her face and she smiled. "Oh, Jake. I was worried. Thank God you . . ."

Her voice trailed off as her gaze went beyond him and fixed on the pool.

"Come on," he said, his heart heavy, wearied by more than the effort of forcing his legs to support him. "Let's get moving."

"No, wait. Jake . . . isn't that Fredo?"

He nodded. "Yeah."

"But he was over there . . . on the side . . ."

"He's taking a farewell dip in his pool."

He saw the look in her eyes—shock, revulsion, and the most painful of all, crushing disappointment. He sensed a sudden distance between them, felt it growing, as mentally and emotionally she began backpedaling from him, staring at him as if he were a stranger.

And there was nothing he could say that would make this right—nothing that wouldn't cause a greater harm.

Now it was Graham popping through the entry, holding a flare, a panicked look on his face. "I think I heard a siren!"

Grabbing Angel's arm, the doc pulled her into the entry passage, then stopped as he saw what was floating in the pool. Jake steeled himself, but Graham shot him an unreadable look, then turned away.

Jake followed the glow of Graham's flare as they hurried to the first floor. He was glad for the banisters on the stairs—they allowed his arms to help his legs up the incline.

Up ahead he could hear Angel's voice as she made her way through the dining room into the living room.

"Oh, my God . . . Oh, my God . . ."

Jake called ahead: "Drop the flare in the front room, Doc, and head for the car. If the cops come before I catch up, take off."

Neither Graham nor Angel replied, but when Jake turned the corner into the living room, he found the flare lying on the rug in a spreading circle of flame.

In the distance, he heard a siren.

Jake put all he had into his legs, hurrying out to the front yard and down the grassy slope to where Graham was supposed to have brought the car when the shooting began.

More than one siren, growing louder now.

He had a bad moment when he thought they might have left without him, but no—the station wagon sat at the curb, idling, its passenger door open. Jake threw himself into the front seat beside Graham.

"Two blocks straight ahead with your lights out, then pull to the curb."

As the wagon lurched forward, Jake turned and saw Angel huddled in her blanket on the backseat.

"Are you all right?"

"No," she said, her voice low, hoarse.

He wished he could see her face in the shadows.

He said, "Angel—"

"I don't want to talk right now," she said in that same voice. "About anything."

Jake turned and faced forward again, feeling a cold void in his gut. Was there no way he could make her see . . .

No. No way.

Graham pulled into the curb as directed. "What now?"

"We wait," Jake said.

A short wait. Seconds later the mansion was surrounded by flashing red lights. When the last siren had wound down, Jake pointed straight ahead. "All right. Keep the lights off, head up another couple of blocks, then turn right and put your lights on."

They got to Black Horse Pike, made their way back to Route 9 and the motel, where they dumped the wagon and switched to Jake's Jeep.

And still Angel hadn't spoken a word.

They began the drive back to Brooklyn. A two-hour trip, but Jake knew it was going to feel like two days.

28

HOME AGAIN

"I want to go home," Angel said.

The first words she'd spoken since Ventnor.

Graham had pulled to a stop in front of his rehab center. He twisted in his seat to face her.

"No, Angel. I want you to stay with me. I know I don't have to tell you about post-traumatic stress syndrome. You shouldn't be alone."

Angel's silence was an acquiescence of sorts.

Jake cleared his throat. His mouth was dry. He was almost afraid to speak. "You got a place where I can bunk for the night, Doc?"

He couldn't imagine making such a request under normal circumstances, but he didn't want to let Angel out of his sight. If he had to, he'd sleep curled up on a rug by the door, on guard in case any of Fredo's men assigned to watch the house hadn't got word that their boss was dead.

"No," Angel said. "I don't want him here. If he stays, I go."

It's like I'm not here, Jake thought.

"Angel," he said. "I only—"

"Jake . . . please."

She turned toward him and the reflected glow from a nearby streetlight lit her face. She had her eyes closed as she spoke.

She doesn't even want to look at me.

"I know I owe you," she said, her voice tight. "I'd be in the middle of an all-night gang rape right now if it weren't for you. And probably a day or two from now I'd be dead, or wishing I were. So you saved my life. I'll always be grateful for that. But what we had before . . ."

Her voice choked off and Jake watched with dull dread as a tear made a gleaming trail down her cheek.

"Angel—"

"No. Let me finish. We can never have what we had before, so I think it best we make a clean break here and now."

"But why?" Jake's heart ached as he played out the charade.

"Why?" She opened her eyes now and stared at him. "*Why?* That's what's so scary. You don't even know."

"Because of Fredo?" Jake said. "What else was I supposed to do? Leave him alive so his lawyers could get him off and he could come back and finish what he started with you? God knows how many others I killed tonight—"

"I think I counted fifteen bodies," Graham said.

Thanks for nothing, Doc.

"—and you're all bent out of shape about one, who happened to be the worst of the lot."

"I don't care about the others," Angel said. "I can accept their deaths because they were trying to kill you to keep you from getting to me. You had to defend yourself. You gave back in kind. It's terrifying that you're such an efficient killing machine, but without that skill, I'd be dead. Fredo told me that you were a killer for hire before you were shot. I think I could have found a way to accept even that, because I could tell myself that you'd changed, that the man who'd done those things didn't exist any longer. But what you did to Fredo tells me you haven't changed."

"Why is Fredo any different from the others?"

"Because of the utter cold-bloodedness of it. He would have been taken in by the police. I would have testified against him and put him away forever. But you took an unconscious, completely helpless man and threw him facedown into the pool. I know you did it for me, and as I said, I will be eternally grateful for all you did for me tonight, but I can't be with a man who could do something like that. Don't you see? What you did tonight was something Fredo would do."

Jake's throat constricted. He felt his world, all hope for a new life, tumbling into ruins around him. And still, there were no words he could find to make it right.

Angel turned to her uncle. "Can we go in now . . . before I fall apart completely?"

Graham handed her a set of keys. "Go ahead. I'll be right in."

She turned back to Jake and he saw more tears streaking her cheeks. "Jake, I did love you."

He wanted to reach over and draw her into his arms, but he knew she didn't want him to touch her.

With a sob, Angel lurched from the car and stumbled to the front door.

Jake reached for his door handle to go after her, but Graham grabbed his arm.

"Don't. Not now—not tonight. Give her some time."

The implications of the words hit home then and Jake stared at him. "I don't get it, Graham. What do you mean, give her time? This is perfect for you. This is just what you've wanted all along: Angel and me apart."

" 'Was'—it *was* what I wanted, you're right. But now, after what you did beside that pool . . . Well, I can't believe how . . . how wrong I was about you."

"You're leaving me in the dust."

"Don't pull that on me," Graham said. "I'm a doctor, remember? Angel has no idea what she did to the back of Fredo's head—she was in a fugue state at the time—but I know. I know head injuries, Jake, and there's no way Fredo was alive with his skull stove in like that. You knew it, too. You knew he was dead when you put him in the pool."

"You can't tell her she killed him," Jake said with alarm. "Not ever."

"I know that. But what amazes me is that you know that, and you're willing to take the lumps to protect her, even at the cost of losing her. Dear God, you really do love her."

Jake felt tears welling behind his eyelids. "I do. But what she said about me being like Fredo . . ." The words caught like broken glass in his throat, but he forced them out. "I'm terrified that she's right. That I haven't changed."

"You're wrong. You—"

"Listen, Doc. If Fredo had still been alive, I'd have done just what I did: float him facedown in the pool."

"Maybe. Maybe not. We'll never know. But tell me: Would the old Jake have done what you did with Fredo's corpse if he knew it might cause him to lose something he wanted very much?"

Jake said nothing, but he knew the answer to that.

Maybe at some point the distinction would be a comfort.

"You *have* changed," Graham said. "Now you must hold on to that change. Nurture it. It will pay off in the long run."

"Right."

"No—listen to me, Jake, understand what I'm telling you: I'm telling you you're not completely healed and, of course, as your doctor, I want to know why. That means further tests, which will require your recurring presence at the center. Understand? Meanwhile, I'll wait a bit, then start to work on Angel. I can't say I'll turn her around, but I can soften her up. The rest is up to you . . . if you want her bad enough."

Oh, I want her, Jake thought. Like I've wanted nothing else in my life. He felt torn between hope and despair. Did he really still have a shot with Angel? After what she'd said, he couldn't really believe it.

But he wasn't ready, either, to let all hope die.

"Okay, Dr. Graham. I'll be your guinea pig a while longer. We'll give it a shot."

"Wonderful," Graham said. "Can I drop you anywhere?"

"Thanks, but I think I'll walk for a while."

"Are your legs strong enough?"

Jake opened the door and stepped out. "They'll carry me." When he turned to shut the door, he saw Graham's outstretched hand. He clasped it. Graham's grip was firm, and he didn't let go.

"Where are you going, Jake?"

"Not sure. I don't know how Mr. C's going to take the loss of his nephew. He may want payback, or he may want to thank me for getting rid of a loose cannon. So I think I'll lay low until I see what shakes out."

"Whatever you do, I want you to check in with me in two weeks. I'll have a battery of tests set up by then."

"Will I see Angel?"

"If I have anything to say about it—yes."

"Then I'll see you in two weeks."

Graham finally released his hand and Jake slammed the door. As he walked away, he looked up at the windows of Graham's house. He thought he saw a curtain move, as if someone had been watching him and had stepped back when he turned.

Or was that just wishful thinking?

Turning away again, he kept walking.

Where to from here? he wondered. He was out of the hit game. What else did he know?

He'd worry about that later. Right now he simply wanted to walk.

Because walking was something he never again would take for granted.